"Good work," he said, nodding toward the man's lifeless eyes. "You came closer than most." Silas rubbed a streak of blood from his cheek with the back of his hand. A shallow cut burned there for a second or two before the skin sealed itself perfectly, healing in moments, leaving no sign that there had ever been an injury.

The collector's attack had taken Silas by surprise. It would not happen again.

# JENNA BURTENSHAW

# BLACKWATCH

## THE SECRETS OF WINTERCRAFT

GREENWILLOW BOOKS
An Imprint of HarperCollinsPublishers

Blackwatch
Copyright © 2011 by Jenna Burtenshaw
First published in 2011 in Great Britain by Headline Publishing, an imprint of Hachette Livre UK. First published in hardcover in the United States in 2012 by Greenwillow Books, an imprint of HarperCollins Publishers; first American paperback publication 2013.
The right of Jenna Burtenshaw to be identified as the author of this work has been asserted by her.

Library of Congress Cataloging-in-Publication Data
Burtenshaw, Jenna.
Blackwatch / by Jenna Burtenshaw.
p. cm.—(The secrets of Wintercraft ; 2)
"Greenwillow Books."
Summary: Will the sinister and soulless Silas Dane abandon Kate Winters, who can pierce the veil between life and death, when she is pursued by the Blackwatch squadron of spies and assassins?
ISBN 978-0-06-202644-6 (trade bdg.)—ISBN 978-0-06-202645-3 (pbk.)
[1. Fantasy. 2. Dead—Fiction.] I. Title.
PZ7.B94569Bl 2012 [Fic]—dc23 2011045278

13 14 15 16 LP/RRDH 10 9 8 7 6 5 4 3 2 1
First Edition

 Greenwillow Books

*For Adam,*
*my wonderful brother.*
*With love.*

# CONTENTS

# 1

# HUNTED

A month had passed since the Night of Souls, the night Silas Dane had left the city of Fume as a traitor and begun his new life as a fugitive. He had murdered a councilwoman, slain many of her wardens, and threatened the lives of the council's twelve remaining members. In that one night he had gone from being one of the High Council's most trusted men to being an outlaw, no better than any of the smugglers and thieves he had brought to justice in his time.

Word of his treachery had spread to every town in Albion. The High Council wanted him caught, but no matter what had come as a result of his actions, the memory of that night still made Silas smile.

At night, heavy mists spread across the open wilds of Albion as the darkest weeks of winter closed in. Bitter winds blasted in from the north, and every morning a new layer of frost clung to the trees. Silas's crow soared high overhead as

Silas rode deep into the wild counties, making his way between small settlements that peppered the landscape. For the first time in twelve years his life was his own, and he found himself enjoying his freedom upon Albion's open roads. For now that freedom was enough.

The settlements were lawless places, beyond the reach of the High Council's rule: roughly built clusters of houses, trading posts, and inns whose residents made anyone feel welcome so long as he brought silver or goods to barter with. Silas had visited some of those settlements disguised in a traveling robe taken from the body of an unlucky thief who had challenged him upon the open road. There he blended in among other nameless strangers, hiding his gray eyes beneath a hood during the day and conducting all his business at night. Wherever ale flowed, people talked.

As snowstorms moved in steadily from the frozen north, Silas was forced to stop camping in the open each night and began renting rooms within the eastern villages instead. His most recent room was inside a run-down inn clinging to the edge of one of the larger villages. He had heard that Whisperers—information sellers—often visited there and hoped to overhear news of the search that had been mounted against him. During his second night, spent hunched in its darkest corner listening to whispers shared over flagons of cheap ale, he was not disappointed.

Just before midnight a tall man entered the inn with a

thick scarf wrapped around his neck. He walked like a soldier and swept his eyes past every face in the room, scrutinizing everyone. Silas lowered his eyes and turned away. After weeks spent in the company of strangers, he had just spotted a familiar face.

Silas tried not to look interested as the man nodded in greeting to a hooded stranger sitting three tables away and went to join him at his table.

"There's been no word from any scouts on the rivers or at the coast," Silas heard him say. "None of the dockworkers has seen or heard anything of Silas Dane along the eastern or southern coasts. Either your information was wrong, or he has paid them well for their silence."

"He will head to the Continent eventually. Keep searching. I want to know the moment he is seen."

"Have you considered that he may not even be heading for the sea? He may not have even heard of this woman."

The hooded man shook his head slowly. "The council have known about her long enough," he said. "It will not be long before Silas hears about her, too."

Silas leaned farther over his ale glass, trying to identify the speaker. He was dressed like any other common man, but beneath his plain brown coat Silas caught a glimpse of a bright red boot, polished and pristine. Those boots belonged to a councilman. If there was a councilman in that inn, a consignment of wardens would not be far away.

Silas scanned the room and identified two men he had not seen the night before. If there were wardens there, they had not recognized him so far.

"Dalliah Grey is an enemy to our country," continued the councilman. "We have reason to believe that she will try to contact Dane when she discovers he has turned against us. Dane may have murdered a councilwoman, but Dalliah Grey committed far worse crimes before she was driven out of our lands. If the two of them join forces against us, the consequences could be disastrous."

A burst of laughter broke from a group of smugglers close by, and Silas made use of the distraction. He stood up, walked straight past the two men, and pulled open the inn door to step out into the snow-filled night. A black carriage stood waiting to his left with two wardens on board, sitting exposed to the elements with their shoulders hunched against the falling snow. Neither of them looked his way as he headed to the right, slipping into the dark.

If any wardens planned to attack, their training would force them to attack there, while their target was in the open, out of sight of any witnesses.

No one came.

The inn door creaked open five times to disgorge various breeds of drunks out into the street until, on the sixth, the councilman stepped into the open with the man he had been speaking to close behind him.

"The longer Dane remains at large, the less generous I shall be," said the councilman. "Find him. You have had long enough."

The man nodded. "As soon as I hear anything, you'll be the first to know."

Silas's hand stood ready upon his blade as the hooded man walked to the carriage and the wardens cracked a whip to drive their horses on. The man stayed by the inn door, counting money out of a small coin purse and into his pockets. Silas moved silently up behind him.

"How have you been, Derval?"

The man reached for his dagger in surprise.

"There will be no need for that," said Silas, pulling his hood back a little to expose his full face.

"Silas?" The man relaxed at once. "You have the luck of a demon, my friend," he said. "Do you know how many wardens were just here?"

Silas led him back into the shadows, where they could talk unseen. "What are you doing here, Derval? I hear you have been hunting me. And not very successfully."

"I have far better things to do than hunt you down," said Derval. "I like living too much, but the High Council don't need to know that, do they? Where there's fear, there's coin, and you've got them all quivering in their boots since what happened on the Night of Souls. Twenty wardens killed, half the city swears they saw spirits of the dead, and a councilwoman finally got what she deserved, from what I hear."

Silas nodded slowly. "How is the hunt progressing?"

"It's not," said Derval. "The council doesn't know where you are, and if anyone else does, he's not talking."

"So the councilmen have decided to head out into the wilds themselves?"

"This was an arranged meeting," said Derval. "He chooses the location. I spin him a lie or two, and I get paid. It works for me."

"I don't believe in coincidences," said Silas, keeping a close eye on the street, still primed for an attack. "Since you are here, I need something from you."

"What kind of thing?" asked Derval, suddenly suspicious. "I'm not giving you my horse. Not after what happened last time."

Silas smiled. "I need information," he said. "This woman the council are worried about. I want you to tell me everything you know about Dalliah Grey."

"From the sounds of it, she is as bad as you. Trouble," said Derval. "Word is, she caused Albion a lot of trouble a few hundred years ago. Got on the wrong side of the council, killed a few of them, messed with things she shouldn't."

"A few hundred years ago? Why are the council worried about her now?"

"Because, according to our councilman friend, the old girl *isn't dead*," said Derval. "Now, I have an open mind, you know that, but even I think the High Council have got it wrong with this one. Five hundred years later, and they're convinced this woman is still going strong, with a grudge against Albion even longer than yours, I'd bet. All that business in the city square a few weeks ago jogged a few memories within the council. I wish I'd been there to see their faces when the veil opened like that. Some of them think Dalliah Grey was involved, and it's got them worried. Let's face it, if there were a five-hundred-year-old woman out there with a grudge against me, I'd be worried, too."

"And the council believe she is still alive?" asked Silas.

"They sound convinced," said Derval. "Something to do with the veil, so I've heard. The old councils tried everything they could to kill her off when she was in Albion last, but nothing touches her. She bleeds, she heals. Just like you."

"Where is she now?" asked Silas.

"On the Continent somewhere. All I know is the council don't want you crossing the sea to find out. But if they're worried about this woman, she can't be all that bad. She sounds like an interesting one, if you ask me."

Silas emptied his pocket and pressed a coin pouch of his own into Derval's hand. "This is for your silence," he said. "If I find out you have told the wardens about me, I will hunt you down, slit your throat, and watch your blood drain out of your lifeless body drop by drop. Do you understand me?"

"As always," said Derval. "You keep the money coming

and I keep my mouth shut. It is always a pleasure dealing with you, my friend. I hope we will meet again soon."

Silas nodded with respect, and a slight smile flickered across his eyes. "With luck, we will."

The two men clasped hands in farewell, and Silas skulked away from the inn as quietly as he had arrived. His horse was stabled in a blacksmith's yard. He unhitched the stall gate, saddled the restless beast, and rode out of the village without looking back.

Silas spent the whole of the next day on the move, staying away from the main trails. He rode his horse over snow-covered hills, through frosted fields, and alongside frozen rivers. It was no weather for traveling, but Silas did not suffer the cold like ordinary men. His body was unnaturally resilient. His heart beat more slowly than that of any living creature, he had the well-honed strength of a lifelong soldier, and his bones, muscles, and skin could repair any injury in a fraction of the normal time.

Silas's endurance was the product of an experiment that should have sent him into death twelve years ago. Instead, he had survived, with part of his soul bound to the veil between worlds and the rest linked forever to his mortal bones. The energy of the veil sustained his life while tormenting his mind with visions of the half-life, where souls could not die. Silas had heard of only one living person who shared his condition, and the High Council's fear of the woman called Dalliah Grey was enough to help him make a decision. If Dalliah's soul had indeed been damaged the way his soul had been, he had to meet her.

It took him two days to find a hidden dock where smuggling ships set sail for the Continent. Once there Silas convinced a captain to allow him passage on the next vessel to leave that night by offering up his horse in trade. Given enough time, he could hunt down anything, and his reputation as the High Council's most capable collector was known as far as his name had traveled. If he could find Dalliah, one of the council's oldest enemies could well become his greatest ally.

The ship set sail just before sunset onto a calm ocean, and as soon as he was at sea, watching his homeland drift out of sight, Silas knew he was doing the right thing.

The journey to the Continent would have taken only a few hours in fine conditions, but the northern countries were in the middle of a freezing winter. Ocean currents were carrying sheets of ice southward along the center of the Taegar Sea, forcing ships to push their way through and making the journey a slow and treacherous one.

Silas spent most of the journey out in the open on deck. Hours had passed in slow, silent solitude, and when the evening shifted into the dead of night, he had made his way into the cargo hold. Now he crouched down, cleared a space on the dirty floor with his hands, and pulled open the neck of a black drawstring pouch. Rows of fat leather sacks swung from bars lined up above him, each one swaying gently, following the slow motion of the ship as it cut through the icy waves. He could hear chunks of ice grinding against the hull, scraping at the wood like a thousand fingernails as he emptied the pouch's contents onto the floor.

A handful of coins rattled out first, then a silver ring and three rolled notes. Two of the notes were sealed with buttons of wax, but the third had cracked open and was busy unfurling itself slowly across the floor. Silas pocketed the coins and the ring and picked up the open note. The seal was dark green and stamped with a rolled scroll, the mark of Albion's High Council. He struck a match and held the flame close to the paper to read its words:

ORDER IS HEREBY GIVEN FOR THE CAPTURE OF
SILAS DANE,
TRAITOR, THIEF, & MURDERER.
COLLECTORS MAY CLAIM A SUBSTANTIAL REWARD OF
GOLD AND LAND
UPON PRESENTATION OF THIS DANGEROUS CRIMINAL TO
THE WARDEN OF THE WATCH.
NORTH TOWER, HIGH COUNCIL CHAMBERS, FUME.

Silas looked over at the dead man who had owned the pouch. His body was still warm, his neck twisted awkwardly against the floor. Collectors were resourceful and persistent, but he had not expected one to find him on the open sea.

"Good work," he said, nodding toward the man's lifeless eyes. "You came closer than most." Silas rubbed a streak of blood from his cheek with the back of his hand. A shallow cut burned there for a second or two before the skin sealed itself perfectly, healing in moments, leaving no sign that there had ever been an injury. The collector's attack had taken Silas by surprise. It would not happen again.

He allowed the match flame to catch upon the corner of the page and consume it in a burst of heat and embers. "The council does not give gold to dead men," he said. "You should have known better."

Silas stood up, grabbed the collector's wrists, and dragged him roughly across the floor. Then he unhooked an empty leather sack from its hanging place, wrestled the body into it, and hooked it heavily back into place. No one would find it until the ship arrived at port, and by then he would have already left it behind.

Silas left the sack swinging with the rest and made his way to the front of the hold, where a trapdoor led up to the main deck. He climbed a short ladder, grabbed the door's handle, and pushed it open, letting moonlight spread across his face. The deck was rough and untidy, tracked with deep scratches and stained with everything from wine to animal dung. The smugglers did not care what they carried, so long as it brought them a profit at the end of the journey. There had been eight men upon the ship when it left the dock, including Silas and the captain, whose clothes bristled with hidden weapons; he trusted his own crew as little as he trusted the strangers who had paid their way on board.

Silas carried a weapon of his own, a sword forged of blue-black metal that was still sheathed beneath his stolen robe. He stood out in the open, listened carefully, and made a note of every man's position on the ship. The captain was pacing in his cabin; he could hear his boot steps scraping on the floorboards. The helmsman was at the wheel, and two young men bundled in thick clothes and arguing loudly with each other were climbing among the rigging. The sixth man was in the galley cooking potatoes and old beef, another was snoring in his sleep, and the eighth would give Silas no more trouble: the dead collector, swinging gently in the hold.

He checked the position of the stars. The night was clear, and moonlight shone upon the floating ice, making the frosty surfaces shine like ghostly lights as the ship traveled northeast. Silas knew the journey well. They were following the wide sea channel that spread like a scar between Albion and the Continent, heading for the northern Continental town of Grale. He had made that journey many times during his time in Albion's army, and so far it seemed the captain was keeping his word. The ship was set to reach Grale within the hour. They were right where they were meant to be.

As the moon moved steadily across the sky, the ship's heaving sails caught a favorable wind and sliced more swiftly through the frosty waters. None of the crew questioned the whereabouts of the missing passenger—he could have fallen overboard and no one would have cared—so while the smugglers ate their midnight meal, Silas patrolled the ship instead, looking for anything else that was out of place.

If one collector could follow his trail onto that ship, a second could have found it just as easily. He stood at the back of the ship, behind the helmsman's tied-off wheel, and looked back toward Albion. His homeland's dark cliffs had long since retreated over the horizon, but between the ship and the distant coast, Silas spotted something moving in the water. It was a low black shape, far enough away to be indistinct, even to his sharp eyes. Something was following the ship. Silas made sure he was out of sight and watched.

It could have been a whale. Small whales often traveled along the Taegar Sea in winter. But as the shape drew closer, a square of black cloth flapped silently above the waves, and Silas spotted two shadows crouched beneath it, struggling to keep a small sailing boat on course. The ice may have been enough to slow the large ship down; but its hull left clear waters behind it, and the little boat was maneuverable enough to nip safely between any chunks that passed its way.

Silas walked through the shadows and stepped up onto the ship's guard rail. He balanced there perfectly, pulled off the stolen robe, and let the icy wind rip through the long leather coat he was wearing underneath. He looked down at the churning ocean. The water sliced and foamed beneath him, black and fast. He waited until the time was right, then stepped casually off the rail and plunged feetfirst through the air, down into the freezing ocean.

The water swamped his head, and the ship's powerful wake captured him and pulled him down into the depths. He opened his eyes, waited for the current to release him, and remained underwater, reorienting himself in the direction of the little boat's hull. The weight of his sword fought against the water, and the ocean blurred his vision; but he did not need clear sight for what he was about to do. His sharp ears lifted tiny sounds from the water, listening for the creak of ropes or the echo of the men's feet shuffling across the boat's oiled wood. Dull thuds carried toward him, and Silas's heartbeat throbbed glacially slow as he stretched out his arms and swam silently toward his enemy.

No breath left his lungs as he reached the boat and hung beneath it, keeping one hand pressed against the wood, feeling for the movements of the people above as vibrations against his fingertips. One man was talking loudly enough for Silas to hear his voice, and he concentrated upon it until the words became clear.

". . . enough to bring down a walrus, that one. Don't think I'll need it, though. Good old-fashioned cunning . . . that's what'll finish him in the end. I'll bet he hasn't seen the likes of me in his lifetime, no matter how tough they say he is. Hey! You even listening?"

Silas felt a hard jolt reverberate through the boat. The other passenger yelped but did not answer.

"Ignorant rat! I never shoulda brought ya along. You're as useless as a pig at a rabbit shoot. Maybe I should throw ya over the side right now and test those weedy little arms of yours. What do you say to that?"

Silas placed his other hand on the hull and pulled his feet up into a crouch. The hull was slippery, but he held on and moved along it in a silent crawl until he was as far from its occupants as it was possible to be. His gray eyes broke the surface of the water, and he pulled himself up, making the boat rock and shift as he climbed aboard.

Two pairs of terrified eyes glared at him in the dark.

"It can't be!"

The collector reached for his blade, but Silas was faster. He took five steps across the boat, sent the sword spinning into the sea, then wrenched the man's arm behind his back before throwing him casually over the side.

"Hey! S-stop!" the man yelled as the boat left him behind. "Come b-b-back!"

Silas ignored him. In water that cold the fool would be dead within minutes, so he turned his attention to the second passenger, who was now cowering beneath a blanket, a useless sword quivering in his hand. Any apprentice who gave up a fight so easily deserved to be run through by his prey.

Silas drew his own sword and wrenched the blanket away in his fist. A young boy looked up in terror, dropped his weapon, and held his grubby hands out to protect his face. Silas glared down at him and dragged him to his feet. This was definitely not an apprentice. He was scrawny and weak, a slave boy brought along to do whatever the collector did not want to do himself.

The boy looked down at his feet as his master's pathetic shouts faded into the distance. Silas studied him carefully. The smugglers' ship was moving away, and the little boat was starting to drift off course.

"Can you sail?" he demanded.

The boy nodded quickly.

"And do you know how to reach Grale?"

He nodded again.

"Then get to work. Give me any trouble, and I'll put you over the side just like your master. Understand?"

Silas released the boy, who set to work immediately, checking a compass that was sewn into his left sleeve and adjusting the sails to carry them steadily across the waves.

"Keep the sail up," ordered Silas, wringing the seawater from his clothes and drying his skin as best he could on an old blanket. "Follow the ship until you see land, then turn in toward the cliffs. I do not want to be seen."

Under the boy's guidance, the little boat cut swiftly through the waves while Silas stood at the front, looking out over the ocean to where the distant shores of the Continent would soon be moving into sight. A single lantern slung from the great ship's bow glinted ahead of them as the boat kept pace. Silas whistled once—a long, piercing call—and was answered by a deep cackle from somewhere among the huge sails.

A small shadow dropped toward the sea, and a bedraggled crow skimmed the surface of the water and flapped up to land upon Silas's shoulder. Its feathers were scruffier than usual, and a white line of feathers upon its chest was dull and dirty. It did not like being upon open water, and it huddled close to Silas's neck, fluffing itself stubbornly against the freezing wind as distant lights gradually sparkled into life upon the horizon.

While many of Albion's main towns clustered along the central spine of the country, most Continental towns clung to the coast, as if trying to escape from the sprawling forests, mountains, and lakes that dominated its territory farther inland. Every western town had guards posted along its beaches in case of an attack from Albion, but Grale's guards were far less particular about whom they allowed in their waters compared with those posted in the larger towns farther south. Grale was too far from anything to be used as a useful landing point for an invading army, and anyone who risked traveling there had nothing but the pungent smell of fish and smoke to welcome him. War or not, there was still silver to be made, and Grale was still open for illegal trade.

At night the town looked shabby and bleak. The glowing lights came from lanterns slung along wires above Grale's empty streets that hummed like strings of bees whenever the wind blew through them. The rough faces of Grale's once-white buildings had been stripped back by centuries of powerful sea winds, and the people who lived in them were as cold as the streets they walked during the few sunlit hours of their darkened days. The town stood humbly at the mercy of the elements, and its residents were opportunists, every one of them devious and unpredictable. Silas had endured dealings with them before.

"Pull in the sail," he ordered. "Now."

The boy obeyed. They were too close to the coast to risk their boat's being seen, and before Silas could even demand it, the boy had a pair of oars at the ready, preparing to row them to the shore himself.

"No," said Silas, noticing that the oars were the same thickness as the boy's scrawny arms. "I plan upon arriving sometime before next week. Give them to me. You keep watch for lens lights."

Grale had been a trader's port before the Continent's war with Albion had begun, and the people there could still be persuaded to barter with smugglers who did not plan to stay too long. The smugglers' ship's arrival would already be expected. Special provisions would have been made for them at the docks at a designated time, but Silas's boat would be given no such privilege. If just one man saw the boat out there on the waves, the rest of them would know about it in moments and decide what to do about it.

Silas rowed swiftly. The sooner he was out of sight, the better.

The land rose into looming cliffs on either side of the wind-lashed town, each one topped by a stone watchtower. The boy shivered in silence as they crept in toward them. Silas was concentrating on avoiding the clutches of rocks that rose stealthily out of the rising waves when something glimmered up ahead, a flicker of light where a light should not have been.

Halfway up the cliff face, a shadow moved. Silas kept moving. Another stroke of the oars . . . two . . . three, carrying the boat closer to the shore. The hairs on his neck began to bristle. He looked up, saw nothing, and then a sound high above him left no room for doubt. There was the thinnest rattle, a scrape of metal against stone, and a gentle hiss as something fell out of the sky.

Silas was already on his feet. He grabbed the boy's arm and pulled him over the side of the boat. The crow fluttered up into the darkness, and Silas hit the water on his back as a weighted net swamped down onto the boat. The ropes caught upon the mast and tented across it like a dead jellyfish. The air filled with arrows. Silas released the boy and plunged underwater.

More arrows ripped past him, but his attackers were shooting blind. They had expected him to strike out for the shore and were misjudging his position by a good few feet. He treaded water to stay close to the surface and heard a squeal of fear nearby as the boy slapped the water uselessly with open palms, battling to stay afloat.

The frequency of the arrow strikes allowed Silas to calculate how many enemies were nearby as he swam back toward the frightened boy. A black-shafted arrow stabbed into his arm, and he pulled it out without flinching, filling the water with a swirl of blood. He grabbed the boy's ankle and pulled him down under the water. The sea foamed with air as the boy flailed and fought against him, but Silas kept hold of the boy's foot and dragged him along, heading for the rocky shore.

The arrows stopped. Silas swam faster. Whoever was up there would be making his way down to the waterline. At last his hand came up against a cold mass of cliff rock. To his right was a huge expanse of rock, solid and black; to his left was a path leading up into the town.

The sea rose and fell against the coast, pulling the two swimmers' hands away and forcing them back again. Above them four shadows ran along the sheer side of the cliff, suspended by ropes that let them swing between two distant ledges with ease. Silas knew that technique. He had seen it before; it meant that those men were not just ordinary guards. They were something far worse.

"Blackwatch."

The Blackwatch soldiers were the elite of the Continental army, every one of them highly trained in stealth, infiltration, and assassination. Silas had encountered many of their agents in the past, but he had definitely not expected to see them there. If the Blackwatch was in Grale, his search for Dalliah Grey was going to be more difficult than he had anticipated.

Soon the men moved out of sight, and Silas pulled himself out of the sea and dragged himself up onto the rocks at the base of the cliff. The boy was right behind him, and the moment he slithered up onto solid ground, Silas grabbed him by the scruff of the neck and hauled him to his feet.

"They *knew*," he said coldly. "They knew I was coming. How did they know?"

The boy did not answer.

"What is this?" Silas dragged on a leather cord hung around the boy's neck and found a glass lens hanging there.

The boy cried out as loud as his pitiful lungs would let him. "Here! He's here!"

Silas grabbed him by the neck and loomed over him. "You have chosen the wrong side, boy," he said. "Pray that you never see me again."

The boy's eyes widened in fear, but he was not looking at Silas, he was looking behind him. Silas saw a shadow move in the reflection within the boy's eye. He watched it carefully, saw the gleam of a blade shining in the moonlight, and dodged smoothly as it stabbed toward his back. The man wielding it stumbled, the boy ran, and Silas killed his attacker instantly with a swift snap of the neck.

With one man dead, Silas reached for the rock face and pulled himself up the cliff, hand to hand, making for a ledge a few feet above him. The rocks were slippery and smooth, but he reached the ledge, got to his feet, and drew his sword, ready to defend himself. The ledge was part of a curved pathway sliced into the cliff rock, and Silas followed it upward to gain the advantage of higher ground as the rest of the Blackwatch closed in.

The sea roared against the coast as he climbed higher. His crow screeched a warning through the air, and he stopped. Spotting a bowman posted up ahead, watching the waves, Silas moved along the cliff face, staying out of sight, and took the bowman by surprise. The man loosed an arrow, missed his target, and was dead before the arrowhead found its way into the sea.

More Blackwatch agents moved in, surrounding Silas on both sides. There was nowhere to go. Arrows flew, but Silas was fast on his feet, dodging every one until a second net edged with weighted blades was launched toward him from the dark. The rope tangled around him, capturing him beneath it. Silas fought to free himself, but the rope had a metal core that could not be cut. He stopped struggling as his enemies gathered around him. He waited, choosing his moment.

"Secure him."

Silas did not see who had given the order, but he had no intention of letting anyone see it through. He waited until the men crept close enough. Only six of them were left: five with bows or swords raised, and one, the leader, standing behind them, silhouetted in the moonlight. He waited until they were close enough, and then he stood up quickly, making the net lift with him. The Blackwatch scrambled to secure the edges, and Silas lashed the ropes, using the blades as weapons against them. Two men fell when the blades slashed their throats, and a third fell to a thrust of Silas's sword. He wrenched the net up over his shoulders and threw a fourth man into the sea, leaving only the leader and his last man standing close by.

"Silas Dane," said the leader. "Welcome back."

Silas knew that voice, thick with the deep tones of the Continental north. The voice of an enemy. It had been twelve years since he had heard it last.

"Bandermain," he said.

Silas's fingers flexed around the hilt of his sword. He was eager to fight, but this was no time for bloody reunions. The Blackwatch never worked alone. For every group Silas had fought in the past another had always been posted nearby, and he did not have time to fight them all. He had been betrayed by a child, and the enemy had found him before he had even set foot on land. His arrival upon the Continent was not going to plan.

The last Blackwatch agent raised his bow ready to let loose an arrow. Silas looked out across the black ocean, and as the bow snapped, he bolted straight for the edge of the cliff path. The arrow snicked behind him, dangerously close to his neck. The bowman quickly readied another and Silas's feet left the ground as he leaped from the path and launched himself far out into the air. The north wind streamed against his face, and the sea beneath him bristled with rocks as he brought his arms up into a deathly dive, plummeting down into the waves.

Silas plunged hard into the shallow water and was buffeted by the tide, which sent him slamming back into the cliff. The rocks sliced his arms, and the force of the ocean racked his body hard against the coast.

The remaining Blackwatch looked down from the path, not daring to follow their target into the sea, but there was no sign of life in the water.

Silas was gone.

# ← 2 →

# JUDGMENT

Kate Winters sat at the back of the empty meeting hall, staring at a pair of slim wooden boxes that stood side by side on a small semicircular stage at the front of the chair-filled room. One box was painted white, the other black, and both were tied together with two wire baskets hooked onto their sides, each one standing half as tall as a man.

"There they are," she said quietly. "Those boxes are going to decide everything."

Edgar kept a wary eye upon the hall's main door, his fingers tapping restlessly on the back of the chair in front of him.

The meeting hall was the largest building in the sanctuary of the Skilled's underground cavern and one of the oldest. Like most of the buildings there, part of it was built into the cavern wall, but the stone outer walls were curved slightly, making it stand out from the rest. It was a communal space, set aside only for important meetings and events, and it stood empty most of the time.

Edgar shifted in his chair, leaned back, and stared up at the vaulted ceiling, where paintings of all the Skilled who had lived and died there in the last twenty years were pinned into place. "This place gives me the creeps."

Kate did not look up. She could already sense the pale ghosts of the people those faces had belonged to, trapped within the veil between life and death, unable or unwilling to leave the living world behind. She tried to ignore them, but since the Night of Souls, it had become difficult to block them out.

"We shouldn't be here," she said. "When do you think the others will start to arrive?"

"We've got plenty of time," said Edgar. "You'd think they'd at least let you sit in on the decision. If anyone deserves to hear the verdict, it's you."

From the moment Kate had arrived in that cavern a few long weeks ago she had walked into an atmosphere of hate and suspicion. She had hoped that someone among the Skilled would help her make sense of the strange, unfamiliar world her new abilities had allowed her to see, but instead, she had spent her first days being questioned about the murder of Mina Green, the Skilled's leader, who had been killed while Kate was in her care.

No one believed Kate when she told them Silas Dane was Mina's true murderer. Instead of helping her, the Skilled had taken her uncle Artemis away and would not let her speak to Edgar or his brother, Tom, for three days. The veil could be terrifying to an unprepared mind, and Kate had been left to face the confusion of her visions alone. She was woken often by nightmares creeping into her dreams and was haunted by whispers of spirits that were drawn to her, every one of them pleading with her for release, as she had managed to free so many others on the Night of Souls.

Kate was tormented by memories of days that had passed since she had been stolen away from her home. She wanted to forget everything that had happened since the night her family's bookshop had burned. She didn't want to remember the deaths she had witnessed or the sight of the veil tearing above the city square as she had risked everything to save her uncle's life. She had seen a councilwoman's soul leave her body to be dragged, screaming, into the deepest levels of the veil. Kate had even glimpsed the edges of death itself, before Silas had carried her soul back into the world of the living. Now even he had left her.

Kate would have given anything to return to the bookshop and her old life. She wanted to be ordinary again, invisible. Life had been simpler there. Now she was an outsider, a criminal, and an object of fear.

Silas had been right. The Skilled did not understand her; they feared her. They worried about why her silver-sheened eyes looked so different from theirs, and they refused to do anything except ignore her. Even Artemis, who rarely bothered to hide his personal dislike of the Skilled, remained strangely distant, and he seemed to spend more time with them than with her. Kate felt exhausted, empty, and alone. Everything had become a battle. She did not want to live like this any longer.

During the past few days an informal trial had been ordered to determine if Kate truly was responsible for Mina's death. The Skilled consulted the veil and argued with one another over the best course of action to take against her, but no one was interested in what she had to say. Deliberately or not, she had brought death to that cavern. No one wanted someone like her living among them.

For now Kate was free to move about the long underground street that was the Skilled's home, but she was not allowed to leave it. The vast tunnels of the City Below were off-limits to her. She was forbidden from using her abilities at any time, and it had been a whole month since she had seen the sun.

What most of the Skilled did not know was that Kate was a Walker, meaning that the world between life and death was open to her senses all the time. Walkers did not simply look into the veil as the Skilled could; they *entered* it, sending their spirits deep into the half-life, the shadowed realm between the living and the dead. For the Skilled, dealing with the veil was like looking through a window that kept them safe and separate from what was going on around them. Walkers were different. When they connected with the half-life, frost spread across their skin and their consciousness separated from the living world, throwing their spirits completely into the unknown.

"What do you think the verdict will be?" she asked, trying to distract herself from the souls drifting gently near the ceiling.

"They'll have to admit you didn't do it," said Edgar. "This is all just for show. You've lived with them for a whole month now and you haven't had the urge to go around stabbing anyone, have you?" He lowered his voice a little. "There are a few of them *I* wouldn't mind seeing off if the opportunity presented itself. I think spending all that time with Silas has rubbed off on me."

"This is serious," said Kate. "It isn't a joke."

"Leave the worrying to me," said Edgar. "It'll go your way. You'll see."

Kate's eyes flashed with silver as she looked down, and Edgar stared at her secretly. He still wasn't used to seeing her eyes do that, and it usually meant trouble.

"It's happening again, isn't it?" he said.

"It's not too bad." Kate glanced briefly at the ceiling. "It's those pictures. They attract the shades sometimes. It makes it harder to shut everything out, but it's okay."

A door creaked open at the side of the stage, where three chairs had been set, facing out toward the rest.

"Watch out!" whispered Edgar.

The two of them slid off their chairs onto their knees as a man's voice carried across the hall.

". . . it is not only a matter of our laws, of course. It is the message it would be sending. Of that we must be perfectly clear . . ."

Kate crawled along the chair legs as quietly as she could, and Edgar scrambled after her, heading toward an antechamber with an old stone tomb sitting in its center, separated from the main hall by an open door.

"I do not have to tell you how dangerous this situation is." The man continued as Kate ducked around the door and Edgar pressed in against the other wall, crouching out of sight. "From what I have heard, the great majority of votes are going to lean the same way. If today goes the way I expect, you may find that it is time for you to make a hard decision."

Kate looked out through the gap between the door's hinges. The man speaking was Baltin, one of the most respected members of the Skilled. The other had his back to Kate, but she recognized him at once.

"Is that Artemis?" whispered Edgar, looking around the door frame. "What's he doing here?"

"Are you ready?" Baltin placed a hand on Artemis's shoulder.

Artemis looked out across the hall. "Yes," he said quietly. "Bring them in."

Baltin nodded to the open stage door, and someone behind it began ringing the low bell, announcing that a meeting was about to begin.

"What now?" said Edgar. "We can't stay here. Someone will see us."

"Shh."

Two minutes passed before the hall's main doors swung open and people began filing in one by one. Kate recognized each of them from her time in the cavern. She knew every face, where each lived, and exactly what all of them thought about her. A few of them were polite enough whenever she was nearby, but not one of them had ever taken the time to speak with her. She was an enemy living within their walls. Edgar may have been confident that they would find her innocent, but Kate was not so sure.

Of the eighty-eight people who lived in that cavern, just over half chose to regularly attend meetings in the hall, and this time it looked as if every one of them had shown up. Not all of the Skilled wanted to take an active role in Skilled business. Many just wanted a safe place to live away from the wardens, but as those who were interested in Kate's trial took their seats, quiet chatter filled the room. Kate waited for Artemis to step down from the stage, but Baltin gestured for him to sit in one of the seats upon it instead.

"They're letting him stay," whispered Edgar. "That might be a good thing."

The Skilled hardly ever let ordinary people sit in on their meetings, but to let one take pride of place on the stage was unheard of. A shocked whisper spread through the gathered people as Artemis sat down. A small woman claimed the second chair, leaving the central one free for Baltin.

To Kate, that woman was the most dangerous person present. She was the magistrate, there to record everything that was said in that room and make sure whatever was decided was carried out quickly and completely. Kate had long given up hoping that things were going to go her way. Whatever punishment she was going to face, the magistrate would be the one to see it through.

The woman eyed the crowd carefully, and Kate stepped back. She had questioned Kate many times, but it did not seem to matter how honest Kate was or how much she protested her innocence, she would not listen.

Baltin raised his hands for silence, and as the crowd quieted down, a sense of anticipation settled over the hall. "I am sure we all know why we are here," he said. "Just over four weeks ago three of our old friends came to us for protection: Edgar Rill, whom many of us know and trust like a son; Tom Rill, whom we have known and trusted equally as long; and Artemis Winters, our reluctant friend from the north, who has done us great service in the past despite his long-held suspicions of our people. For that, we welcome him here among us today and honor him as we would a brother."

Gentle applause rippled across the hall. Artemis looked down at his feet and did not even raise his head to acknowledge their respect.

"Now," said Baltin, "to business."

The magistrate attracted his attention with a rap of her ink pen on the arm of her chair.

"Yes, Greta?"

"Where," she asked slowly, "is the girl?"

Baltin smiled at the crowd before turning to her. "She is safe in a guardian's care," he said. "Once she is—" He stopped and corrected himself. "*If* she is charged, she will be taken swiftly to the lockhouse, where she will be passed over to your hands. Until then she remains under careful watch. You have my word on that."

Kate and Edgar looked at each other. The magistrate recorded Baltin's answer on her page and then looked around the room like a hawk searching for prey.

"I never liked her," whispered Edgar.

Baltin turned back to his audience as Kate looked out again. "As I was saying," he said, "there was indeed a fourth visitor to our home, one who is perhaps a little less welcome than our three friends."

*"She is a murderer."*

Baltin squinted down at a man in the first row. "Excuse me?"

"We all know what she did. There's no point in dressing it up. She *killed* Mina, and Seth, too! Or have we all forgotten what happened to him for trying to bring her to justice?"

Kate's heart sank. Silas Dane had claimed a second victim

in that cavern on the same day he had taken Mina's life. Kate had not known his name.

Baltin raised his hand for quiet.

"That is a separate matter altogether," he said. "It is not why we are here today."

"We all know she did it," said the man at the front.

"Perhaps," said Baltin. "But for now we are here to vote upon her guilt or innocence of the crime against Mina Green. Nothing more or less. Those of you whose votes may be tainted by any other concerns should leave this hall now. No one here shall think the less of you. Indeed, you shall be respected for your honesty."

No one moved.

"Very well," he said. "As a people we have always striven to act fairly toward our own. Today I trust shall be no different. We all have had time to reach our decision over recent weeks. Now we shall pass judgment on what we have heard during that time. Do you all have your stones?"

A murmur of agreement went up around him.

"Then let the votes be cast. Innocence"—he placed his hand upon the white box—"or guilt." He placed his hand upon the black. "With order, please. Begin."

Everyone in the hall stood up as one, except for the older invitees, who stood up more slowly and shuffled up the stage steps to cast the first votes, forcing everyone else to snake back in a respectful line behind them. One by one they approached the two boxes, each of them carrying a small cloth pouch in his or her hand. Inside each pouch were two ordinary gray stones, one of which had been left plain, the other carved and burned with a thick black line. Each person had to walk to the boxes with a stone in each hand and then drop them, palms down, one into each box, so no one knew which choice had been made. The number of marked stones in each box would be counted separately, and if the number in both boxes matched the number of voters, the count would be deemed fair and the verdict given.

Kate heard the dull clunk of stones being dropped two by two, and she forced herself to watch. The man who had spoken up made no secret about which box he was dropping his marked stone into, and he strode proudly off the stage as soon as his vote was cast.

"What do I do if the verdict is against me?" Kate whispered once half the people had returned to their seats. She had never dared think about what might happen next. How did the Skilled treat people who were found guilty of murder?

"Let's see what happens," said Edgar, squeezing her hand gently. "Not everyone's an idiot like him. The Skilled are good people. I still think they'll cast their stones the right way."

Artemis, Baltin, and Greta, the magistrate, were not allowed to participate in the vote, but once the final two stones had been cast Baltin was responsible for conducting the count. Kate heard a rattling surge of stones as he opened the boxes' side hatches and the baskets filled one by one.

The people waited in silence.

All anyone heard was the dull tap and scrape of the stones scratching against one another as Baltin took the count from the white box.

Kate found herself squeezing Edgar's hand even tighter. She held her breath. Maybe this was why people weren't invited to their own judgments. The waiting . . . not knowing . . . it seemed endless. She wanted to shout at Baltin to hurry up, just to get it over with, but Baltin was a careful man. He had a job to do, and he would do it right.

An eternity later he moved on to the black box. Kate tried to read his expression, but all she saw was calm determination.

At last Baltin stood up and slowly took his place behind the box. He paused for two breaths until, finally, he opened his mouth to speak.

"The count is fair," he said. "You have all honored yourselves with your honesty. For that, you have my thanks." He turned to Artemis, who was staring at him, his eyes filled with silent desperation.

Baltin looked away. "The verdict is given," he said. "With a count of thirty-eight stones to ten. Kate Winters, by order of this gathering, has been marked *guilty* of murder."

"What?" Edgar shouted out, forgetting that he was meant to be hiding, but his yell was drowned out by the cheers that filled the hall. He tried to stand up, but Kate held him back. "They can't do that!" he said. "This isn't right!"

"It doesn't matter now." Kate tried to calm him down. "Leave it. I don't want you getting into more trouble because of me."

"You can forget that." Edgar tried to squirm out of her hands, but she held on tight.

"You're not going to change their minds!"

"No! I brought you here. I told you we would be safe. This wasn't supposed to happen!"

Baltin's voice cut through the noise of the gathered crowd. "The magistrate shall now verify the count, and I would like to thank you all for your judgment on this day. Be assured, the prisoner shall be brought to justice swiftly and in a manner befitting the nature of her terrible crime."

"What does that mean?" asked Kate.

"I don't know," said Edgar, but Kate knew he was lying.

"Edgar, what does it *mean*?"

Kate forced him to look at her, and she saw terror in his eyes.

## 3

# ENEMIES

Silas heaved himself out of the ocean and limped onto the coastal path. Two small firelights illuminated the cliff face as the Blackwatch lit torches and headed down to continue their search, but Silas did not look back. The path led him straight into the heart of Grale, and a soaking wet stranger on the streets at night was not going to go unnoticed for long. He moved through the dark, leaving a trail of seawater squelching behind him, and passed underneath a series of narrow street arches cut into the long terraced buildings whose dirty walls swallowed the moonlight.

Six arches passed over his head, and at the seventh he saw a man crouching in a doorway. Silas kept walking. The man shifted position, as if to make sure he would be noticed. Silas recognized a Blackwatch tactic when he saw one. That man was a decoy, posted there to make him turn and choose another route, one that would guide him into an ambush. If the Blackwatch thought he was going to play their games they were very wrong.

In one smooth move, Silas kicked a loose rock up from the ground, caught it, and hurled it at the waiting man. It struck him hard on the temple and sent him slumping to the ground. Silas approached the fallen man cautiously. He was unconscious but still breathing. Then came a signal from the dark: the flash of a tiny lens light from the farthest end of the arches. Another member of the Blackwatch was checking in.

Silas checked the man's pockets and found the leather pouch that held his lens. An ordinary guard's lens would have been a small circle made from cut glass with a dull metal frame, but the Blackwatch men were not ordinary guards. Their lenses were fine disks of shaved crystal, faceted around the edges with a flat surface raised slightly out at the center and a thin twist of silver around the edge. With no moonlight to reflect back beneath the arches, Silas slid a match from a slot in the lens pouch, lit it, and raised the lens to his chest, flickering a signal to the waiting man. Silas knew a few of the Blackwatch lens codes but had no way to know if the one he used was still active.

There was no reply. The code must have been old. It had given his location away.

Silas dropped the match, pocketed the lens, and looked up. He was standing in a narrow space between two rows of back-to-back buildings. The sky was a sharp black slit between them, and the gap between the stones was barely three feet wide. He heard footsteps advancing toward him, so he edged farther down the pathway, grabbed hold of a stone raised slightly out of the wall, and pulled himself up. He clung to the wall like a bat, creeping upward and pressing his heel into the wall behind him to gain more height wherever the stones were too smooth to climb. Silas stayed still, clinging on by his fingertips and the toes of his boots as a Blackwatch agent approached.

Once the officer discovered the injured man, he readied a crossbow and searched the alleyway for any sign of life. His target was gone. Silas watched him take two paces into the darkness. He saw the flare and fizz of a match; then *flick-flick-flick,* a lens light signal cut through the dark.

Silas smiled. They had lost him.

Four more Blackwatch officers gathered between the arches as Silas continued his climb toward the rooftops. His fingers ached as he clung to the wall. His muscles were tiring. Something had changed. He had to get out of sight.

He reached the neat black tiles, squeezed up between two matching chimney stacks, and stepped onto the sloping roof. Once there, he checked his position. Grale was a small town, and he was close to its center. The moon cast long shadows from the forests that wrapped around Grale like a horseshoe on three sides, and the ocean was silvery black. Silas could see the covered dock where the smugglers' ship would be spending the rest of the night. He turned away from it and followed the rooftops for as long as they lasted, then threw himself at a post holding up one of the lantern strings, grabbed it with both hands, and slid silently to the ground. He tried to shift his thoughts into the veil as he ran and use it to sense his pursuers' presence before they got too close, but the veil was not there. He could not sense anything.

Silas stopped running.

The veil had been a part of his life every day for the past twelve years. For it to suddenly be gone . . . it was impossible. Unthinkable. He searched for the familiar silhouette of his crow against the sky, but he could not pick the bird out against the background of shifting clouds.

The street opened onto the bank of Grale's only river, a wide, fast-flowing waterway crossed by three old bridges linking one side of the town to the other. Silas followed the bank to the nearest bridge, a stone-built pathway barely a carriage width wide. Crossing it would leave him too exposed, and he was about to return to the cover of the streets when Blackwatch agents emptied out of the alleyways up ahead. There was no time to reach the buildings, so Silas slithered down the bank instead and ducked out of sight beneath the bridge.

The old structure was weak and unstable, with large gaps in its sides where high waters had washed chunks of it away. Years of river debris strangled the stone pillars holding it in place, and old tree trunks had been sunk into the riverbed to support its weakest points. Silt and soil settled around Silas's feet as he waited in thigh-deep water, his black coat camouflaging him in the shadows. The Blackwatch signaled to one another, but instead of searching for him along the riverbank, they backed away and retreated into the side streets. Silas heard them leave and peered out of his hiding place.

A typical Continental welcome, he thought. Nothing has changed.

A scrabbling sound scratched close by, and his crow scuttled through the shadows, head down, like a rat in the dark. He bent down to pick up the bird, which snapped its beak, agitated, as footsteps echoed overhead. Silas stood still, sword at the ready. A wet rope glinted in the moonlight upon the river. One end of it was wrapped around a rotting tree trunk; the other trailed across the water. Two men ducked back underwater when Silas looked their way. How could he have missed them? The Blackwatch agents had not lost him. They had surrounded him.

The sound of straining horses carried from the riverbank. The rope tightened. Silas realized what was happening too late. He tried to run, but the rope was already doing its work. The rotten tree trunk was starting to give, lean, and split. The weight of the bridge was not enough to stop the timber from shifting, and the first stones began to fall, spilling into an avalanche, collapsing in upon the river and crashing down onto Silas's ledge.

The crow launched itself through the destruction as a chunk

of rock slammed onto Silas's shoulder, punching him to the ground. He tried to get up, but there was no time. He threw his arm over his head to protect himself as the bridge fell in, burying him beneath a hail of rubble and sealing him in the dark.

Kate looked out into the meeting hall at the people she had once trusted, people who believed she was capable of murder. Many of them were nodding their agreement with Baltin's words, and some were even applauding the decision, as if some great criminal were about to get the justice she deserved. The sight of so many enemies made Kate feel cold. Artemis had tried to keep her away from the Skilled. He had tried to protect her from their world all her life. Now she knew why.

She looked for her uncle up on the stage. He was just sitting there, silent.

"I don't believe this is happening," she said.

"Someone has to do something," said Edgar. "We need to get you out of here."

He left the safety of the anteroom and stepped straight out into the meeting hall, drawing angry looks and shouts of surprise from people sitting close by.

"Wait!" whispered Kate. "What are you doing?"

Edgar hesitated for a moment, not sure what to do next, until one of the Skilled spoke out.

"You are not meant to be in here," she said. "What's going on?"

Baltin spoke loudly from the stage at the front of the hall. "Is something wrong?"

"Edgar has been hiding in here, listening to us," said the woman as everyone in the hall turned to look at the intruder. "He's not supposed to be here, Baltin."

"Why not?" demanded Edgar. "I care about what happens to Kate, and I know that she deserves a lot better than this, being turned upon by people who should be her friends."

"That murderer is no friend of ours," said the man sitting at the front. "We have no argument with you or your brother, but that girl has brought death to this cavern. She is a threat to us all."

Edgar walked up to the stage. "Artemis! Tell them they're wrong about Kate. Tell them they don't have to do this."

Artemis hung his head, tapping the fingertips of his hands together nervously. "I—I—I—I can't," he said.

"Why not?"

"I can't keep her safe anymore. Not on my own," he said. "This place . . . these people. They understand what Kate is going through. They can help her."

"They think she's a murderer!"

"I know that. But up there, on the surface, the wardens are still looking for her. I can't let the council find her again."

Artemis handed Edgar a folded piece of paper. He opened it and read it quickly. It was a wanted poster, with Kate's face drawn upon in and her name written in thick black letters. Edgar scrunched it up in his fist.

"That doesn't mean anything," he said.

"You told me we could trust the Skilled," said Artemis. "You were the one who said to bring Kate here."

"We didn't have any choice!"

"And I don't have any choice now," said Artemis. "Baltin has given me his word that no harm will come to her. I don't want to do this, Edgar, but it is the only way I can see to keep her safe."

"So you're just going to let them lock her away?" said Edgar. "Just shut her up and forget about her, is that it? Do you really want that to happen?"

"At least she will be safe," said Artemis. "That's all I can hope for her now."

Baltin spoke up and pressed a reassuring hand on Artemis's shoulder. "The girl's guardian has made no objection," he said. "Kate shall be collected and taken to the lockhouse. We will decide her punishment in due course."

The gathered people stood up at once, and Edgar climbed onto the stage, watching them calmly making their way back out into their lives.

"You can't do this!" he said. "I told her you would help her, but you're just as bad as the council! You're treating her the way they have treated you for centuries, all because you're afraid of what you don't understand."

No one was listening. Many of the Skilled looked back at him as they left, their dark eyes flashing with anger. The door in front of Kate's hiding place moved, and Edgar saw her looking out.

Kate was not trying to hide anymore. She was looking straight at Artemis. As far as she knew, he had not even tried to convince them that she couldn't have killed Mina, that she would never kill anyone. Artemis saw her and turned away.

"At least you're ashamed of what you're doing," said Edgar.

Artemis stood up. His clothes were scruffier than usual, and he looked as if he had not slept for days. "Baltin," he said, "there is no need to send your people after Kate."

"The decision has been made, Artemis. I warned you this could happen. You agreed that it was right."

Artemis wrung his hands, struggling with what he was about to say. Kate waited for him to speak up for her, to try to put right what the Skilled had got terribly wrong. Then he raised his hand and pointed directly at Kate's hiding place. "She is there," he said.

Kate could not believe what she was seeing. Artemis could have distracted Baltin or at least said nothing. He could have given her a chance to get out, to explain herself and maybe make some kind of difference to the judgment passed against her. Instead he just pointed at her, handing her over as if he, too, were convinced of her guilt.

Edgar jumped off the edge of the stage and bolted between the rows of seats toward her. "Kate!" he shouted. "We have to go!"

But Kate was not ready to leave.

The air in the meeting hall was changing. Something was shifting within the veil. Kate heard a sound like roaring thunder, the spirits around the paintings in the ceiling looked suddenly clearer, and she felt the veil tugging at her thoughts, fighting for her attention. Dizziness overwhelmed her. The ceiling pressed down toward her, and the walls leaned in. She backed slowly into the anteroom to press her back against the tomb in the center of the floor. It was hard to breathe. The rushing sound of fast water echoed around her, her body would not move, and she heard the screech of a bird from somewhere nearby.

Kate slid down the side of the tomb and sat on the floor. Images flickered in front of her eyes: water, feathers, and stone. She could smell the tang of blood and feel the rough touch of stone crushing in against her fingertips. None of it made any sense. She couldn't stop it. All she could do was let it happen. She wanted to scream, but her lungs would not work. Then Edgar was in front of her. He took hold of her hand, and the veil pulled back. The images faded. Her body came back under her control, and tears were streaming down her cheeks.

"Come on," said Edgar, gently pulling her to her feet. "We'll get out of here."

"Something's wrong," said Kate.

"A lot of things are wrong right now. We have to go!"

"I think it's Silas," said Kate. "I could *feel* him." She looked down at her hands, remembering the pressure of the stone pressing up against them.

"We can talk about that later," said Edgar. "There's nothing we can do about it now. Are you coming?"

One of Baltin's men moved to block the doorway, but Edgar saw a flicker of uncertainty in his eyes when he looked at Kate.

"You've heard how dangerous she is," said Edgar, turning the man's fear against him. "Look at her! What do you think she will do if you get in her way?"

The man retreated at once. Edgar took hold of Kate's hand and pulled her into the meeting hall, where Artemis was shouting from the stage.

"Don't fight them, Kate. Let them help you!"

Neither Kate nor Edgar looked back, and they slammed out the front door side by side.

The Skilled's cavern was dimly lit to simulate the night that hung over the City Above. The lantern light gave a warm glow to the curved ceiling of red bricks and illuminated the two long rows of houses where the Skilled lived. They had been too slow. Flanked by two of Baltin's strongest guards, Greta, the magistrate, was already standing in the street, waiting for her.

"Great," said Edgar, keeping tight hold of Kate's hand.

"The judgment has been passed," said Greta. "The verdict was fair."

"It is more than she deserves," said one of the men. "We should hand her over to the wardens for what she has done."

Edgar whispered to Kate without moving his lips. "If we're going, we have to go now," he said. "Follow my lead."

The two guards flinched when it looked as if Edgar was going to move. Greta took a step closer.

"The cavern doors are locked," she said. "There is no way out."

More of the Skilled were gathering around them, their dark eyes fixed intently upon Kate. Her hands felt icy cold, and beads of water dripped to the ground as the heat of Edgar's grip melted the frost that gathered there as the veil closed in.

"Miss Winters?" Baltin's voice spoke behind her. "It is time to answer for what you have done. Come with us now. You can do yourself no good out here. Let the boy go."

Kate realized that she was holding Edgar's hand so tightly that his fingers were turning white, and she let go.

"That's right," said Baltin, signaling for his men to walk slowly toward her. "Edgar, stand aside, if you please."

"No. You can't just take her!"

"Don't you see what is happening?" said Baltin. "She does not have full control of her link to the veil, and that makes her dangerous. She may not even remember killing Mina. Do you want the same thing to happen to you?"

Kate's pupils sheened with silver as they reflected the lamplight.

"This girl has already gone too deep into things that are none of her concern," said Baltin. "The Night of Souls was . . . there is no other word for it. It was an abomination. The effects of the damage Kate did in that circle are still being felt across the veil. She is dangerous and always will be dangerous. We cannot allow her to make the same mistakes again."

"She used a listening circle," said Edgar. "It's hardly a crime."

"In our world it should be," said Baltin. "She opened a circle, exposed a crowd of innocent people to the dangers of the half-life, and interfered with the fates of thousands of tormented souls. If sheer luck had not allowed her to contain the shades in that circle, the consequences would have been unimaginable."

"But she *did* contain them," said Edgar. "She didn't open the circle. Da'ru did. If Kate hadn't taken control of it, who knows what would have happened? She helped people that night, something the Skilled haven't done for a very long time."

"As I said. Luck," said Baltin. "It all could have ended very differently. Do not forget the blood that was shed because of her. Wardens and a councilwoman all slain. Do you have any idea what could have happened if Kate had lost control?"

"Those deaths weren't Kate's fault!"

"Her actions were reckless, dangerous, and we may only now be beginning to see the consequences. She tore a gateway between the worlds of the living and the dead, one larger than any that has been seen within living memory. An act like that has far-reaching effects. Who knows how many are yet to suffer for what she has done?"

"Rubbish!" said Edgar. "Kate didn't harm anything or anyone, and you're all crazy to think that she ever would."

"That's enough," Baltin said sternly. "You are a guest in this cavern, Mr. Rill. Remember that."

Edgar was about to argue back, but a shade of doubt crossed Kate's mind. What if Baltin was right? What if she had done something wrong? What if she was dangerous? Kate knew too well how close the hundreds of people in the city square had come to death on the Night of Souls. She had seen the current of death with her own eyes; she had watched it claim the life of the councilwoman Da'ru, and she had helped do its work. Baltin was right: if anything had happened to the gathered people that night, she would have been responsible. She could not risk anything like that happening again.

Kate stepped forward and turned to speak to Edgar. "I'm going with them," she said. "It'll be all right."

"No, it won't. They won't let you out again. They'll keep you down here. Kate!"

But Baltin's men were already surrounding her.

Two of them held Edgar back as Kate followed Baltin down the cavern's main street, heading toward a small building that was off-limits to anyone except the one who held the key. The locks on the door were stiff from disuse. Baltin swung open the door and stepped inside the candlelit darkness, signaling for Kate to follow.

Inside was a single room that the Skilled used as a lockhouse. Someone had been inside recently and prepared it for her arrival. There was a bed next to the door, a long table stacked with old books that looked as if they had come from someone's dusty attic, and a row of shelves that ran all the way around the circular wall, holding four lit candles, already burned halfway down.

"For your own sake, I suggest you get used to this place," said Baltin, his voice echoing dully around the room. "You can do no harm in here, and you shall remain here until we decide upon a more permanent solution."

"I haven't hurt anybody," said Kate as Baltin positioned himself between her and the door. "I didn't kill Mina."

"This is not just about that," said Baltin. "We all knew what you were, even before you did. You may not think you have hurt anyone, but the veil does not lie to us. It warned us about you four years ago, and it says that given time, you will. I have people to take care of here. They trust me to do what is right, and *this* is right. Do you really think Mina would not have done the same once she had learned everything she could from you?"

"Mina welcomed me into her home," said Kate. "She trusted me, just like she trusted my parents. They gave their lives to help the Skilled. Do you really think I would break that trust?"

"Children are not their parents," said Baltin. "You may be right about Mina, but look what happened to her. The veil warned us about your . . . unique capabilities. I respect your family, I always have, but I would be a fool to ignore that warning now. I cannot afford to trust you, Kate, and because you agreed to be brought here, I do not think you even trust yourself."

Baltin left the room, leaving Kate standing there alone. He turned the locks tight and rattled the door after each one to make sure it was sealed shut. The moment the last lock dropped into place, he and his men walked away, and silence fell hauntingly upon the room. It was the kind of silence that suggested that someone was standing close by, trying not to breathe.

Kate picked up the nearest candle and held it up. She felt as if someone were watching her. Her skin prickled, and it was only then that she noticed the trails of frost veining along her arms. The veil was closer than usual in that place, and it made her uneasy. This is it, she told herself, sitting down on the bed. This is what you have to look forward to for who knows how long.

A deep whisper circled the room in answer to her words, and Kate shivered. She dared to reach into the veil a little and saw the shadowy forms of shades standing against the walls like statues carved into the stone. Seeing them so clearly no longer scared her, and their presence gave her some small comfort as she sat there on her own. If Baltin wanted her to stay out of the veil, locking her away was not going to do any good. He had to have known that. Sitting in the silence, Kate could not help thinking about what kind of permanent solution he and the magistrate had in mind for her.

# 4

## BANDERMAIN

"Wake him up."

A voice trailed sluggishly through Silas's mind as he tried to piece together what was happening to him. Rope bit into his blood-soaked wrists, and the smell of damp earth was overwhelming. He was in a cellar, tied to a chair and unable to move. That was all he could be sure of without opening his eyes. His mind, taking that as a command, tried to lift his eyelids. One of his eyes was badly swollen and would not budge. The other was wet with blood, and as his eyelashes pulled apart, he took in all the details of his surroundings in a single blink.

A candle flame was burning just inches from the tip of his nose. Behind the flame was a face, watching him, and beyond that were at least three other men, each one armed and staring blankly at the wall behind him. Silas tried to move as his senses gradually returned and pain flashed down his leg. The bone felt as raw as a rod of red-hot iron.

Tiny movements allowed him to test his bones one by one. One of his shoulders was dislocated, making his left arm feel detached and heavy, and every movement sent pain searing through his body. Instinct forced him to stay as still as possible. Most of his finger joints felt cricked and twisted, one of his ankles was broken, and his right arm was cracked in at least two places. He tested his lungs. A crackle of broken ribs rippled in his chest, and he knew not to attempt it again. It felt as if every part of him were bruised, broken, or bleeding. This shouldn't have been happening. He should have been healing.

"You should be dead." The person behind the flame stood up, taking the candle with him. "Why aren't you dead?"

The question was not meant for him. The man with the gravelly voice was talking to himself, studying Silas carefully. Silas did not like to be studied.

The shadow of the man caught in the candlelight dominated the entire room. His shoulders were wide and powerful; his strong arms, well used to wielding a sword. His face bore the thin scars of many battles, and his pale lips were curled up into a look that was half curiosity and half grudging admiration. When Silas had last seen him, this man had carried a two-handed sword upon his back, and while the rest of the Blackwatch wore daggers in their belts, he had still borne the same weapon that had claimed many Albion soldiers' lives. Its hilt rose from its place against his right shoulder, the pommel wrapped in black leather banded with well-worn gold.

"Started traveling with a pack, have you, Bandermain? You must be getting old."

Celador Bandermain was taller and older than Silas and had often proved himself to be a master strategist with the strength and stamina of a bull. The last time Silas had seen him, he had commanded more than half the Continental army. He was an accomplished fighter and an equal match to Silas's strength whenever the High Council had sent him to lead attacks upon the Continent. But that was in another life, before Silas's spirit had been torn away. A lot had changed since that day.

"I always knew I would be the one to bring you down," said Bandermain. "I was right."

Light flooded his face, casting thick shadows across his deeply set eyes, which gave away nothing of the thoughts that lay behind them. He was wearing the long red coat of a high-ranking member of the Blackwatch, and many strangers might have thought him handsome on first glance; but there was an edge of danger to his face, an edge worn only by people who had killed and who loved to kill. It was a trace of darkness that could be sensed only by another killer, or by anyone else during the fatal moment when he realized he had become Bandermain's prey.

"I thought you would be long dead by now," said Silas, using his lungs as little as possible. "Isn't that what normally happens to officers who let the enemy walk free from their lands?"

"That was a long time ago," said Bandermain. "I have learned from my mistakes. I have regained the trust of my leaders many times over, while you, so I hear, have recently lost the trust of yours. Treachery. I never would have expected that from you."

Silas kept his eyes upon Bandermain but said nothing.

"I have heard many rumors about you since you were last here," said Bandermain. "Now I can see that at least some of them are true. Bridges fall. People beneath them die. Every one of them. Everyone . . . except for you."

"Strong bones," said Silas. "Hard head."

"I do not think so. We are not as ignorant as your people like to think we are on this side of the sea," said Bandermain. "We know about the veil, and we know what your High Council plan to do with it." He signaled to one of his men, who stepped forward and unrolled one of Albion's news posters for Silas to read. It was a recent copy, less than a week old, but the main story was one that had been repeated over and over again for many years. "What do you have to tell me about this?"

### War to End
### New Strategies Set into Place
### Continent to Feel Might of Scientific Advances
### Albion on the Attack!

Silas coughed a mocking laugh. "You believe that?" he said. "How many of those have you intercepted? One? Maybe two? *This* is what you are afraid of? I used to look forward to facing you in battle, Celador. Now . . . I just pity you."

Bandermain's fingers twitched, but Silas knew he would not attack a prisoner, not one that could be useful to him. Despite the company he kept these days, Bandermain was no fool.

On any other night not even the Blackwatch would have stood a chance against Silas; but something had changed, and Bandermain was being far too confident considering the bloodied state Silas had left him in the last time they had met in battle. A scar left by Silas's blade was still clearly visible along Bandermain's jaw. Silas had shown him mercy that day. He did not intend to do so again.

"I know what you have become," said Bandermain. "I ordered my men to prepare for a long hunt. Capturing you was meant to be a challenge for them. Yet here you sit, proving yourself to be no more of a threat to us than a fish in a net. I find that interesting, if not a little disappointing."

"You know nothing about me."

"I know that you can heal without medicine, fight and not tire. And tonight I saw you stay underwater longer than any man alive."

"That would be a very interesting trick," said Silas. "But as you can see, you cannot believe everything you hear from across the water."

"You do not sound like a man who is in pain."

"I have had practice."

"I am sure that is true," said Bandermain. "There are people who would be very interested in acquiring you. You are a legend, my friend. Children talk about you in the streets. They play games and take turns to be the one who vanquishes Silas Dane, the 'mighty soldier from the west.'"

"I have no interest in your country's young," said Silas. "Is that where the Blackwatch gathers its information these days? From children in the streets?"

"You would be surprised just how far my spies have reached," said Bandermain. "As things stand, it would be seen as a service to both our countries if I were to kill you right here in this room, but after tonight I think we both know that is not as easy as it appears to be."

Silas felt his broken fingers begin to crack and click back into place. The bones in his right arm racked with pain as they rejoined, but he tried not to draw attention to his returning strength. "The boy in the boat," he asked. "Was he one of yours?"

"No," said Bandermain. "He knows as little about lens lights as you do, but his clumsy signal was enough to attract our attention. He thought that turning you over to us might earn him mercy. That choice was all that saved his life. You should have kept a closer eye on your shipmates, Silas. The captain in particular. We all knew you would leave Albion eventually, and my men were ready to find you when you did. I have had people watching you for a lot longer than you think."

"I'm sure you have," said Silas. "I, however, have had no one watching you. You are not that interesting. In fact my men and I haven't given you a thought for years. We have had far more important things to do."

Bandermain stood tall, failing to hide the anger simmering behind his eyes. "Important things like treachery. Murder. Betrayal?" he said. "My contacts tell me you have had dealings with witches. You have protected them, given up your good name to help them. What did they give you in return?"

"I have protected no one," said Silas.

"Yet on the Night of Souls, Silas Dane, grand champion of Albion's warden army, turned upon his own. The city square of your capital ran red with blood. Isn't that how your council's historians are describing it? There was a time when I would not have believed such stories. You betrayed your High Council, killed your own men, and murdered the woman you had sworn to protect, all to save one Skilled girl that you had been sent out to hunt. That is not the Silas Dane I remember. The enemy I knew valued honor above all else. He would not have turned against his oath without good reason. If his council had asked it of him, he would have slit that girl's throat and let her veins bleed dry. Instead, you chose a different path. It was fine work, I'll admit, but you left yourself open, Silas. It got my attention." Bandermain stepped back and nodded to the guard holding the news poster. "Show him."

The guard rolled up the first poster and unfurled a second, smaller page. Silas knew what it was right away. The paper was rough and yellow, cheaply made. Servants would have sat in their dozens making copy after copy and distributing them out across Albion for as many people as possible to see. It was a wanted poster. He knew it even before he saw the ink, but when the guard turned it his way, he was surprised by the face drawn upon it: a young girl with long black hair and feline eyes. Unmistakable.

"I see that you know her," said Bandermain. "She is the girl you were protecting. Isn't she?"

Silas said nothing.

"Miss Kate Winters. Daughter of Jonathan and Anna Winters. Last Skilled member of the Winters bloodline. This girl was your ally. You killed for her and committed treachery for her. Which leaves us with the question, Why did you leave her in Fume to die?"

Silas looked directly into Bandermain's eyes, letting the deadness of his soul connect with the fire in the heart of his enemy. "I did nothing for the girl," he said. "She is of no interest to me."

"Yet she interests so many others. You knew that when you left her behind. Did you warn her before you turned away and ran?" Bandermain placed his hands on either side of Silas's chair, close enough for him to smell the scent of meat upon his breath. "Did you tell her that she would be hunted down like an animal in the street? Because I would very much like to make that promise a reality. I know that she has something to do with you and your . . . condition. I know she is hidden somewhere within Fume, but she will be of no use to me dead."

"I do not care what you want," Silas said coolly. "The girl seems very much alive to me."

"Your little trick in the city square as good as painted a target upon her back," said Bandermain. "My men are closing in upon her as we speak. They will find her."

It was no surprise to Silas that Bandermain had risen so quickly through the ranks of the Blackwatch. He was by far the Continent's most adept and devious liar, but there, in that room, he was not adept enough. "You don't know where she is," said Silas.

"Then why don't you save us the time of a prolonged hunt and enlighten us? A lot less blood will be spilled that way. I do not want Blackwatch swords tainted by Albion blood any more than necessary."

"Why are you asking me?" said Silas. "'The echo of every word spoken leads to the ears of the watch.' Isn't that what your people believe? You have ears everywhere. Hear everything. Or are you saying they are wrong? Have things changed since you were put in charge? Your men should have the ears of the highest leaders in your land. Instead, they lurk around smugglers' holes, threatening slaves and getting themselves killed by enemies they really shouldn't have challenged in the first place."

Bandermain, his face red with anger, leaned closer, and Silas took his chance. He twisted his right arm free from the ropes, grabbed his enemy's throat, and squeezed it tight. Bandermain did not react, but the Blackwatch agents fell upon Silas at once, and even though his strength had not fully returned, it still took four men to free his hand and tie his arm back to the chair. Bandermain stood his ground as Silas was restrained again. A wide bruise blossomed across his neck, but he did not seem surprised. Instead, he gazed down at Silas with a sinister look of victory.

"Good," he said, rubbing his throat. "Very good. And here I was beginning to think you were going to disappoint me."

Silas's injured shoulder felt as if spikes were being driven deep into the muscle with every movement, but he smiled menacingly, daring Bandermain to come close again.

"We are finished here," said Bandermain. He turned his back and walked to the door with his men following after him.

"You won't find her," said Silas.

Bandermain stopped on the threshold and looked back. "We will," he said. "If the fools you have left her with do not kill her first."

The Blackwatch filed out, and Bandermain's sharp coughs echoed from the walls as they walked away. The lock clicked behind them, and Silas was left alone.

*** 

Kate did not bother trying to sleep. Once Baltin had gone she slid a small package out of a special pocket she had sewn inside her coat. There, tucked inside a neatly folded wrap of black cloth, was a book bound in old purple leather. If Baltin had known she'd had that book, he would have taken it away from her at once. Its pages were as thick as her fist, and her fingertips tingled with cold as she touched the silver lettering on its cover.

# WINTERCRAFT

*Wintercraft* was one of the rarest and most dangerous books in Albion. Within its pages was the life's work of a group of Walkers who had lived centuries before Kate was born (people who, just like her, could enter the veil), along with the many experiments they conducted into what they had found on the other side. The Skilled did not like the practice of Wintercraft. They saw the veil as something to be studied, not entered and experimented upon, and Kate had witnessed for herself the damage the book's knowledge could do. It had almost cost Kate her life upon the Night of Souls, and it had endangered the lives of hundreds of people who had seen it put to work within the city square, but that book was precious to her. She had to protect it.

Many of its pages had been written by Kate's own

ancestors, and her parents had died trying to protect it from the High Council when she was just five years old. That book held answers that the Skilled were unable to give her about what it meant to be a Walker, and even though parts of it were difficult to understand, it had become a comfort to her. Only Edgar knew that she still had it. With nothing else to do in that place, she wrapped herself in the bed blanket and began to read.

The hours snailed by, and Kate found herself dozing over the open pages, dreaming of shades, listening circles, and wardens. Her mind kept wandering back to the time she had spent with Silas, to the faces of the people he had killed and the souls of the people he had helped her set free, and the memory jolted her awake.

She scrambled out of her blankets, reached for the security of her candle, and lit a second one from a box on the room's curving shelf, just in case the first flame went out. The shades had gone, and she had already put out the other lights, not liking the shapes they cast up the walls. A scar on her left arm, a thin line from a cut made weeks before when Silas had stolen her blood, stung a little. "Silas," she whispered to herself.

Then the scratching sounds started.

*Krrrr . . . krrrr . . . krrrr . . .*

It sounded as if something were trying to claw its way into the room.

Suddenly two candles were nowhere near enough. Kate

dragged the candle box from the shelf and held handfuls of them against the open flames, dripping a trail of wax onto the floor beside her bed. She stood the candles up in the molten wax one by one, then held a candle in front of her as she tried to pinpoint the sound. It seemed to be coming from everywhere at once. She pressed her hand against the door, and tiny vibrations thrummed against her fingers. Someone was outside, trying to scrape his way in.

The scratching stopped, and she crouched in front of the door and peered through the middle keyhole. She heard something snap and something metallic ring out against the lock and skid off across the cavern floor. Someone swore under his breath, and Kate pulled back as a metal wire stabbed through the keyhole dangerously close to her eye. "Who's there?" she asked, but no one answered. She moved to the upper lock, hoping to get a look at her visitor's face, but all she could see was a mess of black hair bent forward as its owner concentrated on his work.

Kate tugged her sleeve down over her right hand and waited by the middle lock for her moment to strike. When the wire poked through again, she snatched at the hooked end and pulled hard. The wire threaded straight through the door, and when Kate looked through the keyhole, Edgar's eye was looking back.

"What are you doing?" demanded Edgar.

"What are *you* doing?"

"Getting you out of there."

"It sounds like you're trying to wake up the whole cavern," said Kate. "Just leave me alone. I'm fine where I am."

"Leave you alone? In there? Of course. Why didn't I think of that? I'm sure you're having a great time sitting in the dark."

"I was asleep." She lied to him. "Go away. Before someone sees you."

"Give back my wire."

"No."

"Kate, come on. I'm trying to help."

Kate fell quiet.

"I've got it all planned," said Edgar. "We can get out of here. Find our way to the surface. I've even got supplies. Food, water . . . we'll be fine for a few days at least."

"No."

"Just think about this for a second!"

"I have thought about it," said Kate. "Baltin was right. I don't trust myself. Weird things keep happening around me, and I don't want you to be caught up in it again. Maybe I am better off in here. Go find your brother. Take him up to the surface if you want to. I'm staying here."

"No, you're not," said Edgar, walking away a few steps before coming back. "You think I need lockpicks to get you out? Well, I don't. Baltin has the keys. Maybe I'll just borrow them for a while."

"You can't do that. You'll get caught."

"And what? End up in there with you? It sounds like it's all honey and roses from what you're saying. Why should I be bothered about that? I'm getting that key, and then I'm coming right back here, whether you want to be let out or not."

"Edgar, don't. Edgar!"

Edgar bolted across the cavern. The lights were still dimmed, and the only people about were the watchmen posted at the cavern's two ways out. He crept along the street, glanced over at the main door, and saw a guard sitting with his back to the wall, eating sandwiches and reading news posters smuggled down from the City Above. Just one minute and he could be in and out of Baltin's house, keys in hand. No one would be any the wiser until it was too late. He and Kate would be long gone. He thought about his brother, Tom. Tom had fitted in well with the Skilled. He had even shown some small ability to see into the veil. They were pleased with him, and he liked living there. Tom might miss Edgar for a while, but he was in the safest place he could be. Kate, however, was not.

Edgar made his decision. He crossed the main street, found one of Baltin's windows unlocked, and slithered his way in.

# 5

# CROSSED
# DAGGERS

Kate paced around her room, waiting for Edgar to return.

At last a key scratched in the first door lock. One by one the locks turned and Kate stood in front of the door with her arms folded as it pulled back. But the person who opened the door was not Edgar. It was Baltin, wearing red pajamas and a dressing gown and holding on to the door frame for support. He looked tired, his face an odd sickly green.

"Baltin?"

Edgar was there, holding a lantern a few steps away, and he shrugged his shoulders apologetically.

"Miss Winters." Baltin bowed his head slightly and strode into the room. The bed sagged as he sat down upon it. "Close the door," he ordered as Edgar followed him inside. "Close it, boy!"

The door could not be locked from the inside, so Edgar stood with his back pressed against it instead. Baltin shifted his weight on the edge of the bed and sat there with his head in his hands.

"I found him tied up in his house," said Edgar. "He won't say who did it. He told me to bring him straight here. He didn't even call the guards."

"Because the *guards* will be of no use to us," snapped Baltin. "An enemy is loose in this cavern, and I think Kate knows who it is."

Kate thought at once of Silas, but that was impossible. There was no way he would risk coming back to Fume with the wardens out looking for him.

"The veil has pulled away from us," said Baltin. "I can't see into it anymore. Can you?"

Kate could sense the veil all around her, waiting just beyond the reach of her ordinary senses. Nothing had changed so far as she could tell, but if Baltin thought there was something wrong, it was best for her to play along. She shook her head.

"This is worse than I thought," said Baltin. "You have to talk to him, Kate. You have to stop him. Whatever he's doing. He has to stop."

"Who?"

"Silas Dane!"

"Silas wouldn't do this," said Kate.

"He's done a lot worse," said Edgar.

"Silas would have killed Baltin, not wasted time tying him up. It can't be him."

"No one else knows how to find this cavern. He's the only one who . . ." Baltin's voice trailed off, and he looked anxiously around the shadowed room. "He's in here, isn't he?"

"You have the only key to that door," said Kate. "There's no one else in here."

"You're lying. You're protecting him! Why is he here? What does he want?"

Kate grabbed a candle and circled the room once, lighting up every space the flame could reach. "See?" she said. "No one's here."

"Then he is still outside. You called him here. I have to warn people. Get out of my way!" Baltin pushed Edgar aside to peer through the top keyhole. "I'm too late," he whispered.

Kate stepped forward and looked for herself. From the lowest keyhole she could see most of the cavern, right down to the illuminated archway of the meeting hall. There was no one there. Everything was quiet. But when she looked out the one Baltin had used, it was blocked and black.

"He's right outside," whispered Baltin.

"No one is there," said Kate. "There's something stuck on the door, that's all." Kate did not stop to think about what that something might be. She opened the door, ignoring Baltin's protests, and peered around it. A large piece of black-edged paper had been pinned over the lock, and once she had seen it, she noticed at least a dozen others spread around the cavern. Most were scattered loose on the floor, but a handful had been pinned to doors. She pulled the paper down as Edgar joined her outside.

"What does it say?" he asked.

Kate looked at the bloodred letters scrawled thickly on the page.

*You have our demands.*
*Deliver what we require.*

There was a mark printed at the top of the page: a pair of crossed daggers with two letters underneath—*BW*.

"It has to be the wardens," said Kate. "What does *BW* mean?"

But Edgar was already gone. He was back inside the lockhouse, stopping Baltin from leaving the room. "The person who attacked you," he said, "did he say anything else?"

"Move aside, boy."

"Did he give any names? Anything?"

"The veil has drawn back," said Baltin, looking at Edgar as if he were losing his mind. "Silas Dane is responsible for this, and he will be stopped. Nothing else matters now."

"No. This has nothing to do with Silas," said Edgar. He stabbed a finger into the symbol on the poster. "Haven't you heard of the Blackwatch?"

"I don't have time to listen to this," said Baltin. "We all know what is going on here."

"You have to listen! When I worked for the High Council,

people would find posters like these outside the council chambers every few months. The Blackwatch are part of the Continental army. The person you saw tonight was probably a runner. The Blackwatch send them to Albion now and again to remind the High Council that they can send assassins to their doors at any time and to let them know that the Continent is not just going to go away. Sometimes they bring demands; other times they just spread their posters and go. The wardens used to do a good job of covering it up whenever there was a runner in town, but I've never heard of one being sent into the City Below before."

Baltin pointed to the poster in Kate's hands. "So the man who left this—"

"Was just the messenger," said Edgar. "You don't want to be on the wrong side of these people. If you think the wardens are bad, trust me, the Blackwatch are worse."

"But how did the runner get in here?" asked Kate.

"Probably broke his way in. His orders will be to spread the same message all around the City Below," said Edgar. "I'll bet he doesn't even know that the Skilled live in this cavern. If he did, I don't think he would have just upped and left so easily."

Baltin pushed past Edgar and snatched the poster from Kate.

"That makes no sense!" he said. "If these Blackwatch are looking for something, why leave this? Why not just sneak in and take whatever they want? Or just let the runner do it?"

"Because they're looking for something in particular and they don't know where it is," said Edgar. "They want to scare people so they will find what they want for them and flush it out into the open. Fume is much larger than most Continental cities. It would take forever to find something here. Add the City Below to that, and you have months of searching on your hands. The Blackwatch want to find something quickly. They won't want to risk the wardens' finding them before they have it."

"Then what do they want?" asked Baltin. "They didn't make any demands. They didn't ask me for anything!"

Edgar snatched another loose poster up off the cavern floor and pushed it into Baltin's hands. It was written in the same red ink as the first.

*Deliver Kate Winters and be spared.*

"It's you, Kate," said Edgar, turning to her. "They're coming for you."

Kate should have been surprised or at least a little worried. Instead, she just shrugged. "Them and everyone else," she said.

Baltin read the poster over and over again. "That's settled then."

"What is?" asked Edgar.

"There have been arguments about how best to deal with Kate's unique position among us," said Baltin. "This just proves that she is even more of a threat than we first thought. Come inside, both of you."

Edgar stepped forward, but Kate held him back.

"No," she said. "We're not going in there with you. If the Blackwatch are looking for me, I'm not going to just sit in that room and wait for them to figure out where I am."

"What I have to say cannot be heard by just anyone," said Baltin. "If more people knew what I know, they would not be so friendly toward you here."

"Friendly? Every one of them hates me!"

"They do not know everything," said Baltin. "Come inside."

"No." Kate backed away, and Baltin's face grew serious, any pretense of friendship fading at once. Kate felt the chill of the veil descending again, and ghostly shapes moved behind Baltin. She tried to ignore them, but as her mind reacted to danger, the veil stalked across her senses. Her link with Silas strengthened briefly until she could see through his eyes, layering his view of the world like a phantom over her own. She saw his dark cellar prison, felt the misaligned bones shifting in his injured body, and sensed tiny snatches of his thoughts as he made plans to escape.

Baltin was talking, but Kate was concentrating too hard upon what she could see to pay him any attention. Silas's eyes were focused upon the fingers of his right hand. The tendons rippled beneath his skin, but something about them was not right. Something snapped inside his hand. Pain lanced up through Kate's arm, and she snatched her own hand away from the wall as the link dissipated.

"Your uncle knew the dangers that would come by bringing you here," continued Baltin. "He knew what had to be done, and I thought you were sensible enough to see it, too."

Kate's arm felt numb. She clenched her right hand into a fist, but the pain there was just a memory. It was over for her, but not for Silas.

"I want to understand what's going on as much as anyone," she said. "I want to help."

"You gave up your right to a free life the moment you started dabbling in things that were none of your concern," said Baltin. "You allied yourself with Silas Dane and you still expected to find friendship among us? The only reason you were not thrown out of this cavern the first night you arrived was because of threats like *this*." Baltin crumpled the Blackwatch poster in his fist. "You are a threat to everything we have tried to protect for hundreds of years. The veil responds more to you than it does to any of us, and it is clear we are not the only ones who have recognized it. This is not just about you anymore. Do you know what could happen if the Continental leaders got their hands on you? I would give you to the High Council myself before I would live to see that day."

"Hold on," said Edgar. "That's a bit harsh, isn't it?"

"If we had recognized Kate's ability when she was

younger, things might have been different. As it is, her mind has been opened to the veil without proper training or care. With ancestry like hers that could be disastrous. When we thought Kate had not inherited her parents' Skill, we were relieved. The Winters family's abilities are legendary. Because they are Walkers, their spirits can enter the veil directly, but their link can become so strong that they do not just step into it, they can *attract* it. If their spirit is powerful enough, the veil can become unstable around them, letting it bleed freely into the living world. When that happens, just being close to them can send living souls into death."

"You think Kate can kill people just by standing next to them?"

"Given the right conditions, yes," said Baltin. "It has happened before. The Skilled have tried to prevent the Winters blood from being passed on for generations. Now Kate is the only Skilled Winters left. Exposing her mind to the veil unprotected was like pouring oil on a flame. Silas Dane ignited something inside Kate that will never stop burning. If she is not controlled, she could well be the death of us all." Baltin turned to Kate. "Why do you think Artemis never told you the truth about your family? He knew this could happen. Silas Dane ruined you, Kate. He made you dangerous and uncontrollable, just like him. It amazes me that you do not see that."

"I know what I can see," said Edgar, trying his best not to look as unnerved as he felt. "You're scared."

"Of course I'm scared. I'm scared for all of us!" said Baltin. "You may not have seen what Kate really is, but I am not a fool. I know the signs: the change in her eyes, the way the veil shifts when she is nearby. I know what she is. Kate's kind can be dangerous as much as for what they don't know as for what they do. All it takes is one mistake, and people will die, just like Mina."

"Mina was stabbed," said Edgar. "The veil had nothing to do with it."

"If Kate were allowed to explore her abilities and develop them, she would eventually *use* them," said Baltin. "That must not happen. If she is kept in the dark, there is at least a chance that the veil will draw back from her permanently. Her link with it may simply . . . wear off."

"Wear off?" said Kate. "That is what you're all hoping for?"

"If it doesn't, people like these Blackwatch will keep hunting you," said Baltin. "They will force you to influence the veil in their way, and that will put us all in danger. You could be a brutal weapon. We cannot let that happen."

"So, I'm meant to stay down here in that room until I'm 'cured.' That's what you're saying?"

"I wish it were," said Baltin. "This attack changes things. We do not have time to wait anymore."

Baltin moved before Kate realized what was happening. He ducked behind her and pressed a short blade up against her throat.

"What are you doing?" demanded Edgar.

"Making sure I have your attention. I never wanted this situation to come to this, but I have a responsibility. I have to do what's right. Now, step inside."

Edgar did not move. Baltin's hand was shaking, the blade brushing against Kate's skin. He did not look like the kind of man who had hurt someone before, but he was nervous enough to make a mistake and cut her without meaning to if things got out of hand.

"All right," said Edgar. "Let her go."

"Get inside!"

Edgar raised his hands and stepped inside the room. "What are you going to do?" he asked.

"What someone should have done weeks ago." Baltin reached into Kate's coat and pulled *Wintercraft* from her hidden pocket. The silver studs on the book's dark purple cover glinted in the dim cavern light. Kate wanted to snatch it back from him, but her instinct for survival told her to wait.

"You did well, hiding this from me," said Baltin. "No one knew you had it. Even the spirits kept your secret, but I do not need spirits to tell me what an observant man can see with his own eyes. These secrets are not yours to keep."

"Does Artemis know what you're doing?" asked Edgar, blocking the doorway.

"Move!"

"He doesn't, does he?"

"I said move!" Baltin pointed the dagger at Edgar in anger, and Kate got away from him as soon as the weapon left her skin.

Baltin faltered, not knowing what to do or whom to threaten next. Edgar grabbed his opportunity, threw himself at Baltin, and tackled him to the floor. He pinned him on his side and forced him to stay still as Kate prized the dagger from one hand and *Wintercraft* from the other.

"*Guar—!*" Baltin tried to shout for help, but the struggle had stirred dirt up from the floor, and he choked upon it, his shout becoming a hacking cough.

"This book is mine," said Kate. "Don't touch it again."

Baltin coughed harder, his cheeks flushing deep red.

"Is he all right?"

"He's fine," said Edgar. "Help me lock him in."

"Wait!" Baltin wheezed as they each pulled an arm and dragged him along. "Think about what you're doing!"

"I've thought about it," said Edgar, lifting a bunch of keys from the pocket of Baltin's dressing gown. "You attacked us. We defended ourselves. Sounds fair enough to me."

"You don't understand. Kate can't leave this cavern, especially not with that book. She can't!"

Edgar closed the door, sealing Baltin inside.

"You don't understand!" Baltin's fist hammered on the other side of the door, and Edgar left the key hanging in the middle lock.

Kate looked in through the upper keyhole. "You turned Artemis against me," she said. "What did you say to him?"

Baltin's eye appeared at the lock. "I told him the truth," he said. "He would not believe it until we showed him what we knew. Artemis is a logical man. He could not deny what he had seen with his own eyes."

"What did you show him?" asked Kate.

"We showed him the veil," said Baltin. "We opened his eyes . . . gave him proof! He knows that you are not a simple girl any longer. He knows how dangerous you will become."

"Why didn't you show me this?"

"Because the veil would never show you what we can see," said Baltin. "You cannot witness your own future, Kate. We can."

"Don't listen to him," said Edgar. "We can go, right now, before anyone realizes he is gone."

"What did you see?" asked Kate.

"We gave you a chance," said Baltin. "If you run now, we will have no choice but to hunt you, for your own safety and to protect the future of Albion."

"You were going to kill me."

"I was willing to do what must be done!"

"I don't know what you saw in my future, but I know I won't be spending it here, however long it lasts," said Kate. "Good-bye, Baltin. Tell Artemis he'll never have to worry about 'protecting' me again."

"Wait!" Baltin shouted as Kate turned away from the lockhouse. "Guards!"

Kate kept her eyes straight ahead, walking along a street she had once thought safe, not wanting Edgar to see the tears on her face. "There's no place for me here," she said. "They can keep the veil and Artemis to themselves. I don't want anything to do with them anymore."

Kate could hear the dull thuds of Baltin's fists hammering on the inside of the lockhouse door as she and Edgar walked away. It wouldn't be long before one of the guards heard him, and when they found him locked inside with their only prisoner missing, there would be no convincing them that she was not a threat. Any safety that had existed in that place was gone now.

"Are you serious about leaving Artemis behind?" asked Edgar, following her along a path between two houses and emerging in a small rock garden on the other side.

"He'll turn me over to them the moment he sees me," said Kate. "And you can't come either. What about Tom?"

"He likes it here," said Edgar. "He'll be safe enough. And I'm not letting you go out there alone."

Kate did not say anything. No words would be enough to say how grateful she was to have at least one person left whom she could trust. Edgar hoisted his bag onto his shoulder, and Kate hurried along with her head down as the guards' warning bell sounded behind them.

"They've found him," said Edgar. "Let's go."

# ← 6 →

# ALLEGIANCE

With the Blackwatch gone Silas tried to free himself from his chair, but his body had other ideas. Going for Bandermain's throat had hurt him more than he wanted to admit. His muscles screamed out whenever he tried to move them, and his broken bones grated together, forcing him to stay still. He should have been able to loosen his ropes and break his way out of that place easily. Instead, he was stuck to that chair like an animal caught in a trap.

The room he was sitting in was an ordinary cellar. The floor was thick with decades' worth of coal dust and dirt, but there were clear spaces around the edge of the floor where boxes or old pieces of furniture had been sitting until recently. Bandermain's men must have emptied it in a hurry, and it was clearly not meant for holding someone securely.

For years the worst fate for any soldier of the Albion army was to find himself in the hands of the Blackwatch. He had heard stories about the mistreatment of prisoners under Blackwatch guard during past campaigns into Continental territory and had known dozens of men who had been taken by its agents. Only two of them had ever found their way back, carrying gruesome stories that helped make the Blackwatch legendary among those who were sent out to face it.

Silas was not worried for himself—the Blackwatch was no threat to him—but he was concerned by what it planned on doing with Kate. If the Continental leaders finally got their hands on a powerful member of the Skilled, they could turn the tide of the war spectacularly against Albion. They knew Kate's name. They wanted mastery of the veil, and now they knew exactly whom to hunt to get it. What greater prize could Bandermain present to his masters than a girl who was able to demonstrate the power of the veil. The Blackwatch would not stop until it had what it had set out to collect. Trouble was heading into the heart of Albion, and Kate was going to be right in the middle of it.

Silas tried to reach out for the veil, but again he felt nothing. Kate was a weapon just waiting to be found, and he could not do anything to help Albion so long as he was tied up in someone's worthless cellar.

Blackwatch voices filtered down through the thin floor of the room above. A door slammed shut, and Silas could hear harsh coughs and a conversation unfolding between the floorboards overhead. Bandermain and his men were close by. He stayed still and listened.

"Send in more men," said Bandermain. "Call them back from border patrols. Use the ship, and tell them not to return until they have the girl in custody. We are close enough to the attack to risk a few lives. Concentrate our efforts upon the capital, but do not neglect the northern cities. Send men everywhere we have the manpower to reach, and make sure all agents are aware of their responsibilities well ahead of time."

"They have already been informed," said another voice.

"Have they found their way into Fume's understreets?"

"All entrances to the City Below are being monitored, sir. Runners have been sent down into the tunnels, but our agents are holding back until the posters are distributed, as ordered. If our intelligence is correct, we should have control of the main gathering points by dusk tomorrow."

"'Should' is not good enough," said Bandermain. "Those people live underground like ants. They will put up no significant resistance. I want to know the moment we have those gathering points."

"Yes, sir. There are birds in flight as we speak. We are expecting fresh reports very soon."

"Good work," said Bandermain. "Keep me informed."

The situation was worse than Silas had believed. The Blackwatch was not just interested in acquiring Kate. Her capture was simply the first stage of a much larger plan, an invasion. He had to act. If he could do nothing else, he could at least try to slow them down.

"You . . . outside," he said loudly.

The cellar door opened, and two Blackwatch officers who had been standing guard walked in.

"Bring Bandermain in here," he said. "Tell him I am ready to talk."

Bandermain took his time answering the summons, and when he finally returned, he came alone. "I am here," he said. "So talk."

"How does it feel," asked Silas, "to be the one who captured me? Think of the glory that will be yours when you present me to your leaders."

A flicker of pride crossed Bandermain's face. There it was, thought Silas. There was the adversary he knew so well.

"You and I both know that our leaders are more concerned with outdoing one another than bringing an end to this war," said Bandermain. "I have no interest in earning the praise of fools any longer. There are greater battles to fight, and you are far more valuable to me than you could ever be to them. They would parade you through our towns in an iron cage and invite children to spit at you through the bars. You would be the freak of Albion, captured and weak. I have more respect for you than that."

"I can see that," said Silas. "Not many people have enough respect to crush me with a bridge. Perhaps I will return that 'respect' to you one day."

Bandermain smiled. "Under normal circumstances, I doubt even a bridge would have been enough to stop you," he said. "I have learned that you are unusually weakened here. The veil does not favor my country as powerfully as it does your own. While you are here, you are disconnected from it, and whatever abilities you have acquired clearly rely upon the veil for their strength. You have left your home at a dangerous time, Silas. Albion's connection to the veil is not what it once was. The veil is falling. The link your country has enjoyed for so long is decaying as we speak. You may not be able to hear your little spirit voices here, on my land, but imagine what will happen when the whole of Albion is plunged into the half-life. Your people will no longer be able to tell the difference between the living and the dead. Spirits will walk the land for every living soul to see. There will be chaos. Your people will fall into madness and turn on one another. Albion will die, and the Blackwatch will be there watching, while your country's arrogance brings about its destruction."

"You know nothing about the half-life," said Silas.

"You would be surprised," said Bandermain. "It is interesting what you learn when you have the right friends. If you have knowledge that can be of use to me, I suggest you share it with me now, while my patience lasts."

Silas considered his options. Bandermain had always been skeptical of the veil. He had called those who believed in it fools and witches, but now he was talking about the veil's falling as some kind of inevitable event, rather than as an irrational fear or a fantasy. Silas had to know more. He had to earn Bandermain's trust, and to do that, he had to give him what he wanted. He had to make a sacrifice. "I know where Kate Winters is," he said.

"Where?"

"Somewhere your men will not find her. At least not on their own. If you want her, you will tell me exactly what is going on here. No lies." Silas sat back in his chair, sending a stab of pain needling along his spine. "Now, are we going to talk?"

"You are in no position to make demands."

"I think I am in an excellent position," said Silas. "I have information you need. Tell me why you want her, and she is yours."

Silas's face was unreadable, and as his demeanor changed so did the atmosphere in the room. He did not need the veil to affect the environment around him. Threat clung to his words and spread around the room like smoke, making it feel small and airless, as cold as a place cut deep underground. Bandermain reacted to the change at once. His eyes narrowed briefly. Fear, Silas knew, was a powerful weapon. "I did not need the veil to incapacitate your men," he said. "I did not need it to lead them across Grale on a chase through the night, and I will not need it to put an end to your life when the time comes."

"You cannot even stand on your own," said Bandermain.

"And even if you could, killing me would not help the girl."

"I do not doubt that," said Silas. "You are not that important, Celador. Your men are sworn to obey the orders of the Continental leaders, but I doubt even they would waste so many of you scouting along the coast just in case one enemy were to swim ashore. You have already admitted that your goals are no longer the same as theirs, and you are not known for your ability to think for yourself. You are the sword, not the hand that wields it. You are a man who takes orders, which means that someone else sent you here. Who was it?"

"Where is the girl?" demanded Bandermain.

"I think I am not the only traitor in this room," said Silas. "Your men will see it too before long."

"My men know exactly why we are here," said Bandermain. "They are loyal men. Loyal to me and to our country. We know what we must do, even if our leaders do not."

"Kidnapping a young girl," said Silas. "Since when have the Blackwatch begun hunting the innocent?"

"She is not innocent. The Skilled are no more than a valuable resource to be found and exploited. They are secretive and underhanded, and she is the only one left alive who has dared show her face in public long enough to let her identity become known. She is wanted by your High Council, yet she has no interest in helping them. She is affiliated to no one, and that makes her useful."

"Useful to whom exactly?" asked Silas.

Bandermain clenched his fists, and when he opened them again, Silas caught a glimpse of his open palms. The left hand had a deep cut sliced across it, one that could only have been made by the slow cut of a sharp blade. The skin was healing slowly and someone had stitched it together neatly with thin black thread.

"What happened to your hand?"

"War is bloody. Or have you hidden away from it for so long you have forgotten?"

"That is not a war wound." Silas opened his own hand, revealing an old white scar that matched Bandermain's cut exactly. "Who gave you that cut? Who are you working for, Celador?"

"Someone who hates Albion as much as I do," said Bandermain. "Someone who has a deep interest in you and your life, as pitiful as it has become. You may enjoy living in the gutter like vermin while your country falls apart, but I still have a hand in influencing the direction of this war. Albion will die much sooner than you think, and my men and I shall be the ones to strike the final blow. I serve my country in my own way. *That* is honor. Perhaps you will recognize that before the end."

Bandermain walked to the door and faltered in the doorway. One of his knees gave way, and an officer stepped forward to support him; but he leaned against the door frame and waved him away.

"What's wrong with you?" asked Silas as a bone in his own neck snapped back into place. "Old wounds giving you trouble?"

Bandermain ignored him and gave an order to his men. "Have the carriage prepared," he said. "We are leaving now."

"Yes, sir."

"I have been told that your injuries are likely to heal within a matter of hours," he said, turning to Silas. "You will tell me what I need to know long before then."

"You still have not told me why you want the girl," said Silas. "It is a simple enough question."

"You will find out once we have her," said Bandermain. "In the meantime, there is someone who is very interested in meeting you. Where we are going, you will be made to talk. You are going to help us win this battle, Silas. Your time is over. Albion will fall, and you will watch it burn. You can be sure of that."

Bandermain left the room, and the moment the lock clicked into place Silas fought against his bonds and studied his surroundings again, determined to find a way out. Three of the walls were plain slabs of solid brick, but the fourth had a patch halfway between the floor and ceiling that was partly boarded with wooden slats. Now that the sun was rising higher he could see tiny flecks of light seeping from the other side, cutting through the dark. He cursed out loud as his broken ankle realigned with a sickening crack. He tested it carefully.

The bone was still knitting together, but it was strong enough to stand on. One of his arms was still useless. His right leg was heavily bruised, and the muscles were tender, not nearly ready to mount an escape. One arm and one leg would have to be enough to get him over to those boards.

Silas twisted his right wrist out of its ropes and untied his useless left arm, then delicately slid it between the buttons of his coat to keep it still. He wrenched loose the ropes around his ankles and pushed himself up, forcing his crushed thigh muscles to work. There were times in his life when he had cursed the veil and hated it for healing his body and prolonging his life; now it was all but gone he found himself willing it to return. The last thing he wanted was for his knees to give way and to have Bandermain find him crawling around on the floor.

Silas turned the chair and used its back to help him limp over to the boards. Every step was an effort, but he could smell fresh air on the other side. He pulled one of the boards away and looked into a narrow space that slanted toward strips of sunlight caught behind what looked like a small wooden hatch. He pulled more boards from their nails until the entire space was exposed, and he looked up along an old diagonal coal shaft.

The building was silent. There was no sign of any Blackwatch agents close by, but there was no way he could climb that shaft with a damaged shoulder. At least that was something he could fix for himself. He slid his arm gently from its support, gritted his teeth, and slammed his shoulder hard into the wall. The bone jolted back into its socket with a sickening thud, his shoulder muscles exploded, and he growled with pain, grinding his fist into the stones as he waited for it to subside.

The coal shaft was cluttered with dead leaves and litter that had blown through cracks in its upper hatch over many years. As soon as he was able, Silas squeezed into the shaft, then slid along on his side and pushed with his good leg until he was clear of the cellar. The walls and floor were filthy, but he had enough of a grip to make it all the way to the top, only to find that the wooden hatch was locked and its catch rusted shut. He held on to the wall, twisted himself around, and, raising his good knee, aimed straight for the lock. One kick and the door shattered outward, exploding into the cold light of midmorning. No guards came running, so Silas dragged himself out, legs first, into the middle of a quiet alleyway. His crow was already waiting for him, looking down from the windowsill of a building close by.

"Making yourself useful, I see," said Silas.

The crow flew down, but he batted it away.

"Keep watch," he said. "Stay high. Do not let anybody see you."

The crow obeyed and soared up high above the rooftops. With the way clear, Silas held on to the cracks in the walls, using them to support himself as he made his way slowly down the alley. Every step was a torture, but he kept going.

He needed somewhere to rest and heal. Four streets away he found it.

The Blackwatch house he'd escaped from had been built in a quiet part of Grale, and Silas had found it easy enough to stay out of sight whenever someone threatened to walk his way. The crow stood out against the gray clouds, circling high above a fenced-in patch of frozen grass. Iron gates hung ajar within the tall black fence, and beyond the gates Silas saw the pale gray shapes of headstones set into the ground. He pushed through into the silence of a large cemetery, left the overgrown path, and headed straight across the graves, toward a circle of old crypts gathered at a central point where four paths met.

None of the crypts was locked, because no one on the Continent would dare desecrate the resting places of the dead; but the door he chose was stiff, and the hinges screeched as he pushed it aside to reveal a small flight of steps leading down into an airless space thick with the smell of forgotten years. Silas summoned his crow from the sky with a low whistle, scraped the door shut behind them, and followed the steps into the dark.

Sunlight streamed through cracks in the forgotten roof, and old stone coffins with heavy lids were lined up along the walls of the small cavern below. Spiders clung to every corner in webs that were old and thick, and the walls ran so far back into the earth that he could not see their end in the dim light. The crypt was quiet and peaceful. He sat on the cold stone floor, and his crow hopped down beside him. Even without the veil he could feel the eerie stillness of the place, and it reminded him of home. "Just a few hours," he said, cracking his damaged elbow joint and pulling his sleeve up to inspect a vicious bruise that was creeping all the way along his arm. He propped himself against one of the coffin platforms and sat facing the door, listening for any sign of the Blackwatch outside.

Slowly the day darkened into a shivering evening. His injuries and his escape had drained him of what little energy he had left, and by the time the moon began to rise, Silas had fallen asleep, safe in the company of the dead.

# 7

# ASHES &
# STONES

Kate and Edgar headed for the cavern's outer wall and
followed it until they spotted a narrow door cut into the stone.
The cavern's only clock chimed out the quarter hour above the
meeting hall; when it fell quiet, Baltin's angry shouts echoed
from the walls. People would start waking up soon, and Kate
and Edgar did not want to be there when they did.

The cavern's rear door was rarely guarded. It led into an
old section of the City Below that the Skilled did not use often,
but it was always kept bolted and locked.

"My lockpick!" said Edgar, holding his hand out.
"Quick!"

"You mean this tatty bit of wire?" Kate pulled the wire
she had taken from the lockhouse door out of her pocket and
passed it to him. "Can you open it with that?"

"Just stand back and watch a master at work."

Edgar dug the wire into the keyhole as Kate slid open the

bolts. The mechanism inside was old and stiff; but the lock soon clicked, and Edgar swung the door open with a grin of pride. "It's a lot easier when someone isn't dragging at it from the other side," he said.

Lanterns emerged from the houses behind them. More shouts went up, and Baltin's voice carried above the rest. "Sound the alarm!" he ordered. "Find her!"

Kate spotted Baltin, still in his dressing gown, striding down the middle of the street, with two of his men behind him.

"Kate!" said Edgar, already squeezing himself and his backpack into the tunnel. A row of dead lanterns was hooked on the wall. He lifted one down and opened the glass case. "Are you coming?"

Kate followed him into the blackness of the tunnel, but a handful of people were already heading their way. Kate closed the cavern door, leaving Edgar struggling to light matches in the dark. He held the lantern under his arm until at last one of them sparked and flared and he managed to light the stubby candle inside, flooding the space with firelight.

"Good-bye, Artemis," Kate whispered to the door. She didn't want to leave her uncle behind. She didn't want to believe that he would choose the word of strangers over her own, but she had no choice. She had to survive. She had to go. She turned her back upon the door and followed Edgar's lantern light into the dark.

Kate did not like the tunnels that made up the labyrinth

that was the City Below. The lantern cast shifting shadows upon the walls, and she tried to ignore the gentle whispers that traveled along the paths. If there were shades down there, they would be attracted to her presence. Without the protection of the Skilleds' cavern, her spirit would shine like a beacon to the dead wandering those passageways, and there was no way she could block them all out.

Most of the tunnels were narrow and grim, with only a rare light to break the suffocating stillness. Some were recently made, a hundred years ago or less; but most were ancient, and a few of them had become unstable, their ceilings held up by wooden scaffolds that she and Edgar had to duck under as they went.

"So far, so good," said Edgar, choosing a direction with confidence whenever they came to a junction in the path, until they reached a point where five tunnels radiated out like a star. There he hesitated. "I think . . . it's this way," he said.

"I thought you knew your way around," said Kate.

"I used to," said Edgar. "The upper tunnels at least, but things have changed a bit since I was last down here. It's harder to know which way to go."

"What about that one?" Kate pointed to a tunnel that was narrower than the rest. There were no old buildings sunk back into its walls to suggest it had once been used as a street. The mouth of the tunnel was held up by a wooden door frame, and the floor was scattered with crunchy grit and earth, as if it had just been opened up recently.

Something scratched behind them, and Edgar spun, holding the lantern high. "What was that?"

"Keep the light low," said Kate, pulling his arm down.

Someone was moving behind them. A soft light flickered into sight, illuminating a corner they had just taken.

"They're right behind us," whispered Edgar.

Kate crept into the tunnel and felt her way along the walls. Edgar was not far behind her, and his light cast her long shadow across the ground, making it difficult to see very far. After four weeks underground Kate's eyes had been given plenty of time to get used to the dark, and she did not need to see those walls to know that there was something unusual about them. Those stones had not always been bare. There were holes drilled into them at regular intervals, holes that had once held something. Lantern hooks maybe?

"I don't like this," whispered Edgar. "This path doesn't lead up to the surface. Let's go back."

Kate could sense the veil nearby, like a mist of energy crackling in the air. She could feel the presence of shades within that tunnel, lots of them, all reaching out to her, trying to get her attention. Their whispers spoke quietly in the walls, willing her along. She concentrated on where she was putting her feet. No matter where that tunnel led, anything had to be better than being back in the lockhouse.

"We're heading down, not up," said Edgar.

"I know."

"Then shouldn't we go back? Find another way?"

Kate's eyes fogged over, just for a second, and instead of blackness, the tunnel suddenly appeared washed in a dull gray light. The stones glowed gently, as if they were lit from deep inside. She stopped walking. "There's something down here," she said.

"Is it the Skilled? Are they ahead of us?"

Edgar looked back the way they had come. There was no sign of anyone there, and when Kate started walking without him, he hurried to catch up. The movement of their bodies stirred up the stagnant air, raising thick breezes of dust from the floor.

Kate's eyes fogged over again, and this time the feeling would not lift. The link between the veil and the living world was stronger there than in other places she had been, as if something were down there, attracting it. The tunnel widened into more of a corridor the farther they went, and she found thin doors set into the sides, most of them cracked and hanging awkwardly from broken hinges.

Edgar shone the light into the space left beside one of them. "Someone has cleared these rooms out," he said. "There's nothing in there. We could hide inside one of them."

"No," said Kate. "We have to keep going."

They kept walking, following the path to the very end, where it stopped at a dark red door. The handle had been smashed from its fixings, and the door swung open easily against her hand. The two of them stepped inside, and the lantern light shone around an oval room with alcoves sunk into the walls at shoulder height, each one holding a small wooden box no bigger than the book Kate had hidden in her coat.

"Funeral boxes," she said, "filled with ashes of the dead."

Rising dust swirled unnaturally around Kate's feet, and a rush of cold clutched at Edgar's neck.

"Well, that isn't creepy at all," he said.

The room was filled with long tables, each one covered in sackcloths that hid whatever was upon them from view. It looked as if someone were storing things in there. The cloths covered a collection of small shapes that were roughly the same size, but neither Kate nor Edgar wanted to look at what lay beneath them.

"We're safe in here for now," said Kate.

"I'm not spending more than five seconds in this place," said Edgar. "Baltin will track us if we stay still." He unclipped the lid of one of the boxes and curled his nose at the ashes he found inside. "The boxes are full all right, but there's no inscription on the front of any of them. It should at least say who the ashes belong to." He shut the box carefully and did not notice the air shifting beside him as a restless soul filtered through the wall, watching him with interest through eyes that burned like blue fire. Its drifting form sank to the floor and rose behind him, making him look back over his shoulder, but he saw nothing but dust caught in the disturbed air. "Does it feel strange in here to you?"

Kate walked deeper into the room while Edgar looked for some way to block the door. Whatever the things beneath the cloths were, she did not like the feeling she had when she walked past them. It was a pulling sensation, as if each one of them were connected to her by string. Every one of the cloths in that room was fresh and clean. They had not been there for very long. Then she spotted something up ahead. A collection of tools had been abandoned against a narrow door in the wall. The door was broken, and the space beyond it filled with old spiderwebs. As she drew closer, she saw that something had been partly excavated from behind a covering of old bricks halfway up the wall, something made of stone with a curved edge surrounded by a row of small stone tiles.

"Edgar," she said, "I think I've found what the person who opened this room up was looking for."

Edgar made his way toward her, squinting in the light. "I can't secure the door," he said, before realizing what Kate was looking at. "Is that—?"

"A spirit wheel," said Kate.

Only the right side of the wheel had been cleared of its covering bricks. Kate could see half the circular tiles that ran around the central palm stone, but the main carving in the center had been scraped away.

"I've never seen one of these before," said Edgar. "I mean, I've heard about them, but never . . ." He reached out to touch one of the tiles on the right side. "What's that meant to be? A wolf?"

"I think so."

Edgar touched the stone tile, and the wall quivered, making him snatch his hand back. "It still works," he said. "Why didn't they uncover it the whole way?"

"And why did someone wall it up in the first place?" said Kate.

There was something not right about the place. Edgar shivered, and Kate felt it, too.

"Maybe we should ask it something," he said. "We could ask it to tell us the quickest way out. Wasn't that what these things were made for? To give directions?"

"Not all spirit wheels can be trusted," said Kate. "This one has to have been bricked up for a reason."

"It's got to be worth a try," said Edgar. "I've brought enough supplies to last us a couple of days, but after that we'll need more. If this thing can help us reach the surface, I say we try."

Edgar pressed his palm against the center of the circle. The hidden tiles rattled gently behind the wall, but other than that, nothing happened. There was no movement, no illuminated symbols, or at least nothing either of them could see. "It's broken," he said. Then a faint glow like gentle firelight spread along his outstretched arm, and one of the tiles shone with a splutter of inner light before fading again.

"The closed eye," said Kate. "That means no. The open eye means yes."

"So it heard me! It's saying it's not broken, right?"

"I still don't think this is a good idea."

"I suppose we have to stick to yes and no," said Edgar. "Unless you know how to read the rest of these things." He kept his hand against the wheel and concentrated on his question, speaking the words slowly and clearly out loud. "Are we heading the right way to reach the surface?" He waited a few seconds and looked at Kate with expectation. "Anything?"

"Nothing."

The wall shuddered, Edgar snatched his hand away, and the circle of tiles began grating slowly in a clockwise direction. A handful of them sank back and rotated as they passed the cleared space in the wall, and they kept moving steadily, refusing to settle.

"It's not meant to work without someone's hand on it," said Kate.

"What do we do now?"

Old mortar sprinkled down from the spaces between the bricks as they rattled against the force of the vibration behind them. Kate and Edgar stepped back to a safe distance, knocking against one of the tables and sending one of the covered shapes rolling out from beneath its cloth and cracking on the hard floor. It was a soft crack. Whatever it had been had offered little resistance, smashing instantly. Kate looked down. Beside her feet was an upturned skull, its empty eye sockets staring up at her.

Edgar raised his lantern as the spirit wheel kept turning, and the light cast soft shadows from all the cloth-covered shapes in the room. "They're all skulls," he whispered. "Someone is collecting skulls down here!"

Then the wheel stopped, Kate and Edgar looked back at the wall, and a dull light glowed behind the covering of bricks. Edgar walked up to it and pressed his cheek against the tiles, trying to see where the light was coming from.

"How do I read it?" he asked.

"The important symbols glow," said Kate. "What can you see?"

"There's only one," said Edgar. "It looks like . . . a snowflake, I think."

That got Kate's attention. "Anything else?"

"No. Why? What does it mean?"

"It must be confused," said Kate. "Ask it something else."

Edgar pressed his palm against the wheel again and spoke out loud. "Where can we go where no one will find us? Where will we be safe?"

The stone tiles trembled a little, and then the wheel ground into action. The tiles turned heavily on their clockwise path, and the snowflake carving settled at the three o'clock position, where Kate could see it clearly. All other movement stopped at once, and the fiery glow brought the symbol to life even more brightly than before.

"Still the snowflake," said Edgar. "This is a waste of time."

"It's my name," said Kate. "It means Winters."

"Maybe it wants to speak to you."

The open eye tile flickered weakly.

"Ask it something," said Edgar.

"No. I'm not touching it." Kate had used spirit wheels before, but this one was different. Just by being near it she could tell that it was darker, more powerful. A feeling of sadness spread from it and filled the room. She could feel it clinging to her soul. The whispers in the walls returned, and Kate could hear the spirit in the wheel speaking to her in a voice that was distant and strange, but the words made no sense to her.

"All right then," said Edgar, who could hear nothing. "I say we leave this creepy room of death behind. We'll find our way up on our own."

The whispers in the room grew gradually louder. Kate's eyes were drawn back to the wheel and to the illuminated snowflake that burned brighter as she concentrated upon it. Then the tiles began to spin.

Edgar stared. The tiles quickly gathered speed, then one . . . two . . . three of them settled together where the snowflake had just been: a bird, a dagger, and a pointed mask. Each symbol burned fiercely in the dark, but for Kate, looking at that spirit wheel was like staring into a void. The symbols appeared to float upon a black mist, her mind emptied of every thought, and darkness spread around the edges of her vision, leaving nothing but the image of the wheel. Her body slipped into a dead calm as a half-heard voice whispered through her mind. The wheel wanted her to listen. It wanted her to touch it, to connect with it.

Bird. Dagger. Mask.

She stepped forward, barely aware of what she was doing, and pressed her hand into the center.

The moment her palm made contact with the stone the three symbols' images came together powerfully in her thoughts, overlapping with a burst of memories that flooded past her eyes faster than she could acknowledge them. She tried to concentrate. She tried to understand what the wheel was trying to say. The less she resisted it, the clearer the images became.

The symbol of the bird flickered over memories Kate had of Silas and his crow, showing her what the bird was meant to represent.

"The bird is Silas," she said out loud.

"Silas? What's he got to do with anything?" asked Edgar, as Kate gripped his hand tight, using him to anchor herself to the living world.

*The dagger dripped blood. Kate saw it gripped in the hand of a dangerous man dressed in red with a long scar trailing across his jaw. She did not recognize his face, but she could sense that he had taken many lives before, and there was a small body, bloodied and still, curled up at his feet. She tried to see more, but the details blurred if she concentrated too hard, and she did not need to see whose body that was to get the wheel's message.*

"The dagger means danger," she said.

"Silas is in danger? Why is it telling us that?"

"I don't think it's about Silas. I think it means us."

"No surprise there, then. What about the last one?"

*Only the mask was left, but the images that came to Kate did not make any sense. She could see a town full of white buildings, a ship sitting in a covered dock, and a line of black cliffs with waves crashing against the rocks. Beyond them were a wide green forest and two spires of a much older, darker building rising in the distance. It looked like two tall towers that had been built side by side, and it was surrounded by a wide patch of stony ground with a few scattered pockets of green earth.*

*The wheel took her closer to the spires, right up to a boarded window that had once been painted black. One of the wooden panels had fallen away, and she could see into a room that seemed warm and inviting. A small fire was burning in the hearth, the floor was covered in deep wool rugs, and there were dozens of beautiful mirrors and old paintings standing up against the walls. Kate looked closer at those walls and saw words carved into the bare stone. Names and dates had been etched into the spaces where the paintings had once hung.*

*Her senses sharpened within the veil. She could feel someone close by, watching her. She turned away from the window and found herself face-to-face with an older woman, maybe sixty years old, with black hair that was clipped smartly short and gray eyes that had seen many more years and held more memories than Kate could imagine.*

A hand squeezed Kate's shoulder, and she jumped, pulling her hand away from the wheel and breaking out of the vision to find Edgar standing where the woman had been.

"Are you all right?" he asked.

Kate nodded, and Edgar blew out his lantern.

"What's wrong?" she whispered.

"The corridor," Edgar said quietly. "Someone's out there. They've found us."

# ← 8 →

## THE SECRET IN THE SKULL

Kate could not see anything in the darkness. All the symbols on the spirit wheel had stopped glowing, and it had returned to its dead state. She pulled Edgar down behind one of the tables as the door opened and voices bled into the room.

"There is a spirit wheel in there," said one figure, its shadow filling the doorway. "If Kate went near it, it could be dangerous to be in the same room."

"I don't care! She is out here somewhere, and I won't go back without her. If there's even a chance she's in there, we have to look."

"That's Baltin and Artemis," Edgar whispered close to Kate's ear. "What's Artemis doing out here?"

"This room is a restricted space," said Baltin. "I can go in, but you have to stay outside. You must stay back."

Kate heard a whispered argument between the two men, and then a lantern swung into the room. Its sudden light was blinding, and Baltin squinted behind it, edging his way in.

"Kate? Edgar?"

The spirit wheel thrummed with energy as Baltin drew closer. Kate could feel it reacting to his presence.

"Stay out there, Artemis," said Baltin. "It's not safe in here. The floor is unstable. You have to know where to put your feet."

Kate and Edgar held their breaths in the dark. Baltin was lying. That room was as safe as any other in the City Below. They ducked beneath one of the covered tables before Baltin's lantern light swept too close. He moved down the rows, oblivious to the two pairs of eyes watching his boots walk by.

Baltin stopped a few steps from the spirit wheel and shone his light onto the ground. He had found the fallen skull. Kate looked between two of the tables and saw him slide his fingers into the eye sockets and lift the skull unceremoniously up to his face for a closer look. Fragments of bone splinted to the floor from the damage caused by the fall, and he kicked them aside as if they were worth less than dust. "I told them to clear this place up," he muttered quietly, "not that this one will be any good to us now." He dropped the skull back onto its table and left it rocking awkwardly on its side. "Waste of time."

Baltin ran his hand around the exposed part of the half-excavated spirit wheel.

"Anything?" Artemis's voice carried in from the corridor.

"Nothing," said Baltin, holding his light up to the symbols. "No one has been in here."

Fear climbed up into Kate's throat. Baltin had been in that room before. He had noticed something that was out of place. The symbols were in a different position, and from the look on his face, he was quickly understanding why.

"She made it work," he whispered.

Baltin turned quickly, scowling beneath deep eyebrows as he searched the room for signs of life, holding the lamp out in front of him. Kate and Edgar stayed still as he lifted the corners of the cloths one by one. If he came much closer, they would be forced to move, and any sound was likely to give them away.

"How did you make it work?" he whispered. "What did you do?" Baltin kept moving, his light spreading dangerously close. They had to move.

Kate had only the fleeting light of Baltin's lantern to see by, but it was enough to notice a few seconds' gap between his lifting one cloth and reaching for the next—not enough time for them to slither between tables, but there was another way. Kate pulled Edgar close to her and whispered in his ear, "Follow."

Kate saw Baltin thrust his light beneath the next table, and before he could drop the cover and step toward theirs, she crawled as fast and silently as she could out of the back of her tablecloth with Edgar rolling out behind her. Baltin's light shone into the space they had left, and the two of them stayed completely still until it pulled away and he moved on to the next.

They were out in the open, exposed in the wide space between the table and a stone wall. Kate did not want to stay there, and as soon as Baltin was far enough away, she tugged Edgar's arm and began crawling back toward the spirit wheel. Baltin had his back to them, and Artemis was still blocking the doorway they had entered. Their only choice was the broken door.

"Baltin? What are you doing in there?" asked Artemis.

"Quiet!" Baltin snapped back.

"There are other tunnels to search. We should keep moving."

Artemis was becoming restless and continued to question Baltin, eager to move on. Kate used the distraction to get to her feet. She could move more quickly and quietly that way. The spirit wheel was right ahead. The symbols were so dark and lifeless it was easy to think she had imagined them glowing with light. She did not know how close she was to the table beside her until her hand brushed against the cloth and a rush of energy rippled against her skin.

She could feel the shape of the skull under her fingertips, but it was too late to pull her hand away. Sudden images flooded her thoughts, confused and garbled, as if the spirit the skull belonged to were trying to share everything it remembered with her at once. Baltin was just on the other side of the cavern, but frost glittered across Kate's fingers and swept past her wrist. The spirit in the skull was dragging her into the veil, and she had no choice but to let it happen. The images kept coming, faster than thoughts, as the frost reached her eyelashes and she was drawn completely in.

*"The wheels are all we have left. This is the right decision. We have already waited too long."*

*Kate was standing in the same oval cavern, only now it was washed with candlelight. Groups of oozing candles burned in the alcoves cut around the room. The tables were gone, replaced by four separate circles of wooden chairs, legs roped together, each circle leaving a single space leading into the center of the room, where an ornate spiral had been carved into the floor.*

*Most of the chairs were empty, except for the three that sat closest to the wall where the spirit wheel should have been. But instead of a circle of ancient carved stone, there was a deep hollow cut into the stones. Three people were hunched over on the chairs, drawing sharpening stones along bright silver blades and talking quietly, not wanting to be overheard. They all wore simple gray robes, each with a belt that had books hanging from it, tiny books the width of fingers, each one perfectly bound in silver and black.*

*Kate looked down at the hand that had touched the skull and saw a silver blade grasped between her fingers instead. But they were not her fingers. She was looking down at a woman's* hand some years older than her own, a hand that was well used to digging in the earth, with a bracelet of herbs knotted around her wrist, a talisman Kate recognized as one worn by those often dealing with the dead. The sight of the strange hand shocked Kate. This had happened to her before, but that did not make it any less terrifying. She was inside someone else's memory, witnessing an event as it had once been seen through that person's eyes, the eyes of the woman who had once owned the skull.

Kate felt the woman's heartbeat rise as she walked toward the three men and one of them looked up.

"Is he prepared?" he asked.

"There was some . . . resistance," said the woman, her words vibrating in Kate's throat as if she herself were speaking them. "He has been restrained."

"Good. No one wishes to relive last night's events. It was wise to take action."

"Are you sure he is ready?" asked the woman.

"We need the wheels," said the tallest man. "We have already waited too long. The city will fall in the end, but after what we have done . . . it is our duty to put it right."

The woman bowed her head curtly, then turned to lead the three men out of the cavern. As they made their way into the corridor, a cry of anguish echoed through the tunnels nearby.

"Let us hope our friend has been restrained tightly enough," said one of the men, and Kate was sure she heard a smile in his voice.

Once she was inside the corridor, Kate saw it as it had been in its prime. A few brass lanterns hung from hooks along the wall, and between them was gathered a collection of far more gruesome artifacts: a human hand, severed at the wrist, that looked as if it had been preserved in yellow wax; a skull with no teeth whose eye sockets had been filled carefully with mud; and a group of perfect bones—human, Kate guessed—all of them long, stripped and polished, with initials carved neatly into the very centers of their length.

Kate tried not to notice the other dead things, but if the woman had seen something, it had become part of the memory, and she had no choice but to look at the strings of dead bird skeletons spread wing to wing and the long sticks of wood pierced with rows of teeth and smeared the dull color of old blood.

The man's shouts sounded louder now, and there was a light up ahead, leading off into a room that Kate and Edgar had not seen on their way to the spirit wheel, one that had probably been sealed up long ago in her own time. She tried to pull away from the memory, but she did not know how to break herself out of it. Without someone to help her, she was trapped.

The woman continued to walk steadily toward the room, no matter how much Kate willed her feet to stop. She could hear the men talking behind her, but she did not know what they were talking about. The woman was as transfixed as Kate was upon the light of that doorway, and her memory did not recall what the men were saying. Kate felt her footsteps slowing as they neared the threshold of the room, and she dared to hope she would be spared the sight of what lay inside. Then the moment of hesitation passed, and the woman stepped out into the light.

What Kate saw in that room was to stay with her for the rest of her life. She had seen something like it long ago in a printed picture—she couldn't remember where—and her mind instantly registered two things: this was a moment that meant something, one that was set to be a turning point in Albion's history, and she knew then who those people were. The bonemen. Keepers of the dead. Men and women who had once been trusted to bury and care for Albion's dead in the vast tombs beneath Fume, people who were generally seen as having done good work, not the kind who hung bones on their walls, carried blades, and restrained others so they shouted out like that.

The picture Kate remembered was an artist's view of the bonemen's last collective deed before they disappeared from history. Their final funeral. The interment of the man thought to be their leader. No one knew his name. In the picture at least sixty bonemen were standing around a coffin in an otherwise empty room, their heads bowed to represent the ending of an age that was to die with that man. It was a beautiful picture, drawn in black ink, but Kate now knew that it was a lie.

The bonemen were gathered there, surely enough, but the room was not the plain one the artist had depicted. The floor was alive with energy. Thirteen freshly carved spirit wheels were laid flat on their backs, creating a stone mosaic upon the ground, and soft light spread from their symbols like a blue mist floating just above the floor. It looked as if thirteen individual listening circles had been opened at once, creating thirteen separate tears between the living world and the veil.

More mud-eyed skulls watched from the walls, and in the center of it all was not a body in a coffin but a man who was still very much alive. He had been stripped bare to the waist and was lying on top of one of the spirit wheels with a plank of wood along his spine to keep him still. Two of the bonemen knelt on either side of him, painting inky symbols across his chest. His eyes were tar black, but when they moved, Kate saw that they had the same sheen of silver as her own eyes. He was a Walker, and a powerful one, just like her.

But none of that could help him there. Kate could feel the combined will of the gathered bonemen dominating the thirteen wheels. Not even a Walker could fight against a force of energy like that, but it did not stop the man from trying. Kate could feel him reaching out to the wheels one by one, his spirit searching for a way to close them but finding none. Then he shouted again, his voice black with anger.

"Dalliah!"

The bonemen with the ink finished their work, and everyone in the room turned to see a woman entering the room. She was younger than most of the people there. She wore the same gray robes as everyone else, but her long hair was knotted into ragged plaits, and her face was drawn and thin. She did not walk forward but looked down at the closest spirit wheel as if it were a snake ready to snap at her ankles should she take another step.

The man in the center considered his words carefully, knowing that he had only one chance to stop what was happening. "Dalliah," he said, battling to keep his voice calm. "Wintercraft caused this mistake. Wintercraft will put it right. This is not the way forward. This is not what we do."

Dalliah drew her own silver blade and handed it to the boneman beside her. "It is now," she said.

The boneman crossed the spirit wheels, gripping the blade at his side.

"The veil is not meant to be used this way," said the bound man, watching him approach. "There is no guarantee this will even work. We do not know enough. We need more time!"

The boneman with the knife knelt down and placed his hand across the bound man's mouth, and Kate felt the energy in the room shudder as the silver blade was lifted and the point stabbed down. The man's death was swift and silent. Kate caught a glimpse of red blood pooling near the boneman's feet and watched it bleed down into the carvings of the central spirit wheel. The memory flooded with the woman's emotions, guilt, grief, fear, and doubt all wrestling for Kate's attention while she looked on in horror. Then the memory turned and focused upon Dalliah, who was watching the man's death with quiet reverence. There was no guilt or grief on her face. Her gray eyes were empty of any emotion as she began to whisper a short verse, one that Kate had read before.

*"A circle made of blood and stone, to bind the words of soul and bone. A meeting place for those who seek the spirit sleeping underneath."*

*Kate felt two conflicting bands of energy spill out across the floor, one seeping from the dead man's blood, the other being spread by Dalliah herself. The two forces joined together above the dead man, and as the gentle mist of his spirit rose up to be carried into the current of death, her energy acted as a wall, forcing his spirit down. Down into the spirit wheel. Down into the stone. The blood bled deeper into the wheel, and once the spirit was trapped, the energy within it died instantly. The wheel became dull and dead, with only the faintest vibration of energy at its core suggesting that there was anything unusual about it at all.*

*The room fell silent then. All eyes were on the bloodstained carvings, until the man's murderer stood up, his blade slick with blood, and spoke for them all.*

*"Did it work?"*

*"It worked," said Dalliah, sweeping her eyes around the people, a dangerous smile lighting up her face. "Now for the rest."*

*"The rest?" The voice came from Kate's throat as the woman stepped forward. "We were told one would be enough," she said. "We have taken one life. We are finished here."*

*Dalliah met the woman's eyes, and cold fear washed through Kate's soul: fear of what that woman was and fear of what she could do.*

*"We are finished only when I say," said Dalliah. "Do it."*

*With those words twelve more blades flashed into action. Kate saw a handful of bonemen turn suddenly upon the others, stealing lives and binding souls into the spirit wheels with more spilled blood. The walls echoed with their victims' screams, and the wheels flickered out one by one as the bodies of the dead lay across them. It all happened too quickly for anyone to react, but the horror of what the woman was seeing choked through the memory as she stumbled back, turned, and stood face-to-face with one of the men she had brought to that room.*

*Kate saw the dagger and the silent apology in his eyes. Cold silver plunged deep into her chest. Kate felt the blade grate against bone, the explosion of heat and fire as the dagger found her heart, and the shuddering pull of eternity as the final wheel claimed its soul.*

Kate opened her eyes to blackness. She thought she was screaming; but the frost of the veil still had her throat, and no sound came out. Her hands flew to her chest, but there was no dagger, no blood. Her heart was racing, and she did not know where she was. She was lying on her back on a cold floor with something soft underneath her head.

She sat up and felt deep grooves sliced into the floor beneath her fingers. For one terrifying moment her confused mind thought she was still inside the bonemen's room, sitting on top of a spirit wheel. Then logic took over. She was no longer inside the memory, but she was not in the skull room either. The walls of this place felt closer together, and someone was crouching nearby, breathing nervously in the dark. "Edgar?" she whispered as soon as her voice returned.

Something shuffled beside her, and she heard the scratch of a match. Light flared across Edgar's face, and he held a finger to his lips to warn her to be quiet. They sat in silence while the match burned down and Edgar lit another, shielding the flame with a cupped hand.

"I think they're gone," he whispered at last.

"Where are we?" asked Kate.

"Something happened," said Edgar. "You fell."

Kate sat with her arms clutched protectively over her chest where the dagger blow had landed, her forehead throbbing with a dull ache that was gradually getting worse. Something tickled against her left eyebrow, and when she rubbed her hand across it, her fingers came away dark and wet.

"Don't touch it," said Edgar. "You hit the table pretty hard before I caught you. Here, put this against it."

Edgar pressed something soft into Kate's hand, and her head stung as she tried to stop the trickle of blood.

"Did Baltin see us?" she asked.

"He should have," said Edgar. "I think—I think there was something else in the room with us. One of the funeral boxes smashed on the floor when you fell and the spirit wheel started moving again. Baltin shouted at Artemis, and then he just stood there, staring at the wheel like he was obsessed by the thing. That place just didn't feel right. I got us out as quick as I could, once he had left. You're heavier than you look, you know." Edgar smiled before the match flame scorched his fingers and fell to the floor, flickering out. "Better save the rest of these," he said.

"I'm sorry for what happened," said Kate. "I didn't even know the skull was there until I touched it. I think there was a shade inside it. It showed me memories. Horrible things."

"So long as you're all right, that's all that matters," said Edgar. "How does your head feel?"

"Sore."

"I don't suppose it showed you anything useful, did it?" asked Edgar. "At this point I'm willing to take any help we can get."

Kate considered telling Edgar what she had seen, but it did not feel right to talk about a group of murders that had happened so close to the place they were sitting, no matter how many hundreds of years ago they might have happened. "Nothing important," she said, though with the possibility of shades still lingering close by, she felt uncomfortable saying those words out loud.

"Maybe we should stay here for a while," said Edgar. "Get our bearings before we head out again."

"We're lost, aren't we?"

Edgar let the question hang in the darkness between

them, saying more than any answer ever could.

After what Kate had seen she was glad to be able to stay still for a while, but the longer they sat there, the more the silence and gloom of being underground spread around them like thick fog, threatening to steal her senses one by one.

Baltin had found one of the missing spirit wheels and had been collecting skulls in that room for a long time. Bonemen skulls, including those whose spirits had long been sealed away inside Fume's spirit wheels. The thought of what the bonemen had done to those people chilled Kate, but the idea of the Skilled digging up old bones unsettled her, too. Baltin had reacted far too strongly to one small disturbance in the veil and had been willing to kill her to prevent it from happening again.

The veil plucked at the edges of Kate's consciousness as the wheel's warning weighed heavily on her mind. And even there, sitting in the stony shadows of their tiny hiding place, she did not feel safe.

# THE
# MESSENGER

Silas woke not long after midnight to the earsplitting sound of lightning striking close by. His chest burned. His heart, usually steady and unnaturally slow, raced up to a speeding irregular beat, and his skin blazed with heat. Pain spread like veins across the left side of his chest, stabbing into his heart like a core of flame. The intensity of it took him by surprise and he clutched a hand to his body waiting for the feeling to pass. He had felt the stab of metal many times before. When he opened his shirt to inspect the skin, he half expected it to be stained with blood, but his palm came away clean.

Remnants of fading memories disturbed him: old memories of betrayal and death. Somehow, Kate Winters had shared that pain with him. The link between them had flared for a moment, and her soul had called out, dragging his consciousness back into the veil. The effect had been potent but brief. Already the connection was lost.

Rain streamed down in rivulets through the ruined roof, and Silas stood up, shaking his wet hair and feeling the strength returning to his body again. He tested his arms by clenching his fists and feeling the healing muscles stretch beneath his skin. He had to move. Pure luck was all that had prevented the Blackwatch from finding him in there, and a thunderstorm was not going to stop them from continuing their search.

Silas climbed the stairs to the crypt door and opened it to a bitter blast of icy wind. Outside, the sun had not yet begun to rise, the rain was already freezing where it had collected on the ground, the paths were slick with fresh ice, and scatterings of hailstones had blown up against the crypt walls. The ground crunched beneath his boots as he stepped out into the cemetery, and heavy clouds crossed the sky like purple bruises streaked with sulfurous yellow and crackles of blue. He smelled the air. It was too late in the year for storms. The land was too cold, yet the clouds still hung steadily within the arms of the mountains, hurling rain down onto the cold houses below.

He turned up his coat collar, and his crow flew out of the crypt and huddled on a bare tree branch, fluffing itself up for warmth. A bolt of lightning shook the ground, striking somewhere in the forest to the south. Ignoring the spearing rain that needled down around him, Silas walked back through the cemetery toward the iron gates. The Blackwatch had taken his sword during his capture. They had emptied his pockets and left him with nothing. The last of his silver was gone, as well as his hidden blades, everything that could have been of some use to him; but the short time he had spent in their custody had given him something more useful than any of those things. They had given him an idea.

With the early hour and the rain pelting down hard, Silas had the streets to himself. There was no sign of the Blackwatch anywhere on the southern side of the river, and many of the lantern strings over the streets had snapped or been blown out by the wind. A few early risers were standing at their windows watching the unseasonal weather, but those who saw him backed away from the glass as he walked by.

Silas's mood matched the ferocity of the sky. He made his way toward a small row of shops, found one that specialized in trade goods, and broke his way in while barely breaking stride. There was a rumble from the upper floor, and a short man ran down the stairs still in his nightshirt, wielding a dagger, determined to defend his shop. He stood still the moment he saw Silas standing in the doorway. His face fell, and he lowered the dagger slowly.

"There are some items I require here," said Silas. "You are going to get them for me, and then I will leave you in peace."

"A-all right," said the shop owner, backing up a few steps. "Anything you want. Take it. It's yours."

"I require paper, a pen, ink, and string and a container no longer or wider than a woman's finger with a stoppered top."

The shop was small and well stocked. The man collected

most of what he needed from behind the counter, placed them in front of Silas, and headed off in search of the container. Silas leaned on the counter to write a short letter and bit off a long length of string with his teeth while the man rummaged in a small drawer at the back of the shop.

"Will this do?" He hurried back, holding out a small glass vial between his finger and thumb. It had a small crack running down its side, but it would do.

"Good enough," said Silas. "And I'll take that as well." He pointed to the dagger held by the shop owner, who handed it to him at once.

"Of course," he said, "anything you need."

Silas slid the dagger into his belt, picked up the letter, string, and vial, and walked back out into the street, leaving the relieved shop owner behind.

The wind tried to snatch the paper from his fingers as he pushed it into the vial, stoppered it, and tied the string tightly around it in four strong loops. "Crow," he said. The bird flew down from the shelter of a high window on the opposite side of the street and landed on his wrist. Silas looped the string over the bird's head and tied an extra knot around its middle and across the center of the vial to keep it tucked into place against the bird's chest. The crow snapped its beak in complaint and shook its wings the moment Silas was finished, ruffling the glass among its chest feathers. Silas had never used his crow as a messenger bird before, but if the Blackwatch's tattered pigeons could make it across the sea, he was certain his bird would.

"This must reach Kate," he said. "Do you remember her?" The crow squawked once. "Look for her in the streets beneath Fume, and stay with her until I find you again. I will come for you. Go!"

The crow took flight, cutting through the driving rain and heading out toward the sea. Another streak of lightning lit up the sky, and Silas saw something standing on the other side of the street: a woman, watching him from beneath a gray hood, staring through the rain. Silas started to cross the street toward her, but when he looked up again, she was gone. He stood on the cobbles where she had been and could feel the bristle of the veil within the air. He looked along the houses, but there was no sign of her anywhere.

"I must apologize for your difficult welcome." The woman's voice came from a doorway behind him. Silas turned, and she held out a piece of paper for him to take. "I warned Bandermain he would not be able to keep you against your will. If you want answers, meet me there. I will wait for you. There are things you need to know before we begin."

The eyes beneath her hood were pale and lifeless. When Silas looked into them, he saw nothing, no spark of life, no glint of a soul lying behind their glassy sheen. It was like looking at his own reflection: dead and cold.

"You are Dalliah Grey," he said.

The woman pushed the paper into his hand. Her skin was stained with old soil, and her fingernails were worn back to the quick. "The veil is falling," she said. "We may already be too late."

The woman tried to walk away, but Silas took hold of her wrist and would not let her go. Her skin was icy cool, and he felt the familiar thrum of the veil playing around her like a haze of wild energy, dangerous and fascinating at the same time.

"I will answer all your questions, Silas," she said. "The Blackwatch do not have to be your enemy today, and neither do I."

"What do you have to do with the Blackwatch?"

"Less than they think. The balance of power is shifting. If you trust me, you will regain everything you have lost. Read the note. Meet me there." Dalliah's hand twisted in Silas's grip. Her thumb joint cracked, and her fingers slithered free. "I walked your path centuries ago," she said, snapping her bone effortlessly back into place. "You are still young, Silas. You have not yet seen the world that I know. You should be thanking me, not doubting me. I am the only reason you are still alive."

"It would take more than the Blackwatch to finish me," said Silas.

"Today, yes. But twelve years ago things were very different. You were a different man." Dalliah smiled and backed away. "Answers will come," she said, sensing his curiosity. "For now you should go." She pointed along the darkened street. "The Blackwatch are coming for you."

Silas turned and saw the silhouette of a horse walking across the end of the road. He slipped into the shadows, out of sight of the Blackwatch patrol, and when he looked back, Dalliah was gone. He was about to set off after her when the echo of hoofbeats sounded behind the houses and a lithe gray horse raced out into the street carrying the hooded woman on its back. She snapped the reins once and headed off in the direction of the Blackwatch.

Silas unfolded the paper she had left behind and discovered a map of Grale with a route marked out, leading into the southern forest and ending at a circle marked in black ink. He had not traveled all that way to have the person he was looking for slip away so easily. It would take too long to travel that route on foot. He needed a horse.

Horses and boats were the only viable means of transport between Grale and the other towns along the Continental coast, so the western edge of Grale contained more than its share of stables. Silas moved through the streets, across a river bridge, and along to the largest of the stable blocks, where a group of worried horses were grunting and stamping, agitated by the storm. He opened the stable doors and walked between the stalls, inspecting the beasts inside. Only one of them was calmly cropping its hay, completely uninterested in what was happening outside: a brown mare with white patches between its ears and down its left flank. Silas unbolted the stall and rubbed his palm along the horse's nose. Its eyes were healthy; its ears, straight and alert. "A beast without fear," he said. "You will do."

He did not waste time saddling up the horse. He pulled off its night blanket and led it out into the open. It walked well, and its hooves were well shod. The horse flicked its ears against the rain as Silas climbed up onto its bare back and knotted his hands into its mane. Once up, he kicked firmly, and the horse responded at once. Silas turned it toward the gate, raced it to a gallop, and, clearing the gate in one powerful jump, thumped its hooves down into the cobbled street.

The horse carried him over the river, toward the tree line that marked the southern border of the town. The flicker of a lens light shone to Silas's right up ahead, and another answered it to his left. His eyes searched the shadows. He had been seen.

He drove the horse harder, sending it charging along the cobbles and onto a wide dirt track. Silas kept his eyes on the road ahead as he plunged into the mouth of the forest and hurtled between the trees. He remembered the markings on the map and shifted his weight, guiding the horse down a small side track, abandoning the course the woman had set for him and finding his own way instead. He had no reason to trust a stranger on foreign soil and could not rule out the possibility that he was being led into a trap.

Low branches whipped past his ears as he leaned into the horse's neck, ignoring the thunderous clouds overhead. The horse plowed through the undergrowth, slowing down as Silas took it off the track. It scrambled up the side of a muddy hill, and he led it back onto an overgrown track where it stamped restlessly in a circle, unsure where to go. Silas let his instincts lead the way. He tugged the horse's mane, brought it up on two hooves, and forced it to turn. The horse whinnied, slammed its hooves back down into the earth, and kept going, head down, muscles pumping, eyes wide with the thrill of adventure. Silas looked back—there was no sign of any pursuers behind him— and decided to follow that track as far as it would go.

The horse ran on until its body became laced with sweat; then a glint of light caught Silas's attention in the trees. He was about to turn away from it when he realized that it was too high up to be the flicker of a Blackwatch lens light. Something was glowing at the end of a track up ahead, beyond a turning marked by a pair of old dead trees. Silas led the horse between them. The ground was scarred deeply by carriage wheels, which had left behind long frozen cuts within the earth. Those cuts ran like tiny rivers, flooded with rainwater, and the horse picked its way along the center of the track until it reached a clearing where a high stone wall held a pair of blue glass lanterns on either side of an open gate.

Silas brought the horse to a stop between them. It stamped and worried, not wanting to go any farther, and whatever it was sensing, he could feel it, too. It was like the perilous feeling of standing on the edge of an abyss, not knowing when the ground was going to fall away, yet being certain that a deadly drop lay just ahead. There was danger in that place. That land had known death. The wind swirled through the trees, throwing sharp rain into Silas's face. He dismounted the horse and left it loose at the gate before stepping onto the land alone.

A neatly pebbled pathway cut across a courtyard patched with ovals of frosty earth that were barely visible in the darkness. Silas followed the path, and at its end a great black building came into sight. Moonlight sparkled from the few glass windows the huge house had left; the rest were boarded up, with long tendrils of old plants left creeping unchecked up its walls.

The building was immense. Its central point was marked by two circular walled towers pressed side by side and topped with spires of slate that reached up toward the sky. Everything about the building was old, worn down, yet strangely familiar. The gargoyles set high among the roof eaves were exact copies of those found upon buildings that Silas remembered within Fume. The towers were the same height and shape as some of the memorial towers in the city, and the long windows were made of the same green glass that was set only within its oldest buildings. It looked as if an ancient part of Fume had been lifted up and set there in the middle of a Continental forest.

The house was in darkness except for one firelit window on the ground floor. Silas heard the horses gathering behind him. He turned and saw eight Blackwatch agents lined up on horseback at the gate. He could not see Bandermain among them, and they did not draw their weapons; but each one seemed unwilling to step onto the land. Silas felt the welcome weight of the stolen dagger within his belt, but they all sat there, watching, as he walked steadily along the pebbles and stopped in front of the building's main door.

The woman from the town was already standing there, waiting for him. She raised a hand, and the Blackwatch sank back into the forest, retreating at her command. Two of them climbed down from their horses and pulled the gates shut, closing them against the dark trees as the rain pelted down.

"As you can see, I do not like visitors," said the woman. "The Blackwatch know not to set foot on my land without an invitation. I asked them to follow you and make sure you arrived safely. The forest is a treacherous place."

Silas stood tall, his loose hair slicked down by the rain. "I do not require your protection."

"I disagree. You need protecting from yourself and your own ignorance. You may look younger than your years, but you have still barely begun to live upon this world. It would be foolish of you to ignore me. You cannot afford to let your suspicions cloud your judgment. Especially now."

"Then you are Dalliah Grey?"

The woman placed her right hand to her chest and bowed slightly in greeting. It was an old gesture, one that had not been common upon the Continent for more than two hundred years. "I have had many names," she said. "That is one of the oldest. It is rare for me to hear it spoken out loud."

"That is what happens when you live like a ghost," said Silas. "People forget."

"Good," said Dalliah. "But if they had forgotten me, you would not be here. My name still carries weight back home in Albion. That is good to know."

Anyone standing close to Dalliah would sense that there was something different about her, something powerful and barely restrained living beneath the face of a woman who appeared to be only just reaching the brink of old age. If she truly had lived centuries of life, those years did not show upon her face. She looked strong and fit, her hair was short and perfectly black, but her eyes were haunting, her chest did not rise and fall with regular breaths, and the air around her was thick with threat. It was the same feeling people experienced whenever they were near Silas. He had never sensed it for himself before. It was the aura of a predator.

"Please," said Dalliah, "join me inside. Weather like this is no place for a conversation, and I am sure you have questions."

"Only one, for now," said Silas, standing his ground. "Why did you invite me here?"

Dalliah studied his face and stared into his eyes as if she could read the memories written behind them. "You know that something has changed," she said. "You try to deny it, but you cannot ignore what you have sensed forever."

"And what is that?"

"The girl whose blood runs within your own. The girl who commands the veil more powerfully than any of her ancestors before her. She is in danger. You have felt her within you, even here in these empty lands."

It was true, part of Kate Winters's blood had become bonded with Silas's upon the Night of Souls, but there was no way this woman could know that for certain. He remembered the pain in his chest when he had awoken within the crypt, but he did not trust Dalliah enough to talk about Kate. "I have felt nothing."

"Together we can put right what you have broken," said Dalliah. "Kate Winters is no ordinary young woman, yet she continues to enter the veil with her mind unprotected. No good will come of this, Silas. The girl's life is in danger, and it is all because of you."

Whatever had happened in that skull room had tired Kate out. She lay curled up asleep on the floor of the tiny room, and while she slept, Edgar sat beside her, gently stroking her hair.

He waited for his eyes to get used to the blackness. There was no hint of light anywhere along the tunnel that ran alongside their hiding place, and any sounds made in the distance carried impossibly far, making everything sound much closer than it was. He heard what could have been footsteps, scuttlings, and whispers of wind that were like voices hissing beside him, and he shivered. He did not like the dark. It was just another place for things to go wrong. Anything could creep up on someone in the dark.

A scratching sound skittered close by, and Edgar sent one of his few remaining matches flaring into life. "Just a rat," he whispered as a black rodent ran brazenly across the floor. Edgar liked rats and was happy to leave it to its business until he spotted a second one nibbling at the corner of his backpack.

"Hey!" He snatched the bag out of reach and slapped his hand on the ground. "Go on. Get out!" The rats just stood there, watching him, so he opened his bag, broke a small piece of bread from a loaf he had hidden there, and threw it toward them. The rats set upon it at once and scuttled away before Edgar's match burned out and he lit another.

He put the bag down and opened it carefully in case there was anything lurking inside. Apart from the bread everything else looked untouched; there was a knife, a few apples, a length of thin rope, a chunk of cheese wrapped in cloth, a glass bottle filled with water, a bundle of spare candles, and a couple of pies that were at least three days old. It wasn't much, but it had been all he could find, and it was going to have to last them until they could find some more food. With the Skilled out there looking for them, that was not going to be easy.

At least he knew a good hiding place when he found one. They were inside the front room of a cavelike house that had been dug out centuries ago for use by the bonemen when they worked this far underground. There wasn't much left of it— the rest of the house was already buried—but it was enough to keep them safe. The doorway had been crushed beneath an earth fall years ago, and the only way in or out was by slithering through the glassless window.

Edgar had left the window exposed so he could see any light spread by people searching for them. Kate lay asleep beneath it, her skin sickly and clammy to touch. Edgar had seen her like this only once before, in the first week after they had asked the Skilled for help. She had gone too far into the veil too fast and had trouble separating herself from it again. He should never have suggested using that spirit wheel. Things like that always caused more trouble than they were worth. Whatever Kate wanted to do next, he would help her. He would watch her. He would keep her safe.

Kate was scowling in her sleep, and when he felt her forehead, he found it even colder than before. Edgar shrugged off his coat and laid it over her. He shivered despite his layered sweaters, which were all holey and threadbare. We are going to get out of here, he told himself. We can do this. Just keep heading up. If a tunnel heads up, it heads out. That's all we have to—

A wash of firelight spread suddenly along the wall outside. Edgar stepped over Kate and peered carefully out the window.

Two lamps swung in the darkness, carried by two women wearing brown dresses with hoods over their heads. The women were talking to each other and had large packs slung on their backs, but they did not seem to be in any hurry to get where they were going. Their voices carried softly along the tunnel.

"Which way now?"

The lights stopped moving, and both women held their lanterns up to the wall.

"Left."

The two women headed off around a narrow turning, and the light from their lanterns slowly went out.

"Traders," whispered Edgar. "What are they doing here?"

After making sure that Kate was still asleep, he lit a fresh candle in his lantern, stepped over her, and clambered out of the little window. He crept forward, and when he reached the point where the women had been standing, he looked up at the same patch of wall. There was nothing there. "What were you looking at?" he whispered. Then he found it. Just before the turning that the two women had taken, a collection of deep scratches had been cut into the wall a few inches below the ceiling.

"Path sixty-three," he read out loud. *"TW—E. SM—S.* What is that supposed to mean?"

A sound in the tunnel startled him. He swung his lantern around, and a face came toward him in the dark. "Kate?"

"That light is bright enough to tell everyone where you are," said Kate. "What are you doing?"

Edgar took a moment to hide his sudden fright and stumbled over his words. "Two traders. They, er, passed here and read something on the wall. I came to have a look. How are you feeling?"

"As good as I'm likely to feel down here," said Kate. "Sleep helped."

Kate returned Edgar's coat, and he took the backpack from her hand.

"Take a look at these," he said, looking up at the letters as he pulled on his coat. "What do you make of them?"

"It looks like a signpost," said Kate. "The first two letters could stand for a place, and the last one tells you which direction it is in."

"How do you know that?"

"I read a lot," said Kate. "It's easy to get lost down here. Signposts like this could help the traders find their way around."

"Are you all right to walk?"

"I told you, I'm fine," said Kate. "Show me which way they went, but keep your voice down."

The tunnel wall curved to the left, and Edgar led the way. There was no sign of the traders, and small paths branched away in so many directions it became impossible to guess which route they had taken. Edgar held his lantern high, checking the walls for more directions. The same letters kept appearing over again. *SM—S.*

"At least we're heading somewhere," he said.

The tunnel eventually forked into a wide Y-shaped junction, and sunk into the wall joining the two separate paths was a large black door. It was made of old wood, but it had been rehung on new metal hinges not long ago.

Kate dared to press an ear to the door. "I can't hear anything, but the floor is well worn. Lots of people have walked this way."

"Do we risk it?"

Kate was about to answer when a loud voice echoed down the tunnel to their left. She grabbed the door handle and pulled the door open. "It's our best chance," she said.

The two of them ran inside and closed the door behind them.

"There's no lock," said Kate, searching for a way to seal the door, and when she turned to see where they were, her heart sank.

They were standing on a stone landing at the top of a circular shaft that cut deep into the earth. A staircase curled down the walls, illuminated dimly by yellow lights far beneath them. There was no guardrail to prevent anyone from stepping over the side, and the steps were ancient and uneven. Shadows danced along the staircase, and musty air fogged against their faces as Edgar's lantern bathed the walls in a fiery glow. Part of the staircase led up to their right, but the only doorway Kate could see had long ago been bricked up.

Edgar looked away from the dizzying drop.

"It looks like we're already at the top," said Kate. "The only way is down."

The staircase was just wide enough for the two of them to run side by side. Edgar stayed close to the wall and took care where he was putting his feet, while Kate took the steps two at a time and was already two levels down when someone opened the door they had just passed through. Kate and Edgar stopped where they were and pressed their backs against the wall.

Wood creaked as someone leaned over the guardrail, and footsteps moved above them, descending the stairs. Kate took hold of Edgar's wrist and kept moving, matching the position of their pursuers on each level's curl so they would not be seen if their followers looked down. When the footsteps stopped, Kate stopped. There were bricked-up doorways and short tunnels on the upper levels that might have led somewhere, but she was not about to risk being chased into a dead end. Whoever was following them would expect them to take one of the upper paths. She would not be so predictable.

Hushed voices spoke to one another after the third stop. Kate waited. She looked up and remained still.

At last, soft footsteps moved swiftly away from the stairs, following one of the side paths. The voices grew quieter, and only when Kate was completely sure there was no one else up there did she risk moving again.

"It's quiet," whispered Edgar as they descended another level. "I like quiet. Quiet is good."

They followed the staircase deeper and deeper down, but any doors they came across were blocked up, locked, or, in the case of one particularly ancient door, crossed with a dozen chains with a warning painted on the wall beside it:

Feldeep Prison
No Entry. No Escape.

⇝ ⁂ ⇜

"Nice," said Edgar. "I vote we leave this one far behind."

The stairs spiraled on, and Kate was glad when the bottom finally moved into sight. There were more fiery lights down there, a welcome sign of life, and she led Edgar toward a small wooden sign that was marked with an arrow and the letters SM. They followed the arrow into a low tunnel, which looked promising enough until a battered gate blocked their way.

The gate had been welded together using salvaged metal from at least three other gates, and it leaned at an awkward angle across their path, with the twisted letters *SM* bent into its center. Beside the gate, three long pull chains snaked down the wall.

"What do you think those are for?" asked Kate.

Edgar shrugged in the dark, and something creaked up ahead.

A small wooden shutter was tucked in between two stones, and it flapped open, chased out by a thick plume of pipe smoke. A wrinkled face appeared in the space behind it, and a thick, rasping voice said, "Buy, sell, or trade?"

Kate and Edgar looked at each other, neither knowing what to say.

"I don't have all day," said the voice, dissolving into a glut of choking coughs. "You want in or not?"

"In where?" asked Edgar.

"Stupid kids."

The shutter slammed shut, wafting bitter smoke into Kate's and Edgar's faces.

"Wait!" Kate tried to open the gate, but it was sturdier than it looked.

Edgar reached up for the chains and pulled one at random, sending a tiny bell ringing inside the wall. The shutter opened again, and the face returned.

"Trade then, eh?" he said, squinting at them with suspicion. "Let's see what ya got."

"Er . . ."

"No stock. No way in," said the man. "The Shadow-market's no place to be wandering about without good reason. 'Specially not for young uns like you."

Edgar turned his back on the man and whispered to Kate. "*SM* . . ." he said. "The Shadowmarket! I should have realized it before."

"What's a Shadowmarket?"

"The City Below has four places where people come to trade with one another," said Edgar. "The Shadowmarket is the biggest. If we can get in, no one will be able to find us in there."

"But we don't have anything to trade."

"Maybe not," said Edgar. "Nothing he can *see* anyway." He turned back to the gatekeeper. "Whisperers carry their stock in their memories," he said proudly. "We are here to trade secrets, and unless you are willing to pay for them, we will not be sharing any of our stock with you today."

The gatekeeper grumbled and sank back into his little

room. "Whisperers," he mumbled. "Should've guessed."

A shriek of metal sliding against metal sounded from the gate, and a narrow bar slid out of its locks and into the wall beneath the shutters.

"Thank you, sir," said Edgar, giving the man a smart nod.

"Just keep to the left. And no wanderin'."

With the way clear, Kate and Edgar stepped through the gate and rounded a short curl of steps, where the distant sound of people echoed from the walls.

"There'll be people in the market," said Kate. "Do you really think this is a good idea?"

"Not really," said Edgar. "But maybe we can find someone down here who knows the way back to the surface."

"And how are we going to find someone like that?"

"I said it *wasn't* a good idea," said Edgar. "But right now it's the only one we've got."

The steps took them into a wider tunnel that doubled back directly beneath the gatekeeper's room. A voice bellowed down from above them, and the gatekeeper's face glared down through a hatch in the ceiling.

"Keep to the left," he said. "And watch out for wolves. A few of Creedy's beasts got out last night. Don't blame me if you lose a hand in there." The man's laugh echoed around them.

"Wolves?" said Kate as they walked on. "Is he serious?"

Edgar took the lead, following a trail of candles laid down the middle of the floor. "Let's hope we don't find out," he said.

# 11

# THE
# SHADOWMARKET

The candles led Kate and Edgar onto a fenced-off pathway that curled tightly beneath an archway of earth and opened out onto a covered bridge with a steep drop on either side, plummeting into endless darkness. Edgar kept his eyes straight forward. He ran his hand along the side, shaking nervously as the wooden bridge sprang under their feet.

"This bridge has been here for years," said Kate, sensing his nerves. "It's not going to collapse now."

"That's what the person standing on it when it *does* collapse will have said."

It was the first time since leaving the Skilled cavern that Kate felt that she and Edgar were completely alone. She could not hear any shades. The air felt dank and empty. If the bridge did fall, no one would know. No one would find them.

Edgar walked tentatively across the bridge while Kate treated it like any other path, striding on past him toward a circular entrance cut into a wall of earth and rock. Edgar ran the last few steps and touched the solid wall with relief.

"We're here," said Kate, pointing along the tunnel to an arched door just within reach of the lantern light. "One Shadowmarket and not a wolf in sight."

The door was huge, ancient, and riddled with woodworm. There was no handle that Kate could see, just two dangling lengths of rope where handles should have been. She and Edgar took hold of one each and pulled the great doors toward them.

The first thing that hit them was the noise. The doors opened out onto a mass of people shouting, talking, and arguing with one another. Lanterns made from colored glass were hung along the walls of a long, narrow cavern that looked like a jagged scar cut out of the earth. Long troughs of fire were slung beneath blackened chimney vents in the high ceiling, and the air was thick with the smell of hot metal.

The Shadowmarket certainly earned its name. The moment Kate and Edgar stepped inside they joined a huge bustle of people who were carrying flickering lanterns, shuffling and chattering between clusters of market stalls that stood in groups like wooden islands across the cavern floor. Waxy candles oozed over the stall fronts, creating islands of light that captured the face of everyone passing by in a dancing battle between light and dark.

Traders leaned across their counters, trying to attract the attention of people passing by. The busiest stalls were those selling food and clothes, but even from the doorway Kate could see traders selling more unusual goods. One woman was selling talismans cut from ancient bone, while another had tame rats for sale. Neither of them was attracting much business.

As Kate and Edgar walked forward, adding their hooded faces to the crowd, a hidden mechanism rattled to life within the walls and the huge doors creaked closed behind them. Kate had not realized just how many people lived in the City Below. There were hundreds of them in there, all moving between the stalls with bulging bags hanging from their shoulders.

Kate squeezed her way past a stall selling different kinds of clockworks, whose small counter was covered in clicking, whirring creations, from children's toys to clocks that could tell perfect time or even predict the weather, though what use predicting the weather could be underground Kate did not know.

The next stall took up an entire circle all its own with tables around the outside and a small furnace blazing in the center. Its sign declared its owner a coinsmith, and a red-cheeked woman stood among the tables, chatting to a customer while throwing pieces of metal into hot vats, sizzling them down, and pouring them into presses to forge coins marked with a twisting letter *S*. Young children gathered around to watch steam billowing upward as she plunged the presses into a sump of murky green water and anxious customers haggled with her over whether or not a metal jug was worth smelting into four coins or three.

"What now?" asked Kate as she and Edgar were forced to stop.

"We try to blend in," he said.

Neither of them had anything they could turn into new money, but the farther they walked, the more it became obvious that buying things with coins was not the preferred method of trade within the market. More often people leaned in, pointed to items they wanted, and pressed random items of their own into the traders' hands as payment.

Two groups of stalls down from the coinsmith was a stitchery, where old clothes were snipped, measured, patched, and restitched. Next to that was a carpenter whose stall was almost completely hidden beneath a shell of stacked chairs and stools of different heights. The next cluster included a soup seller whose recipes consisted mainly of mushrooms and roots; a bakery selling hot buns almost as fast as its tiny oven could bake them; and a cobbler who prided himself on the quality of his old leather, selling repaired boots decorated with patches of what looked horribly like mouse fur.

From the high ceiling to the wide people-covered floor everything about the Shadowmarket was big, and like most things in and beneath the ancient graveyard city, it had once been used as something else. Hundreds of small doors were sunk into its walls in rows that climbed to at least twenty doors high. They might have been tombs, but they did not have name stones above them like those Kate had seen in other caverns. Ladders linked the narrow ledges that ran beneath the doors, but many of them were broken, left without rungs, or leaning precariously to one side. No one had any reason to use them anymore.

"If we're quick, I'll bet I can grab us a couple of those buns," said Edgar, breathing in deeply as the smell of warm bread overtook that of the coinsmith's fizzling metal.

"What do you think they are?" asked Kate.

"Apple, if we're lucky."

"Not the buns. The doors in the walls."

"Old tombs, probably," said Edgar.

"And those?" Kate pointed at the ceiling, where the flickering troughs were slung high up on pulleys, casting shaky light across the cavern.

"Cheaper than candles, I suppose," said Edgar. "Someone probably dug them out one day and thought they'd be useful."

Kate was so busy looking upward that she was not paying attention to where she was going or to what was coming toward her. Edgar pulled her into a gap between two mushroom sellers and pressed her against the side of the largest stall.

"What did you see?" she whispered.

Together they looked out between the customers and spotted two dark-eyed people walking through the crowds. Kate recognized Baltin immediately; he was fully dressed, with eyes like thunder. The man walking with him was the one who had spoken up against her in the meeting hall, and both were closely followed by at least six more of the Skilled, all looking warily at the people surrounding them.

Kate had assumed that the Skilled were well known, even liked, throughout the City Below, even though she had never seen them mix with ordinary people. Now she saw the truth. Most people who recognized them as Skilled turned away from them at once. Others whispered to one another or glared at them, and some even spat at their feet, cursing them under their breaths. Traders stood up behind their counters, their faces stern, making it clear that they could expect no service from them that day, and parents corralled their children in close as if the Skilled might snatch them away.

"How did they find us so fast?" Edgar whispered as the two men looked through the crowd.

"The spirit wheel," said Kate. "Baltin could have asked it where to find us."

"All it had to do was send them the wrong way," whispered Edgar. "Is that too much to ask?"

Kate felt the veil shift a little as the Skilled drew closer. Frost pinched at her fingertips, and she pulled them into her sleeves, turning away from the two men. "Something's wrong," she whispered. "We should move."

"Why?"

Kate could feel something building close by, a tiny vibration at the very edge of her senses. Then she heard the scream.

The crowd turned to look toward the source of the noise. More screams joined the first, and a woman standing next to a glove stall pointed up at the ceiling with terror in her eyes. Kate followed her gaze and saw what she was looking at for herself.

"She can see them," she said.

"See what?"

A group of shades was moving across the ceiling and tumbling like spiders down into the people below. There were four of them, doing what they had done for many years: reliving the very last moments their tormented spirits could remember, the moments of their deaths. Those who could see them panicked, and those who couldn't tried to calm the others down. Some people tried to laugh it off, patting the frightened woman on the shoulder and looking at her with pity, and the stallholders were quick to assure their customers that there was nothing to worry about.

"It's the sickness," someone whispered nearby. "It's spreading again."

Kate tried not to look at the shades. They might have

been only shadows of their old lives, but the sight of them plummeting to their deaths over and over again was still eerie. "There are shades on the ceiling," she told Edgar. "How can they see them?"

Someone was already leading away the people who had screamed, and one of the stallholders pointed accusingly at the Skilled. "You did this," he said. "You brought the sickness here!"

Baltin looked down at the stallholder with clear disdain. "We have done nothing," he said.

"My customers are seeing creeps and ghouls and who knows what else, while you and your kind hole up safe somewhere, and you're tellin' me it's nothing to do with you?"

"That's right."

"Why aren't you helping people like her? That's what you're supposed to do, isn't it?"

Someone beside him laughed. "They won't do anything," she said. "They're cowards. Leeches. I won't be takin' their coin."

"We did not offer you any coin," said Baltin. "We have no interest in any of you. We are looking for someone, someone I am hoping you may have seen."

"And why would we tell you if we had?"

"Because the girl we are looking for is dangerous, and if we do not find her, you will have far more to worry about than a few creeps and ghouls."

"Is that a threat? He just threatened me!"

Baltin held his hands up in peace. "I am sure you all have heard about what happened in the city square on the Night of Souls?"

A whisper of fear ran through the crowd.

"Those rich types got what they deserved," said one. "A good scare never harmed anyone. We get worse than that down here every day."

"What they saw was more than just a scare," said Baltin. "It was the beginning of something, something that has to be stopped. We can prevent a great tragedy from happening within this city, but to do so, we need to find this girl."

The man with him held up a poster with a drawing of Kate's face and her name in black letters with smaller writing underneath. It was an official poster, stamped by the High Council, one that had to have been taken from the streets of Fume. Kate sank farther back into the dark. She should have expected it, but seeing it for herself made it horribly real. She was wanted by the council. A price had been put on her head. Who knew how many people were watching for her in the streets above, and how many collectors were already prowling the tunnels of the City Below, hunting for her in the dark?

"The wardens are offerin' the freedom of the city to people who know where she is," said the stallholder. "What are you offerin'?"

"A promise," said Baltin. "If this girl escapes, these glimpses of the dead that you see as an inconvenience will become a way of life before long. You all live and work in the sleeping place of our ancestors. This city was not meant for us; it was meant for them. The veil is weakening. If it continues to do so, life here will not only be difficult, it will be impossible. Not just here but across Albion as well."

"And this girl of yours is part of all that?"

"She does not know what damage she is doing," said Baltin, "but the veil is certainly weakening more quickly in her presence. None of you trust the High Council, and you all know that any freedom they offer you will be taken away as soon as the girl is in their hands. We have always helped ourselves here in the City Below. We may not like our neighbors, but we share these caverns, and we have made them our home. Help us find this girl. Do not allow her to tear apart what we have built here."

With one short speech Baltin's presence in the Shadowmarket had gone from being a threat to being an opportunity. Kate felt as if every eye were about to turn upon her, every hand point her out and deliver her to a man who wanted to kill her. But no one turned, no one looked. The poster was passed from hand to hand around the gathered crowd, and whispers spread back through the market, relaying what Baltin had said to those too far away to hear him speak. The marketgoers soon softened to his words, and as they whispered together, Baltin struck the final blow to any hope Kate had of being left in peace.

"You should also know," he said, "that this girl has been convicted of murder."

Silence fell across the nearest stalls.

"She is responsible for the death of the high councilwoman Da'ru Marr, upon the Night of Souls. She was an accomplice that same day in an attack on two boatmen on the Thieves' Way in which one of them died, and I lost one of my own greatest friends at her hand. Three murders. Perhaps more that we have not yet discovered, and who knows how many more to come?"

The crowd spoke up loudly in answer to Baltin's words, and he held his hands up for quiet.

"Kate Winters is a very devious young woman," he said. "She will lie to you, she may even attempt to bargain with you, but she is not to be trusted. Help me find her, and it will be best for everyone."

Baltin did not wait for the crowd's reaction. He strode among them, his sharp eyes flashing side to side as he walked, eager to snatch any sign of Kate he could find.

"What do you think?" asked Edgar.

"I think we're in trouble," said Kate.

"The market should close soon, and I'll bet it gets locked up at night. I say we wait."

"You think we should get ourselves locked in?"

"It would be safer," said Edgar. "No one would be able to get in and find us."

"Unless they decide to stay in here, too," said Kate. "Once word gets back to the gatekeeper that there's a murderer in here somewhere, don't you think he'll let the Skilled look around once everyone's gone?"

"What do you think we should do then?"

"Stay out of sight as long as we can, then move on."

"Everyone will be looking for us now."

"They're looking for me, not you," said Kate. "We can't just stay here, can we? Follow me."

The Shadowmarket thrummed with noise and chatter as Kate headed toward the walls, where the stalls were much quieter and they could move more freely. Lanterns glowed dimly just above her head, and at small tables set up against the wall people were sitting in pairs, leaning over gaming boards, engrossed in the movements of tiny playing pieces.

Kate kept her head down and walked with purpose, trying not to draw attention to herself. That worked well until a stack of used crates forced her to turn a corner and she found herself face-to-face with the woman who had been pointing up at the shades.

"You can see 'em," she said, snapping her head around to look straight into Kate's eyes. "You're a Skilled! You saw 'em, too, didn't you? It can't be the sickness. Can't be. You tell 'em. Maybe they'll listen to you."

Kate looked up at the ceiling. The shades were gone, but the woman was still staring upward, waiting for them to emerge again.

"No one's going to listen to us, lady," said Edgar. "Just don't go shouting about whatever you're seeing and you'll be fine."

"Fine? You call this fine?" The woman held up one of her wrists, which was shackled by a thin chain to a stall beside her. "They're cartin' me off! Sick, they say. Don't want it spreadin'. If seein' things makes ya sick, why aren't they cartin' young lassie here off, too?" She glared at Kate, suddenly recognizing her face, and waggled a finger at her. "You! You're her! The one Mr. High-and-Mighty was talking about."

Kate started walking away, more quickly this time.

"Sorry," said Edgar. "You must be thinking about someone else."

"She's here!" the woman shouted. "The girl you want. It's her!"

"Keep going," said Edgar as dozens of people looked their way. "Don't look back."

Baltin's voice carried across the market. "Seal the doors. Find her!"

"Don't worry," said Edgar, taking hold of Kate's hand as they hurried along. "No one's going to listen to him."

But they did.

People chattered excitedly as word of the hunt spread

through the cavern. There were people everywhere. Kate headed back to the cavern wall, but she could not see a way out. A few people climbed up onto the stall roofs to act as lookouts, hoping to catch sight of a fleeing girl, but Kate was still walking, forcing her feet to stay calm even though she was desperate to run. So long as she kept her eyes low, few people gave her a second glance.

Ghostly shapes moved at the corners of Kate's eyes, and dim figures wandered along the walls ahead of her. At first she thought they were traders; but their faces were unclear, and their bodies shone gently with faint energy. They were old spirits, shades of people who had died long ago. Their link to the living world was barely strong enough for any of them to appear to her for very long, and they faded in and out of sight, oblivious of the clamoring throng of lives being lived around them. Every one of them was looking at the same place, all focusing attention on the exact same thing.

What looked like the broken stub of an old stone pillar stood out a few feet from the cavern wall up ahead. It was waist high and ground to a flat surface at the top. Kate looked at it for only a second, but *Wintercraft* became heavier as she drew closer to it. The veil had more influence there. The book was reacting to it somehow. Kate could feel it as she had in the skull room, like a window opening in her mind. She did not notice the prickle of frost on her skin or the noise of the market fading around her. Soon her feet were slowing down, shortening the gap between her and the Skilled following behind.

"There's being inconspicuous, and there's stopping," said Edgar, pulling her along. Kate could barely hear him through the pounding of blood in her ears. Her head felt as if it were being squeezed tight by two invisible hands. The veil was everywhere, and for a moment she saw everything that had happened in that cavern flash through her mind.

*The cavern's many doors flickered between being freshly hung and being decayed by centuries of neglect. Many of the shades around her disappeared. They had never walked through the cavern during their lifetimes, but the shades near the ceiling continued falling to their deaths one by one. Kate saw them clearly now: ordinary men and women who had lost their footing on a narrow walkway that once spanned the upper level of the cavern.*

*The veil carried her back farther, until she saw bonemen carrying loosely wrapped bodies across the floor, each one coffinless and nameless, with no friends or families to miss them out in the world. And then there were the fiery braziers, set to burn beneath two distant openings in the ceiling. Their true purpose was soon made gruesomely clear as dead bodies were laid out upon them, set alight, and left to burn down to the bone.*

*People buried in this cavern were not treated with the same care and ritual as those in the rest of Fume. Their charred bones* were bundled together and pushed into the open mouths of the doorways in the walls, bundle after bundle, piled up on top of one another across the centuries. They were the bodies of wanderers, strangers, murderers, and thieves, all pushed onto the Night Train and sent to their rest by towns that did not want anything to do with them or the responsibility of their remains.

This was a tormented place. Fear dripped from the walls, making it cold and uninviting. No matter how many traders and customers gathered in the market, the living could never outnumber the dead that still walked in that place. The tunnels around it were quiet because even shades did not want to come near it. The only souls within its walls were those that were sealed there, trapped within that cavern, forced to walk its stones for eternity. The presence of so many living people in one place acted as a buffer against the anguish of the lingering dead, but anyone who stayed in the market alone—Skilled or not—would soon sense the creeping pressure of thousands of souls still lurking within the dark.

Kate was just a few steps away from the broken stone when a group of people appeared around it. They all were shadowy and indistinct, each one dressed in the same brown robe, and they were talking to one another. Kate could not hear what they were saying; but one of them was clearly in charge, and when he looked up, his image became as solid and real as a living person standing right in front of her. His eyes met hers: instantly familiar, their surface glazed with a hint of silver, just like hers.

*The man turned away slowly, his mouth moving to silent words as something emerged on top of the stone. Kate stopped and stood beside it. A spiral was carved upon the stone's flat, dusty face, and the veil showed her something resting upon it: an open book, solid and real in the shades' time but just a shadow of its original self as its image bled into her own world. It was a book filled with words and warnings, a book that Kate knew very well.*

"I think we should speed up a bit," said Edgar, wheezing beside her. The sound of his voice broke Kate suddenly out of the memory. The spiral in the stone was still there, but the book and the people around it were gone. Edgar looked back toward Baltin's head, which was still cutting through the market crowd, gaining all the time.

"There were Walkers down here," said Kate. "They were working with the bonemen. I think they were trying to use *Wintercraft* in this cavern."

"Not really useful right now," said Edgar. "All we need is to get out of here."

*Kate closed her eyes, trying to separate her mind from the veil, but when she opened them again, the silver-eyed man was standing right beside her.*

*She refused to react. She had seen far worse things than a shade that wandered too close, but part of her knew that the man was more than just a memory and much more than a shade.*

*She recognized him as the murdered man whose soul had been bound into one of the spirit wheels, and despite the centuries that separated their two lives, he was watching her.*

*Wintercraft trembled in Kate's pocket as the man picked his own veil-bound book from the stone and held it in between his hands. The action was clear. He had been one of Wintercraft's protectors in his time. He had guarded the book Kate was carrying, just as she did. She had carried it back to a place it had been used in the past, and the veil was reacting to its presence, its place in history.*

*Any doubts Kate had had that Wintercraft was far more than any ordinary book dissipated in that moment. She wondered how many of its protectors' lives had ended in brutal ways and suddenly feared that her own time with the book could be destined to end in the same way.*

"Whatever you're looking at, it can wait," said Edgar. "We have to move."

Kate turned away from the silver-eyed man, and the veil pulled back from her. The sudden noise of the bustling Shadowmarket returned, and she and Edgar ran together, following the cavern wall, searching for another way out.

Edgar was already out of breath. The farther back they went, the quieter the market became. It was only a matter of time before someone realized what was happening and spotted the two of them. If they kept following the wall, they would end up back where they had started, and Kate did not want to be captured by strangers who thought she was a murderer. People had been hanged for far less. She looked at the doors of the old tombs above her and made a decision.

"Blow out the lanterns," she said, opening the glass door of the little light on the wall closest to her and blowing out the flame. "We have to climb."

"What? You want us to go up there?"

"They're going to find us eventually if we stay down here," said Kate. "We can climb fast and hide behind one of those doors. Baltin knows we can't go anywhere. He won't give up."

The nearest ladder was half rotten, with rungs missing at least every third step. As Kate climbed higher, she looked along the wall and saw Baltin reach the carved stone. The Skilled had split up and were fanning out across the market in pairs. She kept going and stepped out onto the first safe ledge she found. It was darker than she had expected up there, and she followed the crumbling path, clinging to the cracks and bumps in the wall with icy fingers. "In here," she said as Edgar climbed up behind her.

She slid back the bolt on one of the doors in the wall. When she touched it, the rusted metal gleamed fresh and new beneath her hand, as she looked into a memory of how the cavern used to be. A fiery torch flared into life beside her, but instead of firelight, the flames looked silver, casting everything in a cold, washed-out glow.

Edgar felt his way along the ledge as if the light did not exist, and two shadowy men, carrying a large trunk of charred bones between them, emerged from the veil behind him . Edgar felt nothing as the men stepped through him, opened the door Kate had chosen, and tipped the bones inside.

Kate tried to ignore what she was seeing. "In here," she said.

Behind the door was an empty space with a sloping ceiling that dug deeply back into the earth, and Kate was glad to see that there were no bones left inside. Someone must have scavenged from those tombs long ago, leaving nothing but dust behind. Once they had ducked inside, Edgar left the door open slightly to keep a close eye on the people searching for them in the cavern below.

Kate was not interested in Baltin or the Skilled. The veil kept shifting between her world and a time when the little room had been filled with bone. It felt as if something were building in the air around her, beyond her control, desperate to be released.

She squeezed her eyes shut, but it did not stop. She could hear the screams of the falling shades, the crack of bone on bone, the voices of the men gathered around *Wintercraft*, and the sounds of the market still going on outside the door.

A man's shout echoed suddenly across the cavern.

"Did you hear that?" asked Edgar, peering out at what was going on. "It's Baltin. I don't think he knows where we are, but he's not looking well. The rest of the Skilled don't look great either. I think something's wrong with them. Kate?"

Edgar looked back, but Kate did not answer.

Edgar crawled across the dusty floor to Kate's side and found her slumped against the wall. He pulled out his matches and struck one, letting the light blaze upon her face. Her skin was icy to touch, but her eyes were open. He carefully placed his palm against her throat but couldn't tell if she was breathing or not.

Edgar was used to being around the Skilled when they were looking into the veil. Kate usually warned him before she was pulled in too deeply, so he knew this time was different. Fear crawled up inside him and wrenched at his gut. He didn't know what to do, so he knelt beside her and cupped her cold hand in his.

"Kate, come back," he whispered, his voice wavering as the match flickered out. "Please come back."

# ← 12 →
# FATE
# FORESEEN

Silas followed Dalliah into the house. She had refused to speak any further until they were inside. She led him into a wide, richly decorated hall, past two matching staircases with black iron balustrades winding to the floors above, and along a corridor into a smaller room lit with firelight.

The heat in there was stifling after the freezing air outside. The room's walls were covered in framed paintings, and some were even sunk behind glass within the floor, every one of them depicting places that Silas knew very well. They were pictures of buildings, streets, and landmarks that all stood within the walls of Fume. One was a full view of the city square with the lines of Fume's largest listening circle marked out across it in faint red light, another showed the sunken lake filled with floating bodies, and a third showed the council chambers completely consumed by fire, the vast buildings reduced to skeletal remains of charred rubble and ash.

"I have witnessed every one of these events," said Dalliah. "The veil has shown me many things that are yet to be. I have hundreds more of these paintings around this house. Many of the events shown within them have already passed from prophecy into history, but none of the scenes in this room have happened yet. Except for one."

She pointed to a small picture at Silas's eye level. At first glance it looked less detailed than the rest, a swirling mass of gray and black focused around a single point. Then he looked closer and saw that the mass was filled with shapes and forms: shades, drawn within the mist of the half-life with a figure standing in the very center looking up through them. It was a girl with silver eyes, her black hair caught upon the wind.

"I painted that picture many years ago," said Dalliah. "This year, on the Night of Souls, it finally came true."

"You could interpret these pictures in any number of ways," said Silas. "If you wait long enough, anything you see in them will come true."

"Perhaps," said Dalliah. "But historic events are not as isolated as they appear to be. Each one exists as a link in a far longer chain. When Kate Winters stood inside that listening circle, she set in motion a cataclysmic chain of events that will allow everything you see here to come to pass. I have watched history unfold in similar ways many times before. I thought you might appreciate a glimpse into the future of our world."

Silas looked farther along the wall and saw a picture of Albion's monstrous Night Train, the train that had carried people into war and slavery for generations. The great engine lay on its side, its wheels broken and forced from its tracks. Its mismatched panels had been torn away by scavengers, and its front grille was choked with creeping weeds. Another painting showed rows of dead bodies laid out in the streets of an Albion town, and a third depicted the scene of a public execution. Scarred wardens watched over cages full of sickly people who were being released one by one and led into the hands of their executioner, whose silver sword was raised ready to be plunged into the back of a kneeling prisoner at his feet.

"These pictures are not the future," he said.

"The veil has shown me these events," said Dalliah. "The veil does not lie."

"Even if it is true, how could one girl be responsible for any of this?"

"She has already caused the first stone to fall. The rest of our world will crumble soon enough."

Silas noticed a thin table standing along the wall behind the open door. A cloth covering the unmistakable shape of a dead body was pulled over it, and a man's arm hung limply over the side with dried blood tracing along the skin toward a dark stain that had pooled beneath his fingertips.

"The dead speak to me," said Dalliah, "just as they speak to you. I have chosen to listen. One day you will, too."

"Kate would not want to be responsible for this 'future,'" said Silas, returning to the paintings.

"Are you sure of that? You barely know the girl. You cannot presume to know what she wants. She is a Winters, after all. Her family's priorities have often proved . . . unexpected, when placed under pressure."

A door at the back of the room opened. Silas turned, and Bandermain walked in, scraping the tip of Silas's blue-black sword along the floor.

"What the girl wants is no longer important," said Bandermain.

"What is he doing here?" demanded Silas.

"*I* am protecting my investment. I am here to make sure that everything runs smoothly, including you. I remember you being more of a patient man, Silas. If you had waited, my men would have brought you here themselves. Lady Grey has had us watching for you for weeks. It is a shame they could not deliver you here as my prisoner, but you are here nonetheless. I call that a victory."

"Your men could not even keep one prisoner under guard," said Silas. "They are slipping."

"They do not know you as well as I do," said Bandermain. "I doubt any of them would have expected a man with your injuries to escape from that room. When I was told you were gone, I'll admit, I was impressed."

Silas turned to Dalliah, keeping one eye upon Bandermain

as he spoke. "Do any of your pictures include an incompetent Blackwatch officer and his men?" he asked. "I find it hard to believe the future has any use for him."

"Officer Bandermain is here at my request," said Dalliah, crossing the room and standing at Bandermain's side. "He was skeptical about the full extent of your capabilities and did not know if we could trust you."

"I would say no," said Silas. "Men like us do not trust our enemies. We kill them."

"Not in my house," said Dalliah. "Bandermain had to be sure the rumors about you were true before moving to the next stage of our plan."

"*Your* plan?"

"Yes. Bandermain and I have an arrangement. You would be wise to consider joining us."

Bandermain cleared his throat and walked slowly toward Silas, barely concealing his hard-earned hatred of him behind a grimacing smile. It was only when he drew closer that Silas noticed that something about him had changed since the last time they had met. His forehead gleamed with a thin glaze of sweat, his lips were thin and bloodless, and his eyes were shot with red at the edges. His shoulders were hunched slightly, though he still kept his chin arrogantly high, and every breath made his chest quiver slightly, betraying a secret pain. He was hiding it well, but Silas could see that beneath his mask of strength Bandermain was a very ill man.

Bandermain swept the sword up smoothly and balanced the flat of the blade on his cut palm with the hilt laid upon the other. He glanced at Dalliah, and Silas saw her nod slightly out of the corner of his eye. "I believe this is yours," he said.

Silas reclaimed his weapon, taking it from Bandermain and sliding it into its sheath as Bandermain stepped back. It was obvious he had not wanted to return the sword. Dalliah was ordering him to do it. The question was why.

"So the Blackwatch take their orders from you now," he said to Dalliah. "I see you have a new mistress, Celador. To return the weapon that killed your own men . . . I cannot say I would have done the same in your position."

"My men died in battle," said Bandermain, his voice cut with simmering anger. "They were honorable deaths. That is all a soldier can ask."

"There are more important matters at stake here than war and pride," said Dalliah. "Sometimes it takes more than one person to complete a task, Officer Dane. The Blackwatch have proven themselves very useful to me. You will come to appreciate their efforts once they deliver Kate Winters to us."

"Why should that be of any interest to me?" asked Silas. "Do you plan to treat her as well as you did that man back there?"

"The veil has shown me that the influence of her young life promises to be far-reaching," said Dalliah. "If you had known how important she will be, you would never have let her go. The girl's blood lives within your veins. You should not have left her behind."

"She can take care of herself," said Silas. "She means nothing to me."

Bandermain spoke up. "You told me he would try to protect the girl! If he does not care if she lives or dies, there is no reason for him to call her here!"

Dalliah held up a hand to silence him.

"If he truly feels no responsibility toward her, his judgment will not be clouded by his conscience," she said. "He will not turn away from what must be done."

"And what would that be?" asked Silas.

"I am not your enemy," said Dalliah. "We are the same. Equals."

"If that is true, why send the Blackwatch to hunt me?"

"Because I can no longer afford to leave anything to chance. Do you know how many people are looking for you? Securing the Blackwatch was a necessity. If they had found you before I did, they would have delivered you straight to the Continental leadership. I knew you would be weakened here, and they are very effective hunters. I could not risk them finding you first, so I made Bandermain an offer. I secured his services and those of his men for as long as it took us to find you. As you can see, their efforts were successful."

"We knew where you were," said Bandermain. "My

men have had eyes upon you from the moment you left Fume's walls, but we could not approach you within your own country. We had to lure you here, where you would be weakened enough to control. Fortunately I have an asset posted within your capital that you and your council have overlooked for a very long time. One of my agents is stationed within your city walls. His orders are to gather information about your capital's weaknesses, its routines, and the people in power. He has been very useful to me over the years."

"Spies within Fume are nothing new," said Silas. "I have killed dozens of Blackwatch agents myself."

"You hunt your enemies in the shadows," said Bandermain. "This one lives in clear sight. All I had to do was point him in your direction when the opportunity presented itself, and I knew he would lead you to me. The right amount of gold placed in the right hands carries a great deal of influence in Albion society. At first he was just a spy, but the right opportunities taken at the right time allowed him to become so much more. While you were gathering up your own people to send to war, he became a trusted friend of one of your councilmen. In time every decision the old man made was discussed with my agent first. Through him, the Blackwatch were able to hear every secret the council had, secrets they never would have shared with someone like you. I know more about your country's leaders than you do, Silas. When the old man died, he had already named his successor, the indispensable friend who had been so helpful to him in his final years."

"You have an agent on the High Council. Who?"

"Did you not find it suspicious that a High Council member would arrange a meeting with one of your known associates at a place you just happened to be?" said Bandermain. "It was a gamble, sending him there, but when he talked to your friend about Dalliah Grey, you took the bait perfectly. Who do you think has been coordinating the deliberately incompetent search for you? Do you really believe the wardens would not have found you by now unless someone was intentionally leading them away from your trail? My men have been inside Fume for years, watching your people eat themselves away from the inside. You and your wardens have done more damage to your country than we ever could. All we have to do is sit back and watch you destroy yourselves."

"When I return to Albion, your man will be the first to die," said Silas.

"I do not think so. You have already had a hand in the murder of one councilwoman. The wardens will not let you anywhere near the High Council again."

The room flooded with Silas's rage. He was about to challenge Bandermain when Dalliah stepped calmly between them.

"We do not have time for your petty disagreements," she said. "We all are well aware of Silas's history and the fate that befell his former mistress."

"Da'ru is dead," said Silas, "as Bandermain and his men soon will be."

"She and I communicated many times when she was alive," said Dalliah. "There was a time when I believed she might eventually be strong enough to help me complete my work. You cannot deny that what she did was impressive. She did not have the abilities of a Walker, yet she mastered the techniques within *Wintercraft* well enough to bind a soul to her own."

"I was there. I know what she did."

"Da'ru's death was no surprise to me," said Dalliah. "I may not have foreseen it, but I knew it was inevitable. I followed her progress since she was a child, and it was my research that first allowed her to locate the book hidden within a Winters grave. At that time I believed that all of the greatest Skilled families were long dead and that someone like Da'ru would be my only chance to regain what I had lost, but from the moment Kate Winters first entered the veil, I knew I was wrong. Da'ru was a distraction. She was not ready for the world I planned to show her. Kate is different. She is the one we need."

"I do not need anything," said Silas.

"It has not been long since your spirit was broken. You may accept it now, but in fifty, eighty years, when everything you have known has changed, you will not be so accepting of it," said Dalliah. "Only the two of us know what it is like to be feared by the living and turned away by death. Our fates are the same. We will be left to walk this world together long after the last of our enemies and allies are dead and gone. But fate *can* be changed. We can reclaim our spirits and free them from the dark. This is your chance to make things right."

"I am not interested."

"You will be." Dalliah reached out to touch Silas's face, and he snatched her hand away.

"What are you doing?"

"Opening your eyes," said Dalliah. "The veil will answer us more easily upon my land. With my help, you can see what has become of Kate for yourself. If she dies before her time, our hopes will die with her."

Silas felt the energy of the veil gathering around Dalliah and saw frost creeping across her fingernails and along her eyelashes as the veil closed in. He had no reason to trust her, but suspicious as he was, a part of him was interested in what she had to say. She was the only person who knew what it was like to live his life and how much he wanted to undo the damage done to his spirit. He wanted to trust her, so he allowed her hand to rest against his face and let his thoughts lift gently into the veil's cold mist.

*The veil swept icily across the room, allowing Silas to see the energies of life carried deep within the people around him as though a filter had been placed across his eyes. Normally the spirit carried in a person's body was visible as a bright* all-encompassing glow that spread from the core of the body into a pale aura that misted around him. The dead man's spirit shone like candlelight several feet from his body, unable to return to life or to free himself from the threads of the veil Dalliah had used to seal him into a trap. Dalliah's own soul was very different. She barely carried any light at all other than a tiny speck of white light focused in the very center of her chest, offering proof at least that she truly did possess a broken soul, but Bandermain's energy was the biggest surprise.

Instead of the soft light that normally surrounded the living, Bandermain's body was shrouded in a faint, sickly glow. His spirit was there, but it was pulsing weakly, trying to pull away from a body that could no longer support it within the living world. Only Silas's veil sight could reveal the truth. Bandermain's body was damaged to the point of collapse, his spirit, eager and ready to pass into death. With energies like that, he should already have been dead, yet aside from the coughing, on the surface he still looked relatively alive and well.

Bandermain was certainly a curiosity, but Silas turned his attention away from him and concentrated upon searching for Kate instead.

He did not need to look very far.

The spirit of a living Walker who had not been trained to control her influence acted like a powerful magnet to souls within the veil, attracting them toward it and shining brightly like a blazing light. The physical distance between them made no *difference. The veil did not recognize distance or time; everything within it was connected. When Silas focused upon Kate, the veil revealed her to him, her spirit sealed inside an empty tomb of stone.*

She was barely alive, her body huddled limply against the wall. Seeing her there, so close to death, sent a pang of guilt coursing through his soul. He had warned her to leave the city. When he left her behind, he had trusted she would be protected. She was not supposed to be there. Not like that. She was supposed to be safe.

Aware of Dalliah's watchful presence close by, Silas could not afford to reveal his true fears for the girl. He focused all his concentration upon finding her instead. That tomb could have been anywhere within the maze of Fume's ancient underground caverns. There was no way to tell where.

Dalliah's spirit moved beside him, joining him in the veil.

"The Skilled turned against her, just as you warned her they would," she said. "They tried to kill her. She and the boy barely escaped. Now she is overwhelmed. Even death will not find her spirit if it wanders too far. If she survives, the Skilled will find her, and they will finish her themselves. You left Kate to the mercy of the wolves, Silas. This is all a consequence of what you have done."

There were many things in Silas's life that he had reason to regret, but at that moment he regretted nothing more than riding his stolen horse out of Fume knowing that Kate would be hunted once he was gone. He had been alone for too long. He had let his own fears cloud his judgment. Kate had helped him when every other living soul feared him, and he had abandoned her.

"Walkers have lived in Fume for centuries," he said. "None of them were affected in this way."

"That is because none of them lived in times like these," said Dalliah. "Something has changed. The veil is weakening. The barrier between this world and the next is coming to an end."

"That is impossible. The veil cannot fall."

"Everything dies," said Dalliah. "This world will die one day. Even we eventually will cease to live, though it may not be the form of death that we expect. All it takes is the right conditions, the correct sequence of events. Five hundred years ago the bonemen made a mistake. They experimented with Wintercraft and changed the course of history. They were the ones who first tore the veil with their experiments upon the dead and the dying. They were ignorant. History does not record the darker aspects of their work, but I was there. I saw with my own eyes the damage they caused. It took great sacrifices to repair what they had broken. They suffered for their mistakes, and their fate was well deserved."

Silas caught the bitterness in Dalliah's voice when she spoke about the bonemen, and what was left of her spirit flared in anger at the memories her time with them had left behind. He was willing to assume that whatever "sacrifice" the bonemen had made, she had been part of it. She had been with them when they disappeared from history, and it had left a mark upon her.

*He could not tell if it was rage or fear, but it was there.*

*"What has that got to do with Kate?" he asked.*

*"When the bonemen tore the veil open, Walkers helped them seal it again. The veil threatened to overtake all Albion, exposing the living to the half-life and blending the two realms into one. Albion was not ready for that, but our attempt to close the tear was only ever meant to be a temporary solution. As soon as the tear was brought back under control and the living world was separated from the veil once again, the seal we had created started to degrade. In those times, five hundred years were almost an eternity. The bonemen assumed that those left behind would have plenty of time to repair it fully before the tear ever became a threat to the living world again; but the bonemen do not exist anymore—the High Council saw to that—and no one has risen to take their place. The Walkers are dead, and the Skilled have ignored the threat of the veil for generations. They did not carry on the bonemen's work. Recently they have begun to dabble with the remains of the dead, attempting to rediscover and understand the old ways, but it is too late. The Walkers knew that this was coming. They saw the threat from the very beginning, and now there are only two of us left, the girl and I. The Winters family were always the best of us. It does not surprise me that their descendants were the only ones to survive."*

*"If you are what you say you are, why do you need her?" asked Silas. "What does she have that a Walker who has lived for five centuries does not?"*

"She possesses something both you and I have lost," said Dalliah. "The power of a soul can be almost infinite when it is used the right way. We may have lost ours, but Kate Winters's spirit carries all the potential of her parents' family lines concentrated in one young life. The book of Wintercraft teaches the Skilled how to master their spirit, to use its energy as fuel to do what ordinary people cannot do. With the right guidance, Kate could bring the restless dead down upon this world with the force of her will alone. You and I are echoes of the souls we used to be, Silas. We are revenants, neither truly dead nor truly living. We belong nowhere and trust no one. Only we know what it is like to suffer for the mistakes of the past. Kate has not suffered as we have. Her spirit is still intact. She is the only one who can influence a falling veil now."

Silas could see Kate's spirit struggling to reconnect with her physical body and knew there was nothing he could do. He could sense her fear, her confusion, and an emptiness that was growing slowly inside her. She felt betrayed. When Silas first met her, Kate's mind had been clear. Her life had been simple and happy. Now she was lost. The only thing keeping her connected to the living world was the presence of a second soul he had not noticed before. Someone was right beside Kate; someone who had no connection to the veil at all, holding her hand as her spirit wound itself tightly around his, using him to anchor her to the world. It was a young soul, carrying with it the weight of a tormented past. It had to be Kate's stubborn companion, Edgar Rill. At the very least she was not alone.

*"If you need Kate's help to repair the veil, why don't you just ask her?" said Silas, hoping to draw Dalliah's attention away from the girl. "Why involve the Blackwatch at all? You will only drive her away if your men try to hunt her."*

Dalliah pulled her consciousness back from the veil. Silas let his mind return to the painted room, and Bandermain stared at them both with surprise as Dalliah casually continued their conversation.

"There is a sickness spreading across Albion, allowing ordinary people to witness aspects of the half-life," she said. "People have begun to see phantoms and spirits. Many believe they are going mad, and of all of them, the Skilled will soon be affected the worst. I have seen this happen before. As the veil collapses and spreads, the assault of so many lost souls upon their senses will prove too much. Many Skilled died when the veil fell the first time; more will die this time."

"You did not answer my question," said Silas.

"Because it is based upon an assumption," said Dalliah. "We both were cursed with this broken life. The veil is our prison, but when it falls, everything will change. The protections the first Walkers put in place will collapse any day now, allowing the living world and the half-life to exist as one. Our spirits are both bound to the half-life, and when it falls, they will return to us. We will be healed, and our lives will be our own. I do not want to *repair* the veil. I intend to help it on its way."

"How?" asked Silas. "That cannot be possible."

"If we release Kate Winters's spirit in the right place at the right time, we can control the tear within the veil. We can channel the veil through her, focusing everything upon one single point. We can be present at the exact epicenter of the event that will change the world. Every lost soul will be drawn to Kate before the veil spreads fully across the world. Our spirits will be there for us to claim!"

"Release her spirit?" Silas knew too well what that meant. "You intend to kill her."

"The veil will fall, regardless of anything you or I can do," said Dalliah. "It is too late to save it now. This way we can use it to our advantage. We can take back what was stolen from us."

Silas saw the spark of excitement in Dalliah's eyes and recognized her desperate need from dark times he had known in his own life. She was talking about changing the entire course of future history, allowing ordinary people to see into a world that most of them did not believe even existed. It would cause panic and chaos. Nothing would ever be the same if the veil came down. It would be the end of life as everyone knew it. The new age would not be one of science, peace, or exploration; it would be one of fear, and Dalliah was ready to murder an innocent girl to make it happen.

Bandermain did not look at all surprised by what she was proposing. Perhaps he did not fully understand what could come of countless shades' being free to sweep across the world, visible to every living eye, free to follow, influence, and speak with the living. Dalliah was right: everything would change.

The situation was worse than Silas could ever have imagined. He had traveled to the Continent for answers and had walked instead into a nightmare. The veil was falling, the High Council had a Continental spy in its midst, and the woman he had hoped might become an ally was intent upon murder and changing the world for the worst, all for the sake of two broken souls.

Bandermain was watching Silas closely, waiting for him to say something. Whatever arrangement Dalliah had made with him had to have something to do with his illness. There had to be a reason he was still alive, and Dalliah was more than capable of extending a human life if it served her purpose. Until Silas knew more, there was no way to know how far Bandermain would go to honor it.

Dalliah was staring at Silas, smiling as if he were her truest friend. She clearly expected him to see the world the way she did, as something expendable, something that was there to be crushed on their way to getting what they both wanted at last.

"I am talking about freedom," she said quietly. "Death will accept us when the time comes. We can regain our souls, and we will be whole again. Surely that is worth the life of one young girl, Silas. Don't you agree?"

## ← 13 →
## THE WORLD BENEATH

Kate could see Edgar. She could hear him talking to her in the dark, but she could not answer him. He looked like a reflection of himself cast in a pool of water, ghostly and not quite real. She could feel his hand on hers, and she focused upon it, trying to break out of the veil and back into her life, but nothing she tried made any difference.

Kate felt as if she were half awake, being pulled to the threshold of many different dreams. It was hard to focus upon anything. There was no order to it and no reason for her to be connecting with the veil there at all. She concentrated upon her own world and felt the presence of the Skilled in the Shadowmarket, a group of them, each one looking into the veil, trying to find her. She shut her mind to them, but they were too close. Nothing could hide within the veil. They were coming.

Edgar's face moved back in front of her. He kept looking at the door. He knew they were coming, too. "Kate," he whispered,

*"I know this isn't a good time, but I have an idea." He moved away, letting go of her hand, and Kate felt her spirit's link to him break. It felt as if all the air had been pressed from her lungs at once, and the shock of the separation jolted her spirit back into life.*

Kate felt a rush of blood returning to her fingertips. Her body breathed again, and her fingers reached out for Edgar as he went to open the door, as if to hold him back. "What are you doing?" she asked.

Edgar's face sank with sheer relief. He scrambled across the floor and hugged Kate as tightly as he dared. "Welcome back," he said, with a nervous smile. "Do me a favor. Please, never do that again. I didn't know if I had to do something or if— if I just had to leave you to it."

"I'm all right," said Kate. "I can handle this."

Edgar reluctantly let her go.

"You shouldn't have to handle it," he said. "We'll get out of here. I promise."

Kate smiled. It was a doubtful promise but a sincere one. "What were you doing at the door?" she asked.

"We've got trouble outside."

Kate did not wait for her body to settle again. She crawled to the door beside Edgar, and he opened it just enough for them both to see down onto the market floor below. She must have been inside the veil for a long time because all the clocks showed the time as approaching night. The fires in the ceiling troughs had burned down to a faint glow, and lanterns flickered across the cavern as people walked between the market stalls. There were fewer people down there than earlier, and every one of them was busy carrying, lifting, and moving about.

The clusters of stalls were being folded and packed until they looked more like piles of huge wooden boxes than counters and shelves, and the spaces in between the stalls were filled with people pushing small handbarrows or pulling wide carts, clearing the way ahead of them with shouts and whistles. Everyone seemed to have lost interest in Baltin and his men. Kate could not see them at first, until Edgar pointed to a group of people separate from the rest. They were the only people who were standing still, and they had gathered in the light of a candle lantern held by the gatekeeper Kate and Edgar had met on their way in.

"They're packing up," said Edgar. "It looks like everyone locks the stock away at night, but that old guy could mean trouble. I heard him make an announcement a few minutes ago. All who leave the market tonight have to give their names and be counted out. I think Baltin's told him about us. I saw him take ill, the same time you did, but the effect didn't last as long. There'll be people waiting for us at the exits, and if we don't leave, they'll know we're still in here. The Skilled will have all night to find us if the gatekeeper stays here with them."

"Baltin's not going to give up, is he?"

"Probably not. But I have an idea. Down there." Edgar pointed to a large stall that sold well-made wool rugs and shawls. The woman who owned it was loading her valuable items into a handbarrow and padlocking large wooden panels into place around her stall, making sure the rest of her goods were locked up tight. "We're going to stow away in one of those barrows," he said.

Kate looked down at the woman, who was having enough trouble lifting a barrow full of rugs, never mind one with two people hiding in it. "You're serious, aren't you?"

"We hide in one of the barrows and let the traders roll us out of here. Baltin and the Skilled will think we're still hiding in here somewhere, and they'll waste a night searching an empty cavern, giving us a chance to get a head start. It's perfect. Tell me what possible flaw there could be in that plan."

"It's crazy, it'll never work, and it will get us both caught? We'll be spotted before we're even down the ladder."

"Not if we're careful," said Edgar. "That's what I was looking at. See? This ledge we're on leads right along the side of the cavern. Everyone's heading in that direction. There must be a way out over there. If we walk the ledge in the dark, we can get closer to it, climb down, and hide in a barrow. No one will see us. And even if people do, I don't think they'll say anything. They'll just think they're seeing shades again, and no one will want people to think they have the sickness after those people got carted off, will they?"

"What about the Skilled?" asked Kate. "There are shades in here. What if they use the veil to find us?"

"I don't think the shades are being too helpful," said Edgar. "Otherwise they would have found us by now. And if anyone sees us once we're down there, we can move swiftly on to my second brilliant plan—head for the exit and leg it."

"All right," said Kate. "Let's do this your way."

Edgar felt his way out of the door, and Kate followed him onto the narrow path, where she quickly took the lead, picking her way carefully along the ledge and heading along the cavern wall. The traders were still going about their business far below. There were last-minute deals to be made and trading to be done with late customers who refused to stop bartering until the very last item was packed away.

Just being there, looking out across all those people, reminded Kate of the life she used to have, when her days were spent behind a bookshop counter, staring through a window onto a market much like this one. She had never realized how safe she had felt back in her hometown. Life had been easier then. Everything had changed so quickly, and she had barely had time to miss what she had lost. The bookshop had burned. Her home was gone, and now Artemis had turned against her. She could never go back to that life. She wished she had known just how precious it had been when she was living it every day.

Kate tested the sturdiness of each ladder she found, hoping

to find a safe way down, but did not trust any of them. Most were hung on rusted nails, and she had no intention of trusting her or Edgar's life to something that could give way beneath them. Edgar stayed unusually quiet as they walked, until at last, her hand found a ladder that felt sturdy enough to use.

Kate made her way down a few of the rungs and then stopped, hearing people whispering beneath her. She edged lower slowly, signaling for Edgar to stay where he was. They were not the only ones in that cavern trying not to be seen. She was just close enough to make out two old women clinging to the shadows, cupping tiny candles in their hands, and talking under their breath.

"Hey! Don't think we can't hear you creepin' about up there," said one, grabbing Kate's ladder with a wiry fist and shaking it hard. "There's work to be done. Get down here and get on with it."

The women went back to their conversation, and Kate dropped to the ground beside them.

"Go on and make yerself useful," said the ladder shaker, pointing out into the busy crowds.

Kate hesitated, and the two women looked around the cavern before scuttling off, carrying large bags under their arms. Kate waited until they had been absorbed by the crowds and then waved Edgar down.

"Do you think they recognized you?" he asked.

"I don't think so."

The smell of dried tea leaves wafted from the nearest stalls, and Kate tugged up the hood of her coat. "There are no barrows over here," she whispered. "The closest one's next to that vegetable seller. It's too open. We'll be seen."

Two people were walking slowly by a few dozen feet away. One of them was Greta, the Skilled magistrate, and the determination on her face was chilling.

"One of the exits is right there," said Edgar. "We should go unnoticed if we're quick. They can't be everywhere."

Kate kept one hand on the cavern wall and followed Edgar toward the larger of the two exits, where a long line of traders was waiting to push their barrows out and make their way home.

"There," she said, peering past a clothes stall that had already closed up. "What about those two?" She pointed to two large barrow carts stuffed with rolled-up blankets. Each had two large wheels at the back, two wooden legs to stand on, and thin bars pointing out the front, allowing it to be tilted back and pulled along. Each one was so big and heavy that it needed to be pulled by two men, making it an excellent place to hide.

Kate dared to move out among the closed stalls, where most of the market lanterns had already been blown out. The line was moving slowly, and the carts kept stopping and starting, giving plenty of time for stowaways to climb on board.

"That apple seller behind them might see us," said Edgar.

"Not if we distract him."

The floor around the closed-up stalls was littered with loose pieces of wood and sticks. Kate picked up a long, thin piece and held it like a spear.

"Now I *know* you're crazy," said Edgar.

"If we can get this in his wheel, he'll think it's jammed. What's your aim like?"

"Lousy," said Edgar.

Kate brought her arm back, preparing to throw. "Get ready to run as soon as he's looking the other way. Ready?"

She threw the stick hard through the air, aiming for the spokes in the apple cart's front wheel. The shot missed. The stick speared awkwardly between the side wheels and skidded beneath the cart. The apple seller kept walking until the back wheel thumped against the fallen stick and the cart bounced, sending a sack of fruit toppling off the back and scattering apples out across the floor.

"Ha!" said Edgar. "That'll do."

It wasn't exactly what Kate had planned to happen, but it was good enough.

Traders behind the seller helped him rescue his fallen fruit, while Kate and Edgar bolted for the blanket-filled carts.

"You go in that one," Kate whispered. "Split up. Less weight."

Edgar did as he was told. The two of them climbed into separate carts and buried themselves in between the blanket rolls. When the line started moving again, only one elderly man noticed the extra cargo nestled in among the rest.

"Free rides, eh?" he said, grinning through pink gums. "I remember those days. Enjoy 'em while they last, lad. More fool the pullers, I say!" The old man chuckled to himself as he shuffled along the line, but he didn't breathe a word to the traders in front.

Kate tugged the end of one of the blankets over herself as the cart edged closer to the exit. That old man could have walked around the entire cavern in the time it took the cart to reach the gate, and Kate eventually heard people arguing up ahead.

"You're not searching through anything of mine!" said one of the traders. "I've got fine linens among this lot. You're not putting your filthy hands all over them, and you're *definitely* not doing anything with *that*."

"Out of my way." That was Baltin's voice.

Kate felt the cart jolt as someone climbed up onto the side.

"You'll put filthy great holes in everything!"

"No one passes through this gate without being checked."

Kate heard a dull thud as something stabbed into the fabric beside her. The blanket traders yelled in protest, and Kate tucked her knees up, making herself as small as possible, before Baltin slashed at the fabric with what sounded like a blade. She stayed deathly still, afraid to breathe or move again in case he heard her. The traders shouted at him to stop, and he dragged two rolls down from the cart, threatening to send the rest of the stock toppling to the floor.

Kate heard sounds of a tussle as the two traders pulled Baltin off the cart, telling him that there was no one inside it and if he wanted to take his anger out on something, he should go find someone else's stock to destroy. The traders were tough, hefty types, and Baltin was wise enough to decide that he was satisfied with his search.

"Next!"

The traders threw the fallen rolls back onto the cart and, as they pulled away, Kate caught a glimpse of Baltin behind her, stopping the apple seller and demanding to be able to look inside his sacks. The view from her hiding place was limited to the cavern ceiling and anything directly behind the cart. She could not see Edgar's cart anywhere and could only hope that it had been checked and passed at the same time as hers by one of Baltin's men. She could not risk raising her head out of her hiding place to look. Baltin's eyes were badly bloodshot, and he had looked desperate enough to do anything. If he had found her, Kate had no doubt that he could have used that sword on her there and then.

The blanket traders pulled their carts out of the Shadowmarket and into the tunnels of the City Below. Once they were out of the market, most of the traders began heading different ways. Conversations were struck up between those who shared the same tunnels, and the only things any of them really talked about were the sickness, Baltin's behavior, and the sudden interest so many people had in the whereabouts of a missing girl.

Kate closed her eyes and tried to let the gentle movement of the cart calm her after the madness of the cavern, but all she saw when she closed them were the warnings given to her by the spirit wheel: the bird, the dagger, and the mask. She wondered where Silas was and if the High Council was still hunting him.

She watched the ceiling go by as the traders carried her deep into tunnels she did not know and was glad to see that they were heading upward at last. The paths the traders chose curled gently uphill. They headed through old arched doors, past branching junctions, and over a narrow bridge that rattled and creaked as they crossed it. Kate could feel that they were high up, at the top of a dizzyingly high drop, and the carts took it in turns to cross carefully one by one. She wrapped herself in one of the blankets and dared to look out over the side.

The first thing she saw was light, thousands of bright firelights shining from spaces cut into the walls. The bridge hung perilously over a huge cavern sliced through by what looked like a river surging distantly below. The floor of the cavern was too dark to see, but the walls were alive with life. People were living there. Staircases had been built in zigzags between the many levels, and there were at least twenty or thirty floors laid out like a honeycomb, reaching higher than the bridge and down beneath it. She could see rooms cut into the earth, with small fires burning within them for warmth, and there were families there; small armies of children ran up and down the staircases like excitable mice. As the cart drew nearer, Kate could hear flute music echoing gently from the cavern walls and the sounds of people talking carrying from the stones.

Kate had thought the tunnels and smaller caverns were all that made up the City Below, but there, in that place, she realized she was wrong. This was a true city. What she was looking at was a settlement all its own, a place large enough to hold thousands of people yet still not feel crowded. It was a world beneath the earth, an existence completely separate from the world outside.

The pathways were neat and clean. The air was clear, and Kate heard the throbbing heartbeat of spinning fan blades high above her, drawing cool air down from vents cut into the ceiling. She half expected to see light twinkling through them when she looked up, but all she saw was the solidness of rock.

Kate had forgotten all about trying to hide. She could not help staring at the immensity of what was hidden beneath Fume's feet. People were not just surviving; they were happy down there. They were living.

Soon the cart left the bridge and began rolling gently down a winding slope, where it stopped and started a few times. A quick glance up ahead showed Kate why. They were coming to a checkpoint. Three men and three women were talking to the traders who owned a metalworking barrow just ahead. Behind her, more traders were joining the line, and at last she spotted Edgar's blanket-filled barrow a short distance away. She hid beneath some loose blankets as the line moved and her cart was allowed to move up next.

"Residents," one of the blanket traders said brightly. "Back from the market."

"Make any good sales?" asked one of the women.

"Good enough. The rest of the stock got ripped up by some idiot at the door."

"We heard something about that," said the woman. "You're not the only one who has complained. Make sure you salvage what you can."

"Will do."

The cart lurched and drove on without anyone's looking into the back. Kate moved the blanket from one of her eyes and peered out again as it headed across a second small bridge and trundled right up to the front of the lowest houses. She had to get Edgar's attention somehow. They had to get out of the carts before they stopped or they would risk being found. Kate waited as long as she dared. Then once she had passed into the farthest point between a pair of lanterns hanging over the road, she crawled along the blankets, waited for her moment, and jumped.

# 14

# WITHIN
# THE WALLS

Kate ran for the shadows as the second blanket cart rolled by. Edgar was still not moving, so she picked up a stone and lobbed it into the blankets. Edgar shifted the blankets, confused, and Kate waved to get his attention. As soon as he saw her, he scrambled down from the cart and scuttled over to her hiding place.

"What are you doing out here?" he whispered.

Kate pointed to the ceiling. "Do you see those vents?"

"Yes . . ." Edgar said slowly. "If you're thinking of using them as a way out, I don't think either of us can climb well enough to even get up there."

"I know we can't reach the vents," said Kate. "But what about chimneys?"

"Big dark things with fires burning away at the bottom? That's an even worse idea."

"At least we know they go upward."

"And most of them are lit by the look of it."

"Most of them. Not all," said Kate.

She stared at the lantern lights of the carts still moving along the other side of the cavern.

Something was happening on the bridge.

A few of the carts had stopped. Kate could hear traders shouting. They were pointing at something, trying to get the attention of the people manning the checkpoint, but no one was listening.

"What's going on?" asked Edgar.

It was hard to tell from so far away, but one thing they did see was a small baker's cart tilting precariously onto its side at the far end of the bridge. The baker who was pushing it tried to stop it from falling, but gravity took hold. The right wheel gave way, and the cart plunged over the edge of the bridge and plummeted into the distant river. At first it looked like an accident. The baker was shouting, other traders were holding her back from the edge, and then Kate saw a rope dangling from the ceiling with someone dressed in black clambering up it toward one of the vents.

"Look at that!" she said, pointing up at the disappearing man.

"Did he just pull that cart off the bridge?" said Edgar. "Why would anyone—? There's another one!"

A second man was clinging to the wall on the opposite side of the cavern. He waited there for a short time; then he let go and slid down a long rope all the way to the ground. The more Kate and Edgar looked for them, the more men they could see taking up positions around the cavern.

"Blackwatch?" said Edgar.

"I hope not."

"They're tricky enough for Blackwatch. And I've never seen a warden do anything like that. What's that? On the bridge."

The traders were moving again, but instead of heading forward, the carts were rolling carefully to one side to allow something else to pass by. Seven men, dressed in long red coats, strode across the wooden bridge. Every one of them was armed with a bow, a dagger, or a sword, and they advanced right through the traders without being challenged. The guards at the checkpoint looked up as the men marched toward them. One of the guards reached for her weapon, but before the others could react, arrows cut through the air from the men on ropes, and all six guards fell dead to the floor.

"Definitely Blackwatch," said Edgar, already backing away. "They must be stepping up the search. What were you saying about chimneys?"

Kate's thoughts went immediately to Artemis and Tom, back with the Skilled. "Do you think they've already been back to the cavern?"

"No," Edgar said quickly. "Tom and Artemis will be fine. They'll look after each other. Look out. They're coming this way."

The seven men moved swiftly across the second bridge, and the few people who dared to stand in their way were taken down by the wall scouts, leaving the path clear for the seven to reach the main rock face. There was nowhere to go. Kate and Edgar hid in a darkened corner behind a stack of heavy crates as the Blackwatch agents made their way past. Then their boots stopped, and voices carried from somewhere nearby.

"You have had your chance," said one of them. "Enough warnings have been given. The girl was seen in the Shadowmarket just a few hours ago. It would be unwise to hide her from us. Hand her over, or more of your people will die."

A woman's voice answered. "You have made a mistake by threatening my people," she said. "We have told you everything we know about the girl, yet you have returned to us and spilled blood simply to hear the same answer. Order your men to leave, or we will be forced to defend ourselves. My people far outnumber yours. Your men cannot cling to our walls forever."

"We will search this cavern," said the Blackwatch officer. "Your people will not stand in our way. My men have every door, sewer, and rathole under guard."

"You will find nothing."

"If you do not deliver the girl, you will no longer be of use to us. I find people become most cooperative once their leaders are dead."

Kate heard the sound of a blade being unsheathed, and

the woman's voice became tinged with fear.

"Search all you want," she said. "She is not here."

"Find her."

Kate left the safety of the crates and crept into the first doorway she could see. She did not know where she was going. She didn't care, so long as the Blackwatch did not see her. It took a few seconds for Edgar to notice she had gone, and he hurried to catch up to her.

The rooms Kate had found her way into were empty, but there was a fire burning in the hearth, making the chimney too hot and dangerous to climb, even if she put the flames out. She followed the rooms and climbed back out through a small window onto the cavern's main street. The children who had been playing on the staircases were gone, replaced instead by people who were curious to see what was going on down below. Many of them were armed with whatever they had to hand, and they looked ready for a fight.

"Where are you going?" asked Edgar.

"Up," said Kate, making sure *Wintercraft* was tucked securely in her pocket. She did not want to lose it there. "We have to climb."

Kate found a house in the wall that looked old and abandoned. Parts of its roof had fallen in, but she found what she was looking for inside: a fireplace, dead and cold.

"This cannot end well," said Edgar.

Kate was already knotting her hair back, and she leaned in

to look up the exposed chimney, which looked narrower than she had expected. "It looks clear enough," she said. "You'll have to leave your backpack behind."

Kate heard sharp orders being shouted outside. People were being told to open their doors and cooperate fully with the Blackwatch's search.

"Chimney it is then," said Edgar, already wriggling out of the straps and hiding the bag behind an old armchair.

Kate ducked beneath the mantelpiece, slid her arms into the chimney, and stood up inside it, feeling around for something to hold on to. Cool air sank down against her face, and her fingers found the edge of a thin horizontal bar, the first of what looked like a full line that had been put there for sweepers to use. "I think it widens farther up," she said. "There's a ladder on the side."

Kate reached up as high as she could and lifted her foot onto the first rung. Climbing was easy enough once she got started. After she had passed the thin neck of the chimney shaft, the wall sloped along to the right and opened out into a wider space where other chimneys linked with the main shaft. It was not as restrictive as she had first feared. The worst part was the soot. It coated everything and clung to her clothes and skin as she climbed, stirring up blackness in the filthy air. Edgar grumbled beneath her as her feet sent drifts of it scattering down onto his head.

The higher they went, the more chimneys joined with

the one they were in, and threads of smoke trickled out of side shafts that they passed. The fires at their ends must only have been smoldering, but Kate tried not to breathe in case the smoke caught in her throat and a cough gave their position away. She concentrated on getting to the top. She couldn't wait to reach fresh air again and climb up into a city covered by a blanket of stars. The scratching sounds of fires being lit traveled along the side shafts, and half-caught conversations echoed from the walls. Two raised voices sounded close by, and when Kate heard them, she stopped, trying not to make a noise.

Edgar looked up to see what was going on. Neither of them could see anything in the black, but the women's voices were clear enough.

"I'm telling ya, I heard somethin' in the walls!"

"Don't go sayin' things like that. Do you want the Blackwatch to come up here and start beatin' down my door?"

"What if it's her? What's her name? Winters. What if we're the ones who find her?"

"There's nothing there. Just leave it. I don't think we should— *Get your head out of the fireplace!*"

Kate and Edgar froze. Wherever that woman was, there was no way she could see them. More smoke wisped up around them. Kate pressed her face to the arm of her coat to filter the air, but Edgar was not so prepared. His nose burned; his eyes streamed. Kate heard him try to sniff quietly, but it only made things worse. Edgar heaved in a deep breath, he tried to hold it back, but then the walls exploded with the sound of a loud, powerful sneeze.

"There's someone in there! Quick! Call someone!"

"Wait," said the second woman. "Think about this. If it is the girl, we can get a lot more by handing her over to the wardens. The Blackwatch aren't offering much, are they? We both know where the chimney goes. Maybe we can catch her ourselves."

"All right. I'll light the fire. You head up a few levels. Maybe we can smoke the rat out!"

Kate did not care how much noise she made after that. She clambered up the rungs as fast as she dared and followed the shaft along two more steep slopes. Already burning fires spewed heat into the chimney as she passed and the air filled with thick swaths of choking smoke. She had to stop, not daring to climb any farther. Her eyes stung, and her throat burned. There was no way they were going to make it to the surface through that. Edgar coughed somewhere beneath her, and more smoke billowed up from below.

"We have to get out," said Kate. "Go down again. We need to look for an empty shaft."

Edgar held his breath and ducked back into the smoke. Kate heard a thud as she followed him down a dozen rungs, and she almost fell from the ladder in fright when Edgar's filthy hand reached out from a hole right beside her face.

"In here," he said.

It was much harder climbing down a sloping ladder than climbing up. The air there was cleaner and cooler. No fire was burning at the end, and this chimney was wider at the bottom, opening out onto a hearth far larger than the one they had climbed into a few floors below. Edgar hesitated just above the opening, and Kate looked down past him, seeing the glow of candlelight spreading in from the room beyond. She guessed what he was thinking. That room was not empty. She could not hear any voices, but that candle had been lit for a reason.

The walls echoed as a knock rattled the front door. Boot steps scuffed over the floor, a lock clicked, and someone charged inside.

"I need to use the fireplace!" It was the same woman they had heard a few chimneys away, except now she was out of breath from running up many flights of stairs.

"Use it?" said a man's voice. "What for?"

"That girl everyone's looking for. I think she's up there. If I can climb into the chimney and take a look—"

"I can't let you do that."

Smoke prickled Kate's nose as a plume curled in from the main shaft.

"Look, you can hand her over with us if you want," said the woman. "We'll take her to the wardens, not those foreigners downstairs. We can trade her in and finally get out of here. See some sun!"

"My mistress will return once she has dealt with the visitors. She will not appreciate returning home to the sight of your buttocks poking down out of her chimney, will she?"

The woman made an impatient noise, too distracted to be insulted.

"Then just—just take a look for yourself. Tell me if you can hear someone moving around up there."

Edgar tapped on Kate's ankle, warning her to move upward, but the smoke was too thick. If they stayed where they were, they would be seen, and if they moved, they would become overwhelmed by smoke. Edgar's tapping became more insistent and Kate held on tight as something moved in the grate beneath them, and a head came into sight.

"What can you see?" asked the woman.

The head turned, and a man looked up at them in disbelief. "Well?"

The man kept staring. "Nothing," he said carefully. "Lots of muck."

"Can you hear anything?"

"Er, no. There's no sign of anything up here." The man's head returned to the room, and Edgar looked up at Kate, clearly as shocked as she was. "I'm afraid you are hearing things, friend."

"It'd be some find, though, wouldn't it?" said the woman, sounding disappointed. "A free ticket to the outside world at last."

"That is what the wardens want you to believe. They'd have your head on a traitor's pole the moment you handed her over. Too risky, I'd say. It's better forgotten."

The voices moved away. The door closed, and Edgar whispered quietly. "He saw us! What do we do now?"

Before Kate could answer, the man's face reappeared above the grate. They both heard the scratch of a match, and he held the flame out beside him.

"You might as well come down," he said, his voice darker than before. "You have nowhere to go. The Blackwatch have made sure of that. They are lighting all the fires, and I can have this one hot and blazing in a few seconds, so I suggest you do as I say."

The flame burned down to the man's fingertips as he watched them both. When they didn't move, he let the match fall. The flame fizzled and caught upon a knot of twisted bark.

"All right! We're coming!" said Edgar, dropping down into the grate and stamping out the flame. Kate was next, and when the two of them stood side by side within the room, they both felt like scruffy servants who had wandered into a place they did not belong.

The fireplace that had appeared huge from above was perfectly in proportion to the room that it served. Compared with other places Kate and Edgar had seen in the City Below, this one room was more luxurious than anything they had come to expect. It was a bedroom, with a four-poster bed carved beautifully from old wood and covered in layers of intricately embroidered blankets that must have taken months to make. There were colored candles lit in glass holders all around the walls and large wardrobes locked with black keys, one of which had a beautiful red dress hanging on a hook beside it. From what they had seen of the cavern outside, there had been no hint that anyone lived so well there, and Edgar was the first to ask what both of them were thinking.

"Who lives here?" he said.

"Laina Torrigan," said the man. "Leader of this community and the woman I have called my mistress for too long." He was staring at Kate as if she were a work of art, not a soot-covered girl who was walking dirt all over the floor. "But that does not matter now."

The man walked over to a small open window in the wall, unlooped a circular pendant from his neck, and held it out as far as he could, moving it so light flickered from its crystal face.

"What are you doing?" demanded Edgar.

"One of the many tasks I was sent here to perform. Please, sit down. We will not have to wait long."

Kate did not like the look on the man's face. It was a look of triumph, and it made her uncomfortable.

"We're sorry about the mess on your floor," she said, quickly tugging Edgar's sleeve and leading him toward the door. "We appreciate your not turning us in, but we're not

who you think we are. We're just passing through, aren't we?"
She nudged Edgar's arm.

"Yes. Er, thanks for that," said Edgar. "Bye then."

The man watched them all the way to the door. Kate half
expected him to try to block their way, but there was no need.
The door was locked.

"I find it is always best to be prepared," he said, drawing
a long blade from a sheath hidden within his clothes. "For the
past year I have acted as a servant to the lady of this cavern,
but my true purpose here is far greater. I have seen your face,
girl. I know who you are. You are not going anywhere."

"Yes, we are," said Edgar, rattling the door handle. "You'd
better come over here and unlock this door right now, before
things turn nasty."

"Do you think I am afraid of a worm like you?" said the
man. "If your face were not also known to me, you would be
dead already."

"Well, that's good to know," said Edgar. "Open this door!"

"In my own time. Once my countrymen arrive."

"You're with them," said Kate, suddenly realizing how
much danger she and Edgar were in. "The Blackwatch. You're
one of them, aren't you?"

"That is very true," said the man. "We have been looking
for you."

"Kate, head for the window," said Edgar. "I've got this."

"No," said the man. "It is too late for that."

Shadows moved along the pathway outside, and the silhouettes of a group of men passed across the window. One of them already had the key. The door opened slowly, pushed by the point of a long blade, and the Blackwatch's leader stepped inside. Kate and Edgar backed toward the bed, and Edgar stood between her and the advancing men. There was nothing either of them could do. The agent's eyes were vicious, his teeth bared in a wolfish smile.

"The hunt is over," he said. "Your lives are mine now."

# 15

# THE
# PRICE

Dalliah waited for Silas's answer. There was no real choice to make, and he knew it. Even there on the Continent, Dalliah was clearly Skilled enough to work the veil in ways he had never seen. She could easily have used that ability against him to get what she wanted, so the only real question was why she had even asked him at all.

Even if the veil was falling, there was no telling what kind of damage interfering with it could do. There was no guarantee that Dalliah's plan would even work. All she had was a theory, yet she seemed willing to gamble the entire balance of life and death upon a plan whose best outcome would benefit only two living souls. Silas could not deny the reward was tempting. To regain his spirit after so long was something he would do almost anything to achieve. Now it was time for him to take a gamble. He had to buy himself more time.

"I will help you," he said finally, all too aware of what

giving his word to Dalliah could mean. "But *he* should have no part in this."

"Bandermain's presence here is not open for negotiation," said Dalliah. "He will stay because I demand it."

"Why? What use can he be to us?"

"The arrangement we have has not yet been fulfilled. I have offered him something he cannot find anywhere else in this world. He knows where his loyalties lie."

Bandermain's eyes were heavy, and a vein in his forehead pulsed noticeably beneath his skin. His eyebrows knitted together as he rolled his shoulders back, trying to make himself appear strong and healthy.

"Celador?" Silas said as Bandermain's eyes met his with the feral look of an animal. "How long have you been like this?"

"Not all of us are as blessed as you," said Bandermain. There was venom in his voice, and he was about to say something else when the words were lost in a sudden flurry of racking coughs. Flecks of blood speckled on his lips, and he wiped them away with the back of his hand.

"The details are unimportant," said Dalliah. "Officer Bandermain requires my assistance in order to maintain his health for the moment. In return he has pledged his services and those of his men to our cause. The Continental leaders have given the Blackwatch orders to infiltrate Albion and cripple the High Council. I have no interest in getting in their way. They will continue to follow those orders. All I ask is that they follow a few of mine at the same time."

"Whatever you have done for him does not seem to be working," said Silas.

"His welfare is not your concern," said Dalliah. "He has done everything I have asked, and at the end of all this he shall receive his reward."

Bandermain began to speak, but he coughed again, trying and failing to hold back the spasms that strained his lungs, forcing his fingers to claw at the cupboard beside him. As one of the Skilled, Dalliah could have taken his pain away in moments, but instead, she just watched him impassively.

"*This* is how you treat your allies?" asked Silas.

"Bandermain knew what to expect," said Dalliah. "His sickness must sometimes be allowed to carry him close to death if he is to be of any use to me."

"And he agreed to this?"

Bandermain had given up trying to look well and concentrated solely upon breathing instead.

"He is strong enough," said Dalliah. "Every fifth day he must allow himself to move close to death. He has already endured the experience many times. He will survive long enough to see this through."

"He is dying," said Silas. "Any fool could see that."

"I'm not . . . dead . . . yet," said Bandermain, looking up at him.

Silas smiled coldly. "As entertaining as it would be to watch you dance with death, I could gladly save you the suffering and send you on your way."

"You . . . would not . . . understand," said Bandermain. "I do . . . what is necessary."

Dalliah placed a hand on Bandermain's shoulder. At first Silas thought she was going to heal him or at least ease his suffering, but her touch was not a caring one. It was one of ownership. If anything, Bandermain looked worse the longer she stood with him, as if she were somehow actively taking his life away from him.

Bandermain noticeably worsened before Silas's eyes, but he faced the experience with a soldier's steadfast will. Silas was intrigued that the man would allow his soul and his body to be abused in such a way. Whatever reward Dalliah had promised him, it was worth enduring near-death to possess.

"This affliction of yours. Is it contagious?" asked Silas. "Have you been spreading your germ-ridden filth around your own streets?"

Bandermain coughed blood, leaving Dalliah to answer.

"He is infected with the creeping lung," she said.

Silas instinctively took a step back. "You let him walk out among people with the creeping lung? Either cure him or kill him. And burn the corpse before it is cold!"

"No," said Dalliah.

"He is a walking plague!"

"He has only just entered the final stages. There is at least another day before he becomes severely contagious."

"Then cure him and be done with it."

"No. He has agreed to this."

"No one *agrees* to suffer the creeping lung!" said Silas.

"When we met, he was already ravaged by the disease," said Dalliah. "He owes me his life. What he is doing now could well allow the Continent to end this war. He is serving his country the best way he can."

Silas felt something crackle upon the air. The veil was settling across the room, attracted to the promise of Bandermain's imminent death. Frost sparkled upon Dalliah's fingertips and Silas recognized what it was she was doing. The creeping lung was a slow and painful death. Even the most capable among the Skilled had difficulty curing it, and death could drag on for days unless someone showed enough compassion to kill the infected victim. Dalliah was using Bandermain as a magnet, exploiting the veil's attraction to him in order to strengthen her own link to it. There was no telling how long he had been infected by the disease. Dalliah could have been keeping him alive for weeks, strengthening his body just enough to make sure death could not take him.

Dalliah stood listening to something within the veil. Silas felt it reach out to him, but this time he did not look into it with her.

"You were right, Officer Bandermain," she said. "Your men have done well."

Bandermain stood up as straight as his chest would allow. "They . . . have her?"

Dalliah nodded once. "They do."

Bandermain smiled a bloodied grin of triumph. "Then all of this . . . will be worthwhile."

"Congratulations on a successful hunt," said Silas, his words sharp.

"It will . . . benefit us all," said Bandermain. "If Dalliah is right . . . that girl's life . . . is worth more than rubies."

"Her life is not important," Silas told him. "We intend to take her soul."

Bandermain shrugged. "They are one and the same."

"No," said Silas. "They are not."

"With the girl safe, we can begin," said Dalliah. "The boy that she travels with. Do you know him well?"

"I know enough never to underestimate his ingenuity or his stupidity," said Silas.

"The two of them have become closer than I had anticipated," said Dalliah. "Kate has claimed the boy, though neither of them appears to be aware of it yet."

"Claimed?" said Silas.

"It is an old technique. One that might have caused problems for us if I had not become aware of their bond weeks ago," said Dalliah. "When I first knew the Winters family, their Skill was already turning away from the healing and communicative arts in preference of those involving spirit, blood, and sacrifice. When *Wintercraft* was written, they were already descending deeper into areas of veil study that not even other Walkers would dare attempt. Kate is no different. By not training her to control the veil, the Skilled have forced her to act upon instinct instead, a dangerous path. Your bond with her was created through blood, but her link with the boy is equally as important. His presence grounds her to the world of the living, preventing her from realizing her potential and protecting her from the more damaging abilities she does not yet know that she possesses. Her spirit has chosen him as its focus for now. She has become protective of him. He must be removed from her at the right time if she is to do what we require of her. If they are separated too soon, she will be more difficult to control."

"My men . . . know what to do," said Bandermain.

"I do not doubt it," said Dalliah. "Silas, are you ready to do your part?"

"I am."

"Then remain here while I prepare," said Dalliah. "Do not leave this room until I come for you. Will you obey?"

Silas nodded his agreement.

"You know what is at stake," said Dalliah. "We will do what must be done."

Dalliah was a keen manipulator. She expected her orders to

have some effect upon Silas, and he knew it. He trusted her even less than she trusted him. She was too open with her information, too keen to insist that the three of them were equals when one of them was being held deliberately on the threshold of death. Silas kept his eyes upon her as she left the room. She was too calm, too organized. Whatever she was planning, neither he nor Bandermain would truly be a part of it.

"You will get used to her," said Bandermain, sinking down into an armchair the moment she was gone. "That woman is a force of nature."

"She has poisoned your mind," said Silas.

"She has opened my eyes."

"You are weak, Celador."

"As weak as you? You came here of your own free will. I doubt she planned it any other way. The war is there ready to be won, Silas. Your country will lose. Forget about Albion. Your people have already forgotten about you."

"I have pledged my help, and I will give it," said Silas.

Bandermain laughed, his voice dissolving into more racking coughs. "Am I speaking to the man of honor or to the strategist?" he asked. "I know what you are thinking, because I would be thinking the same thing in your position, but whatever you have in mind, you will not win. I do not care what you think of this girl. All I care about is getting what I have earned. Dalliah says she can cure me, and I believe her."

"If she were going to cure you, she would have done it by now."

"The only other choice is death. Three of my men died from this disease before I even knew I had it. If running a few errands for a madwoman can rid me of it, I'll pay that price."

"Dalliah is not a madwoman," said Silas, glancing back at the body on the table. "I would feel better if she were."

"She won't let you ruin this," said Bandermain. "That's why you are here. To be watched. This house is your cage as much as it is mine. You will not leave. Even if you did, she would bring you back."

"I have no intention of going anywhere," said Silas.

"Then that is one thing we have in common at least."

Bandermain sat back in the chair. Silas took a seat on the opposite side of the room and laid his sword across his lap.

"It would be a mercy to kill you," said Silas, breaking the silence that had fallen between them. "Unfortunately for you, I am feeling far from merciful today."

"I appreciate that," said Bandermain.

The two men sat, watching each other.

Silas could feel the veil still hanging within the room as Bandermain struggled for each breath. The creeping lung was a vicious disease, more of an infestation than an infection, caused by tiny insects that gradually ate away a sufferer's lungs from the inside out. Silas had seen people die from it before, and he did not look forward to witnessing it again. It was a common threat out in the Continental wilds, and there was very little travelers could do to protect themselves against it.

Perhaps Bandermain had been suspicious of Dalliah's motives in the beginning, but now desperation had bought her his trust. Men upon the brink of death would give an ear to anything that might earn them even a little more time in the living world. Bandermain's body had become his battlefield, and with Dalliah's help, this sickness was just another war that he fully expected to win.

Silas allowed the veil to creep steadily into his mind. If Dalliah was right and Kate had already been captured by the Blackwatch, there was nothing he could do for her. His crow would arrive too late to warn her about Bandermain's men, but he still had to confirm it for himself. His thoughts slipped gradually into the veil, and while a connection was possible, it was weak at best.

*All he caught were glimpses. Flickers of images seen through the eyes of his crow as it flew across the walls of Fume. He saw the towers and streets soaked with pouring rain as the bird flew on, obeying his command. Sinking back easily into the rhythms and energies of the veil that pulsed like a heartbeat all around him, he let his thoughts fly with the crow. It reacted to his presence, soaring faster upon the wind, speeding toward its destination until Silas reluctantly left it behind.*

*He shifted his focus to finding Kate, and the veil gave*

*him flashes of what her eyes could see. Blackwatch agents were advancing toward her. He sensed her fear and felt echoes of her heart racing within his own chest. Then a different feeling crept across his senses. Something had changed. His body tensed, every muscle suddenly alert, and his consciousness returned to Dalliah's room, where Bandermain was slowly walking across the floor toward him.*

Silas's blade swept up to Bandermain's throat. Bandermain stopped walking. He had no weapon drawn and looked shaky on his feet, but Silas was not willing to take any chances.

"You can do what she does," said Bandermain, wheezing painfully with each breath. "You can see into the veil when she's not here. You're one of them! She did not tell me that."

"Perhaps because it is none of your business."

Bandermain took a shaky step back, and Silas carefully lowered his weapon.

"What did you see?"

"Only that Dalliah was telling the truth," said Silas.

"She has no reason to lie."

"She has many reasons. And most of them are on the other side of the sea, under *your* orders, collecting two young prisoners. The loyalty of your men is all Dalliah is interested in now. They have found what she wants."

"You do not know everything," said Bandermain.

"What did she promise you, Celador? There are many

ways to fight a war. Why are you so interested in helping Dalliah with hers?"

Bandermain turned his back on Silas and waved a dismissive hand as he made his way back to his chair. "Any victory . . . is still a victory," he said, slumping down. "She will give me . . . what no one else can. She can give me my life back."

"She feeds you a handful of good days and forces you to endure the bad. That is not a life. It is torture."

"That is what I was starting to believe as well . . . until you came."

"Dalliah will never cure you," said Silas. "No one can."

"I know that," said Bandermain, coughing again. "She told me there was another way. I did not believe her until I saw you . . . under that bridge, still alive. *You* are the proof. You have shown me what is possible." Bandermain raised his hand, and Silas saw the black stitches across his cut palm.

"Dalliah tried to bind your soul to hers," said Silas. "But she does not have *Wintercraft*. The binding cannot be performed without it."

"She believed that it could," said Bandermain. "It is only a book. Books can be copied, their contents remembered. It has no true power of its own."

"It cannot be destroyed," said Silas. "And it always finds its way back into the hands of a Winters. There is far more to *Wintercraft* than just ink and paper. I see the binding did not work."

"There are some things even Dalliah cannot do," said Bandermain, closing his palm. "But the girl can. She will make sure of it. To live without fear of injury, sickness, or death: *that* is life. You do not know how fortunate you are."

"You would choose to live *my* life. Willingly?"

"I would welcome it. I will see the end of this war. I will live to witness Albion's fall."

"You have lost your mind, Celador."

Bandermain laughed painfully. "If I do nothing, I stand to lose far more than that," he said. "When my men bring Kate Winters to this house, she will be my salvation, Silas, just as she was yours."

# \leftarrow 16 \rightarrow

# WATERWAYS

"Edgar, don't do anything," Kate whispered as six more red-coated men poured into the room. Every one of them had a scarred face and fierce eyes. Their coats were old but neatly patched, and their belts bristled with blades and black pouches. The leader was taller than the rest, and the dagger he held was already stained with blood.

"You both will come with us," he said. "It would be best not to fight."

Two agents stepped forward with ropes in their hands. One of them overpowered Edgar easily, pulled him away from Kate, and tied his wrists together before pushing him toward the door. There was nothing either of them could do. They were outnumbered and outmatched. Kate held out her hands and let them be tied.

"That's right," said the leader. "We'll have no tricks from you, little witch."

The Blackwatch searched Edgar for hidden weapons, found nothing, and pushed him out the door. Kate kept quiet. They did not search her, and she was allowed to walk out into the cavern at her own speed. The people who lived in that place had gathered quickly to see her and her "accomplice" brought out into the light. She heard shouts of anger and surprise as the Blackwatch walked them along the fronts of the houses and down endless flights of steps, but she kept her head high and her eyes lowered.

The Blackwatch took them down to the ground and walked them into a low tunnel that echoed with the rumbling of fast-moving water. There they divided into groups, and Kate overheard the leader leaving orders behind with one of his men. She caught the words *gathering point* and *containment,* but she could not hear enough to know what they were talking about. All but three of the Blackwatch agents remained in the cavern. Kate and Edgar were left with one guard each, and once he was satisfied his orders had been understood, the leader led the four of them deeper into the tunnel.

The darkness was broken by regular clutches of fire torches, and it looked as if the path had been well used before the Blackwatch had arrived. The rumbling sound grew louder the farther they walked; shallow steps led gradually downward, and Kate could smell water in the air. The tunnel exit opened out into a tall vertical crack in the stone up ahead, just wide enough for two people to squeeze through side by side. Kate stepped **through an**d found herself on the bank of a fast-flowing river, one that raced so quickly that it churned up ruffles of foam wherever it touched rocks jutting out from its cavelike banks.

A row of patched-together rowing boats was lashed to metal hooks sunk into the wall, pulled high up away from the water, and beside them a huge creaking waterwheel turned with the flow of the speeding water.

The Blackwatch did not take Kate and Edgar toward the boats. The leader lifted a lantern from the wall and turned left instead, heading to where part of the tunnel had fallen in upon itself sometime in the recent past. They picked their way over a pile of fallen earth and rocks toward a boat that was larger than the others and hidden from the view of anyone standing on their side of the river.

"Get in," said the leader.

The boat was of an unusual design. It was much bigger than a rowing boat, its hull was thick and heavy, and its rear half was completely covered by a curved roof that sealed the deck beneath it from every direction except the front. The prow curved into a wide point with wooden guardrails around it that were hung all the way along with leather sacks. Two interlocked lengths of wood that could have been a short mast stood bare in the very center, and nailed to the floor were wooden chests, each one locked with a thick padlock.

Kate climbed over the side of the boat, and Edgar followed

her in. Both turned quickly to face the men behind them.

"We have a long journey ahead of us," said the leader. "Sit down. Stay still, and you will see the end of this night in one piece."

The boat jolted and scraped as the Blackwatch pushed and forced it down a cleared channel, grating it forward, shove by shove, toward the river. Water surged against the prow as the front half of the boat leaned diagonally into it. Kate and Edgar sat down together on a bench that ran along the boat's exposed left side, clinging to the guardrail with tied hands as water rushed over the deck. Kate heard a shouted order, and the three men climbed aboard, letting the pull of the river do its work.

"Steady! Ready the poles!"

The river dragged the boat forward, pummeling the hull with its force, roaring against the wood until Kate felt sure it was about to burst through. Then the stern lifted clear of the bank and the river snatched the boat up in its watery claws and hurled it down the channel, forcing everyone on board to hold on. The boat bucked with the current, its prow diving deep into the water only to be thrown back up again. The noise was deafening, water pounded hard against the hooded stern, and the force propelled it wildly into a tunnel, where the boat began to shift and turn.

"Poles!" shouted the leader, his voice clear and calm.

The poles were thick enough to be tree trunks, their flat

ends already tattered and shredded from whatever use they were meant to be put to. Kate watched the wall on the right side of the tunnel speed toward them in the lantern light. The dark-haired guard slid his piece of tree through a wide metal ring that pointed diagonally out of the boat and, half hanging out over the water, half on board, screwed metal bolts through the ring to hold it tightly in place.

When the wall came too close, the pole struck it first. Kate and Edgar screamed as the boat shook with the impact and threw them across the deck and into the side of a wooden chest. Mud sprayed across the boat as the pole sheared along the hard earth, leaving deep claw marks in its wake.

"Secure the cargo!" the leader ordered as the boat turned slowly away from the wall, pointing back into the center of the river. "Retract the pole!"

The dark-haired guard dealt with the pole, while the thinner man dragged Kate and Edgar back toward the guardrail. He lifted their arms and clipped their wrist ropes onto hooks meant for holding leather bags. "Hold on this time," he shouted at Kate. "I don't want to have to come back looking for your corpse."

Kate did as she was told, if only to save herself from the rocky water. The Blackwatch used the poles three more times to keep the boat safely on track, but the third time was definitely the worst. Instead of scraping through thick earth, the pole on the left side struck solid stone, splintering its head and smashing into the wall so hard that the guardrail buckled and cracked.

"What do they think they're—*arrgh!*" Edgar cried out. He and Kate twisted their hands out of reach of the grinding rocks, and the boat scraped hard along the tunnel wall. Sparks flew from the metal hooks as the rocks chewed against them, and they turned their faces away from the fiery light.

The Blackwatch fought to bring the boat back under control, but the river fought back. All Kate and Edgar could do was hang on, until the moment of relief when the boat left the wall behind and the tunnel opened into three separate paths, sending them careering down the central flow. The divided current slowed the river enough for the boat to gradually lose speed, and the Blackwatch leader stood at the very front, leaning out across the water as the vessel settled into the river's gentler flow. Kate dared hope that the worst was over, and the two guards used oars to steer the boat smoothly along the very center of the current, eventually making them feel safe enough to let go of the guardrail.

"That's one way to travel," said Edgar as Kate pulled their ropes out of the bag hook.

"It is the only way," said the leader, striding toward him. "I see you have found your voice."

"Hard not to with all that going on," said Edgar. "What are you trying to do? Kill us?"

"Not yet, boy."

"Haven't you lot heard of ladders? It would've been much easier to just climb out of that cavern, you know."

"We will require the use of a boat where we are going," said the leader. "I suggest you keep any further questions to yourself." He turned to the dark-haired guard. "Untie their hands, and give them some food."

"Yes, sir." The guard walked across the boat and slipped a knife deftly through their wrist ropes.

"Where do you think this river goes?" Edgar asked as the guard walked away.

The man stopped and looked back. "We're taking you where all rivers go in the end," he said. "We're taking you to sea."

Silas's crow liked being underground even less than it liked being out at sea. Its feathers were slick with rain and gritty with salt, and the close confines of Fume's streets already made it long for the freedom of the open sky. It hopped in between the bars that blocked the northern entrance to the Thieves' Way and fluttered in, flying gently above the surface of the underground river and following its sluggish course deep beneath Fume, into the lamplight of the smugglers' tunnels.

There were no humans to be seen. The crow blinked, searching for markers to follow. Silas's orders had been very clear: Find Kate. Deliver the message. It remembered the girl who had brought it back to life, but it did not like being away from its master for so long. It could sense the girl's spirit on the river as the flowing water amplified the energies of the veil, letting it sense distant echoes of every soul within the river's sight. Kate was somewhere on the river, and if its master wanted the crow to find her, that was what it had to do.

The humans' lights lit the crow's way as it fluttered along the tunnels like a ghost. Wherever the river split, it chose the path with the fastest water flow, taking it deeper and deeper underground. It dodged fishing nets that drooped from the tunnel roofs down to little anchors in the riverbed and was forced to glide close enough to the surface to feel the chill of the water on its chest feathers wherever the low roof dipped almost to the water. The vial the bird was carrying made its flight more awkward than usual, but it kept going, following a trail of river lights until at last the pounding roar of a second waterway thrummed through the earth.

The tunnel widened, and bridges appeared across the water where the Thieves' Way drew in close to a stronger river. Their waters poured into the same tunnel, both flowing just a few feet apart until the Thieves' Way turned to the left and curled gently away, leaving the other river to speed on. The crow checked the veil and changed rivers. The stronger river was older and followed an ancient path, carving its way through the earth and stone of Fume's deepest foundations on a course it had created over many thousands of years.

The humans who lived this far under the earth lived in clusters of tents in hollows cut into the walls, and the river's steep banks were filled with tiny one-man boats. The crow had traveled this far beneath Fume before, but only at Silas's side. It knew that it was a dangerous place to be, so when the first rock came speeding past its beak, it was ready. The humans on the bank might not have seen a living bird for many years, and their first instinct was to kill. The crow had a job to do, and it had no intention of ending up in a human's cooking pot. It swooped hard toward the rock thrower, raking its claws through the frail man's hair, but the man's throwing arm was faster. A second rock streaked through the air; the crow swerved and felt a tug on its chest as the rock struck the little glass vial, smashed it, and sent its neatly rolled note spinning down into the water below. The bird recovered quickly, flapped away from its attackers with an eerie screech, and followed the river around a corner of jutting stone, leaving them and its precious cargo behind.

The crow flew on. It might not have its message anymore, but it could still reach the girl. It was not long before buildings sprang up along the river: flat buildings that pressed into the walls as if they were being swallowed by the jaws of the earth. Waterwheels slapped the water, the river became straight and fast, and somewhere up ahead the girl was close by. The crow lowered its head and gathered speed. It streaked past a waterwheel next to a bank filled with rowing boats and let the veil lead the way, speeding around turns and on through a handful of branching tunnels until, finally, its target was in sight.

A boat pushed through the water up ahead, its bulbous stern looking like a wooden bubble half sunk in the water. The crow locked its sights upon it, and with two strong beats of its wings it settled into a spearing glide. The boat sloshed clumsily through the water as the crow matched its speed. Then it saw her.

The bird checked for enemies and spotted three men on the deck. The moment all three were looking the opposite way, it made its move: it dropped down onto the hooded roof of the boat and scratched its claws gently into the wood. It opened its wings, stretched them out, and let them settle back into place upon its back. The girl looked up, and the crow sensed the presence of its master within the veil. Somewhere Silas was listening.

Kate elbowed Edgar in the ribs and pointed to the bird perched on the boat's roof, its black wings shimmering in the lantern light.

"Is that what I think it is?" she whispered.

The crow ruffled its feathers, hopped along the roof, and dropped smoothly through the air to land proudly beside Kate. She reached out to touch it, but it snapped at her fingers and lowered its head, eyeing her warily.

The Blackwatch leader crossed the deck to talk to each of his men, and the crow hopped onto the battered guardrail behind Kate, staying out of sight.

"Do you think Silas is nearby?" asked Edgar.

"If he were, I think we would have seen him by now."

Something sparkled on the bird's chest, and Kate noticed what looked like broken glass looped into a string harness knotted around its back. "There's something tied here," she said. The crow allowed her to unknot the damp string, and the broken neck of a stoppered vial hung from it as she brought it down. "I think it was carrying a bottle."

"What? Like a message?"

"Silas might have sent it here to tell us something."

"Well, a lot of good that did us," said Edgar. "Do you think he—"

The Blackwatch leader glared across the boat at Edgar, silencing him at once.

"Who told you to speak?" he demanded, striding over to stand in front of him.

"Er, no one, sir," said Edgar.

"Then be silent."

The crow snapped its beak aggressively behind Kate, but the leader was already walking away.

"If the crow knew where to find us, Silas will," whispered Edgar. "Maybe he can help us."

"Silas isn't here," said Kate. "No one is coming to help us."

"Then what are we supposed to do? I suppose we could set the crow on them. It can be pretty vicious when it wants to be. Ow!" The crow pecked Edgar's ear, and the Blackwatch leader turned again.

"Are you testing me, boy?"

Edgar was about to speak again, but Kate grabbed his hand and spoke first.

"We just want to know why we are here," she said. "Where are we going?"

"That is not your business. You!" The leader turned to the dark-haired man. "I told you to feed them."

"Yes, sir."

The man ducked into the back of the boat and soon reemerged, carrying a bowl of dried fish and soft bread. Kate took it from him before he could get close enough to spot the hidden crow, and he spat at her feet before walking away.

"Nice," said Edgar. "I don't care how your men treat me, but they could at least treat Kate with some respect."

The Blackwatch leader leaned over Edgar like a lion tormenting a rat. "We respect her well enough," he said. "But some of us cannot forget what she is. My men do not trust the Skilled, but they will treat her well because she is worth something to them. You, on the other hand, need to learn your place."

Edgar did not see the punch coming. The man's fist struck his nose sideways, making it burst with pain, but Edgar did not make a sound.

"What did you do that for?" demanded Kate. "Are you all right?"

"Fine," Edgar said, grasping his nose and flinching a little as the man patted him heavily on the top of his head.

"Now you will be quiet," he said. "Or next time I will throw you over the side myself. Do you understand?"

Edgar said nothing, which the man took as agreement. "Excellent," he said. "We will be out of the city very soon. Enjoy the peace while you can."

Edgar would not allow Kate to check his nose, insisting that it did not feel broken, so they sat together, sharing the bread and fish between themselves and the crow, waiting for sunlight to appear in the maze of never-ending tunnels. That sunlight never came. The first glimpse Kate and Edgar had of the outside world was the glow of moonlight gleaming from an arch of metal bars. The underground entrances to the City Below had been sealed off, but the Blackwatch knew about the bars, and they were ready.

The dark-haired guard threw two anchoring lines over the sides of the boat to slow it down and prevent the current from hurling it into the metal at speed. Chains creaked, and the boat shuddered as the second guard jumped out onto the bank and worked at two padlocks holding the bars in place.

Kate and Edgar did not care what he was doing. They were too busy looking out at the beauty of a blue-black sky, feeling the cool touch of fresh air upon their faces, and staring up at the silver moon when it peered out of the fast-moving clouds.

"I never thought I'd be so happy to see the moon," said Kate.

The guard finished his work with the locks, and the bars creaked open. The other guard waited for him to jump back on board, and then the two anchor lines were unhitched at the same time. The current lifted the boat and sent it speeding out of the city's lower walls and out into clear air. The river swiftly left the city behind, carrying Kate and Edgar away from Fume, away from the Skilled and the wardens and the many nameless people who had been so happy to see them captured at last. Their lives as they had come to know them were over. There was nothing else for them to do but look up at the stars as the rain clouds cleared overhead and the river carried them between its darkened banks, away from the confines of the City Below and out into the open world.

Silas sat in silence, watching Bandermain's health deteriorate swiftly right in front of his eyes. The creeping lung was normally a slow, crippling disease, but without Dalliah's efforts to stem its course, Bandermain's sickness was clearly making up for lost time. Soon he could do little more than sit and glare across the room, clenching his fists as he concentrated on his shallow, thin breaths. The sicker he became, the closer the veil drew in around the room, rejuvenating Silas's own body as Bandermain's gave way and allowing him to connect with his crow far across the water once again.

Silas saw a glimpse of Kate and Edgar, both filthy and covered in black soot. He saw the Blackwatch's boat, the river, and eventually the moon as the boat passed quietly beneath it. He could feel the gentle threads of the veil reaching down to Kate, curling around her but unable to fully connect; then he saw her hand resting within Edgar's and began to consider if what Dalliah had said about the two of them could actually have been possible.

The air felt different there in Albion, heavy and familiar. A strange blanket had been laid across the world. The Continent was bare and empty in comparison, but even though Silas recognized the feeling of home, there was something not quite right about it. He allowed his concentration to lift and wander, and then he sensed something else within the veil, a presence that hummed in his mind like a beetle caught within his ear.

It felt as if his mind were passing through clear air that was slowly being devoured by thick black smoke. The source came from somewhere in the east. The boundary between the veil and the living world was being worn away, the difference between the two no longer so easy to sense. Silas could see gatherings of shades congregating at points where the veil was at its thinnest. He could feel their excitement, sense their anticipation as the living world moved nearer and nearer to their grasp.

Silas opened his eyes to the sound of the door opening as Dalliah walked into the room. Outside, the rainstorm had passed, and the land beyond the uncurtained window was already shrouded in night. The veil had made him lose time. He had left himself vulnerable. He stood up at once, but Bandermain remained slumped in his chair.

"We are ready," said Dalliah. "Silas, please follow me. And help Bandermain to walk if he cannot find his way alone."

Silas did not want to help Bandermain, and Bandermain had no intention of accepting any help. He heaved himself up off his chair and slung his heavy sword stubbornly across his back. Silas stood aside to let him hobble out of the room first, and Bandermain was too ill to protest.

Curiosity carried Silas out of the house and back onto Dalliah's overgrown land. High walls surrounded it on all sides, each one covered with the skeletal stems of climbing plants that spidered across the stones, and the ground was cobbled between patches of frozen grass.

Dalliah walked quickly toward a small building in the center of the grounds, and Bandermain stopped twice to cough and compose himself, forcing Silas to stop.

"Keep moving," said Silas, drawing his sword and jabbing Bandermain's back with the blade. "You are wasting time."

Clutching his shivering chest, Bandermain looked up at Silas. "Do not ruin this," he said. "I *need* this."

Dalliah was too far away to hear Bandermain's words. Silas pushed him forward. He had no intention of letting an enemy walk behind him.

"Move," he said.

"I know you don't want to be here," said Bandermain. "Do you think *I* chose this?"

"You are dying," said Silas, forcing him on. "Get used to it."

Bandermain laughed quietly. "You do not have to think about death," he said. "And soon neither will I. I won't let you destroy this for me. Let it happen. We both will be better off."

Silas kept walking.

"When I first found out what my leaders wanted from your country, I thought they were insane," said Bandermain, his words breaking with each breath. "They think your High Council can communicate with the dead. They told me they wanted to learn the secret for themselves, but I did not believe in the veil then. I was not interested in the Skilled. I thought they were witches, fools, and liars. Then I met Dalliah, and I knew that I had been wrong. When she told me about you . . . what had happened to you . . . I thought it was all just Albion propaganda. 'The soldier who could not die.' But you weren't a soldier anymore. You were never sent into battle again. The High Council made you return to the ranks of the wardens. They were keeping you close by."

"I was doing my duty," said Silas.

"And now you are a traitor."

Bandermain laughed, forcing his lungs to spasm. His knees buckled. His hands grasped for Silas's arm, but Silas stepped away and let Bandermain hit the ground. His body twitched, but Silas did nothing. Dalliah stopped and turned.

"Your new friend is dying," said Silas. "Now is as good a time as any to let him get on with it."

Dalliah hurried back to Bandermain's side, crouched down beside him, and laid her hand upon his throat. "I cannot help him here," she said. "Carry him."

"Why is he so important?" asked Silas.

"He isn't. His orders are," said Dalliah. "Help him up."

Bandermain's eyes were wide, and his mouth hung open as he gasped for breath.

"Pick him up!"

"No," said Silas.

Dalliah glared at him in fury, but when she spoke, she sounded calm, managing to keep her temper under control. "This is very simple," she said. "Bandermain is no fool. If the Blackwatch return with the girl and find him dead, they have orders to kill her before she even sets foot within my walls."

"If he passes the creeping lung to her, she will be dead anyway," said Silas.

"We need her alive, and we need him," said Dalliah. "Some of Bandermain's men are not as amenable as he has been. They will not hesitate to kill the girl, and I will not be able to stop them before they do."

"I will stop them," said Silas. "We do not need to appease the Blackwatch."

"That is not your decision," said Dalliah. "When you have lived a few more centuries, perhaps you will understand that there are sacrifices to be made if you are to live any kind of meaningful life. Why do you think I am here and not in Albion? I lived on my home soil for two hundred years before they tried to hunt me. You lasted not much more than a decade. Our presence terrifies those who are not like us. I have been forced to find allies, to trade secrets, and to associate with people I would much rather see with their heads on sticks than sipping from a wineglass beside me. Bandermain is such an ally. If he dies now, Kate will die, too."

Silas looked down at Bandermain. His lips were tinged with blue, his wheezing had stopped, and his body had fallen limp.

"I can slow his death, but I cannot prevent it," said Dalliah. "Carry him."

Silas grabbed Bandermain's arm and slung the dying man over his shoulder.

The walls of the building glinted as they walked toward it. Quartz-flecked cobblestones had been spread across the entire dome-shaped structure, making it look as if it were something rising up out of the courtyard, forcing the cobbles up like a whale breaking the surface of the ocean. Its door was made of swirls of iron and delicate panes of thin glass that shone blue in the rising moonlight. Dalliah unlocked it and stepped back to let Silas carry Bandermain in first.

Inside the building was a single room, circular and small, but with the kind of atmosphere that set hairs prickling on the back of the neck.

"Put him down in the center," said Dalliah.

Silas walked forward slowly, carefully analyzing his surroundings. The wall had no windows and showed its bare wooden frame layered thickly with rows of yellowed bones. Some of the bones were decades old, and others were boiled white and fresh. Every one of them was tied vertically to the wall, creating what looked like a gruesome fence, and hanging down from the ceiling in front of them were long cords holding thin candles and oil lamps, along with narrow-necked bottles and vials filled with what could only be blood.

"What is this?" demanded Silas. "This is not true veil work."

"It is the way *I* work," said Dalliah. "Lay him down."

"Whose blood is this?"

"I have taken samples from many people," said Dalliah. "They are no longer with us now. Your blood is in here somewhere, if that is what you are asking. The Blackwatch had plenty of time to take it while you were in their hands."

"Take them down," said Silas. "All of them."

"Why? I thought you were a soldier. I expect you have spilled more than your share of blood in your time. This is no different."

Silas dropped Bandermain unceremoniously to the floor. "This is very different."

"Why? Because you don't understand it? If you condemned everything you did not understand, there would be very little else for people to do in this world."

Dalliah knelt beside Bandermain and pressed her hand back against his throat. This time the veil answered her. Bandermain breathed in suddenly, rolled onto his side, and spat blood across the floor.

"How many times have you done that to him?" asked Silas.

"More than I thought I would need to," replied Dalliah. "This time will be the last."

Silas looked around at the hundreds of glass containers swinging gently with the movement of air in the room.

"Da'ru wore a necklace filled with blood when she worked the listening circles," he said. "Is this where she learned to do it?"

"I taught her a little of what time had taught me," said Dalliah. "She was my hand across the ocean. She could attempt techniques in Albion that I could never achieve here. She was a useful tool. I learned a lot from her mistakes . . . and from her successes." Dalliah stood up and looked straight at Silas, daring him to say the words that were already on his lips.

"You told her how to use the circles," he said. "You told her where the book of Wintercraft was buried, and you told her to experiment on the veil. On *me*."

"As we can see, it worked very well," said Dalliah. "You should thank me. You have been able to see into a world that few people have ever known. You know the truth about the ways of the spirit. You may have suffered, but look at what you have been given. You have seen beyond the boundaries of our world. It has made you more powerful than your enemies and carried you beyond the limits of humankind."

"Why would you do that?" asked Silas. "What did you have to gain?"

"I needed someone I could trust," said Dalliah, "someone who could survive and thrive and see the world the way I see it. You were my first choice. The subjects who died before you were never meant to survive the procedure. Da'ru needed to perfect her skills. And she did so admirably. You were never meant to lead an ordinary life, Silas, any more than Kate Winters was meant to sell books in a dying town. With your skills, you could have changed Albion a thousand times over. You could have overthrown the High Council and even taken their place if you had wished. I gave you a gift, and what did you do with it? You obeyed orders. You waited. We all are following a path that was laid out for us long ago. Even him," she said, nudging Bandermain's arm with the toe of her shoe. "You were meant to have your spirit torn. You were meant to find Kate Winters and bind her blood to your own. Fate made sure you played your part in history, Silas. You are as much its pawn as any of us. That is why you are here, with me."

Silas looked around at the hanging bottles. There was no way to tell which one of them belonged to him, but if his blood was in there, that meant traces of Kate's could be, too. Silas knew enough about the Skilled to see that something else was going on in that room. The air felt heavy. The longer he stayed within it, the more effort it took to think. "Those vials," he said, "how much of my blood did you take?"

"Enough," said Dalliah as Bandermain struggled to his feet. "That was one of the reasons I chose you. You are an intelligent man, so it surprises me how stupid you can be sometimes. Wintercraft is not a warm and friendly discipline.

Its strength comes from blood, suffering, and pain. Kate Winters is already discovering that for herself. Even you saw it as the fastest way to free your spirit and find peace in death. You did not care what would happen to the girl when you were finished with her. You did not consider what you were opening up inside her soul. There are reasons her family buried that book in the end and why the Skilled were so eager to keep it secret once it had resurfaced. But *Wintercraft* never remains buried for long. Walkers always find their way to its pages. The veil shows us everything. You believe that you have mastered the veil's secrets. You are wrong."

Something sharp prickled inside Silas's chest, like tiny hairs stabbing the inside of his lungs.

"The creeping lung is a very interesting disease," said Dalliah, "tiny creatures that spread and pass between hosts, embedding themselves in human lungs and slowly eating away the tissue until there is nothing left. Did you think you would be immune to it here? Do you still think your body does not need to breathe?"

Silas tested his lungs, making them bristle more sharply with each deep breath.

"What the veil slows down, it can also speed up," said Dalliah. "We may not suffer the ravages of illness and disease, but we can feel the shadow of them living within others. We can make a body believe it is suffering. We can turn it against itself and carry it right to the very point of death. How are you feeling, Silas?"

The first spasm gripped Silas's lungs like a fist. His chest heaved, and he coughed speckles of warm blood.

"Our bodies do not degrade as quickly as others, but they are still quite fragile," said Dalliah. "We need to take care of them. You have been careless."

"This is not possible," said Silas.

"Because Da'ru told you it couldn't happen? Where do you think she was getting her information?"

Bandermain stared at Silas as if he were watching his entire world fall apart. "You told me this wouldn't happen!" he said. "You told me it couldn't affect him!"

"Silas is as healthy as he was the moment he walked in here," said Dalliah. "His body only *thinks* it is ill. He cannot fight it. His mind is not strong enough."

Silas glared at her.

"The girl is supposed to cure me," said Bandermain. "She is supposed to make me like him. But it makes no difference! Look at him!"

"Calm yourself, Celador."

"He should not be able to die!"

"He can't die. But that does not mean he cannot suffer."

Silas gasped for breath. He felt as if he were drowning. His lungs were filling with blood. His body was not healing, and the damage was spreading. He had become used to believing in his body's ability to repair itself and had spent many minutes underwater without any desperate need for air, but this was very different. His body was failing from the inside out. He had assumed, wrongly, that his lungs were no longer of any real use to him. Any energy his body needed was drawn directly from the veil. The veil had kept him alive, no matter what extent of abuse his body had suffered, and he had relied upon it to sustain him. He had not realized how precious his body still was until that moment.

"Pain is the only way to control you, Silas. Da'ru proved that. You are not as strong as you think. Not here. Not anymore. I truly believed we could be allies; now I know better."

Silas did not feel his body when it hit the floor. His mind was focused fully upon his chest and the scratching pain, like needle-thin claws scraping inside it. Silas could hear Bandermain's voice close by and Dalliah answering calmly in reply. He punched the floor, barely aware of the pain cracking across his knuckles as they crunched into the stones.

"You have done well, Celador," Silas heard her say as darkness spread across his vision, leaving only a pinprick of light. "Soon we will be free of our pain. Nothing has changed. The girl's death will save us both."

Silas tried to move, but his limbs were heavy, his body as immovable as a tombstone knotted down by weeds. Then his sight gave out, and all he had was the drifting emptiness of the dark. He reached for the veil, focusing hard upon the circle surrounding him. He could feel Dalliah's energy threading around the room in a gentle pulse, just enough to attract the veil to that room. He should have noticed that. He should have sensed it, but it was too late for regrets. He felt the remnants of Kate's blood vibrating within him: Walker's blood. His cheek rested upon the stones, pressed within a tiny puddle of his own blood. Silas concentrated on that blood, willing it to connect with the circle and the veil. It took every ounce of energy he had left, but he felt the chill of the veil upon his face as frost spread out across his cheek.

"What are you doing?" demanded Bandermain, but Silas was not listening.

Whatever Dalliah had done to him prevented the veil from healing his body, but she could not restrain what was left of his soul. Silas cast his mind out into the veil, fighting the pull of the pain as it struggled to draw him back. Bandermain and Dalliah stood over him, watching as his eyes glazed gray and his body fell still.

"What does this mean?" asked Bandermain.

Dalliah smiled and turned away, walking over to the building's iron door.

"Wait! What about our agreement?"

"You will have what you were promised," said Dalliah.

Bandermain felt Silas's neck, searching for a pulse, but found none. The frost of the veil crept across to his fingers, and he snatched them away. "Witchery," he whispered.

But there was no one left to listen.

## ← 18 →

# INTO
# THE DARK

Kate looked back as the river curled swiftly away from the city and saw its huge torchlit walls stretching in a wide curve in both directions, farther than the eye could see. If there had been any wardens posted at the river gate, they were gone now. Edgar nudged her arm and pointed to something dark inside some leafless bushes lining the riverbank. It looked like a black boot, and there was something glinting near it. A silver dagger held in a lifeless hand.

"So much for the wardens," he said.

Kate watched the walls of Fume being swallowed by the night as the Blackwatch slid the split mast up to its full height and attached a large black sail that billowed powerfully in the wind. The leader took charge of it, and soon the wind was powering them along faster than the river could flow, cutting through the wild counties of Albion and pushing them toward the distant shore.

Once Fume's towers had fully disappeared over the dark horizon, Silas's crow suddenly became agitated. It clicked its beak sharply and shook its head as if something were trapped in its ear. Kate tried to calm it, but nothing she did made any difference. She grabbed hold of it to keep it still, and the moment she touched its feathers she knew something was very wrong. Edgar was huddled beside her, glaring at the Blackwatch agents one by one, so he did not notice the look of shock on her face until she took hold of his wrist, forcing him to look at her. Kate's eyes were fully black, she was breathing heavily, and her skin was tinged with blue.

"It's Silas," she said.

Kate could not describe what she was seeing. She knew she was looking into the veil, but all she could see was darkness, the same kind of void she had seen around Silas when he entered the half-life with her on the Night of Souls. And then she felt it: Silas's presence, as near to her as Edgar was. "He's here," she said quietly.

"Maybe it's just a shade," said Edgar. "There's no reason to think—"

Kate gripped Edgar's hand tightly as images flashed suddenly through her mind. They felt like memories, but they did not belong to her. *She saw a town filled with white buildings and a circular room lined with bones. There was a Blackwatch officer standing beside her, and candles and vials were hanging down from a domed ceiling.* "He's sick," she said as an uncomfortable feeling gathered heavily within her chest.

"What happened?" asked Edgar. "Where is he?"

The two of them fell silent as the thin officer walked beneath the sail and spoke quietly to the leader. He turned and pointed to Edgar, who shrank back against the guardrail.

"This doesn't look good," he said.

Kate released the crow and let it hide in the space between them before the leader handed over control of the boat and walked over to them.

"Stand up," he said.

"Why?"

The man heaved Edgar up by his wrist, and the crow scuttled behind Kate. "Where is it?" he demanded.

"Where's what?"

"There are feathers on this deck. Silas Dane's bird is here. Where is it?"

"I have no idea what you're talking about."

The leader turned to his men. "Find it. Kill it."

Kate stood up before the officers could get close. She grabbed the crow and threw it as far as she could over the side of the boat. Its claws scraped the water as its wings beat hard into flight, fluttering in a wide circle around the lanterns in the sails, out of reach of the arrows that the dark-haired guard sent spearing toward it. The crow cackled up into the night sky, shadowing the boat while staying just out of arrow reach.

The leader grabbed Kate by her coat collar. "What did he tell you?" he demanded.

"Let her go!" Edgar pushed the man hard enough to make him pay attention, and the stronger man struck him hard across the face.

"I have reconsidered the boy's position," he said to his men. "He is no longer welcome on this boat. Kill him."

"You can't do that!" said Kate.

"Do not tell me what I cannot do."

"You could have left him behind! Why bring him all the way out here if you were just going to kill him?"

"My orders were to keep him alive until he became an inconvenience," said the leader. "That moment has passed."

"Don't you think those who sent you here should make that decision for themselves?"

"You have said enough, girl. I suggest you remain silent."

The dark-haired guard acted at once, pinning Edgar against the guardrail and pressing a dagger blade up to his throat. Edgar tried to hold him back, but he was not strong enough to do anything to help himself. Kate tried to pull the guard away, the blade drew a thin bead of blood, and one of Silas's memories forced its way suddenly to the front of her panicked thoughts. *He was standing in front of a dark house, looking at the hooded woman from Kate's own vision. Kate knew that face. She had seen that woman's face twice before: in the memory captured in the skull and in the vision shared by the spirit wheel. That woman had been there when the bonemen died centuries ago, and now Silas was with her, greeting her by name.*

"Dalliah Grey!" she shouted, repeating Silas's words without even thinking about it. The guard held his blade steady, and the atmosphere on the boat changed at once. "You're working for her. Aren't you?"

All three of the Blackwatch looked surprised by the mention of the woman's name. The dark-haired guard's eyes flickered back to his leader, and Kate saw something else within them. He was not just surprised to hear the name: he feared it.

The leader's expression, however, gave nothing away.

"What do you know about Dalliah Grey?" he demanded.

"Enough," she said, lying to him.

The guard still had Edgar pinned down. "This is witchery," he said quietly.

The leader glared down at Kate with suspicion. "Or she overheard one of you two mention the name," he said. "She knows nothing."

Kate glanced at Edgar, making sure he was all right. "I know that Dalliah has met with Silas Dane," she said quickly, piecing together what she had seen within the veil. "Dalliah's one of the Skilled. You don't trust her, but you listen to her. You wouldn't have brought both of us on board unless someone ordered you to do it. She sent you here."

Kate knew she was taking a risk, but there was nothing else she could do.

The dark-haired guard spoke first. "No one said they knew each other," he said. "She was supposed to come quietly. No trouble. Dalliah lied to us."

The leader raised a hand for quiet, never taking his eyes from Kate's face. "Bandermain trusts her," he said. "This changes nothing."

"What about the boy?"

Everyone stood in silence, waiting for the leader to make his decision. "Leave him," he said, "for now."

The dark-haired guard stepped back, and Edgar's hand immediately went to his neck to feel what damage had been done.

"I don't know how you know Dalliah Grey; but one more word out of your friend here, and orders or not, I will kill him myself," said the leader. "You have earned him a few more hours of life at most. I suggest he spend it in silence." He walked away, and Edgar stared at Kate as if she had just achieved the impossible.

"Dalliah Grey?" he whispered as loudly as he dared. "Where did that come from?"

Kate leaned in to check his neck. The guard's blade had left a tiny cut, and when she touched Edgar's skin, it sealed at once. "I think it was Silas," she said. "I saw a memory in the veil. He told me her name."

"Well, I think you've just made those guards afraid of you."

"It's Dalliah they're afraid of, not me."

"That's not what I saw," said Edgar. "You stood up to them, and it saved my life. Thank you."

The crow continued circling high overhead as the boat made its way through the wide river channels on its way to the coast, and the Blackwatch officers took shots at it whenever they thought it was straying too close. When they began to reach villages and other large settlements that were scattered across the eastern wilds, Kate and Edgar were sent into the covered section of the boat while the Blackwatch officers posed as traders, talked their way through the river gates, and sailed the boat on.

Slowly the night lightened into dawn. Kate managed to sleep for a short while, resting her head on Edgar's shoulder, and Edgar was leaning back against the guardrail, snoring loudly, when a sudden explosion jolted them both awake. Edgar grunted and blinked, bleary-eyed. "What's happening?" he said.

The two of them shielded their eyes from the brightness of the midmorning sun, and a streak of red flame burst into the sky above the boat.

"A fire flare," said Kate. "They're signaling someone."

The land on either side of the river was covered in frosted green trees that glimmered in the rising sun, and where the river wound between them Kate noticed something strange about the horizon. There were no hills in the distance, not even a single smoky plume from a fire marking an outlaw settlement or the beginning of another village. The horizon was dark, bleak, and completely flat.

"Edgar," she whispered, pointing through the trees, "Edgar, look. I think I can see the ocean." Half afraid and half amazed by what she was seeing, she stared out to the east. "I've never seen the sea before."

The morning sun glittered upon the water, illuminating the cresting tops of distant waves and making them sparkle with light. It looked as if the sea were higher than the land, its waves rearing up ready to swallow the wilds in one mighty flood, even though the waters were still and calm. In that eerie place between the land and the sky a greater danger sat like a black scar upon the water. The silhouette of a ship was anchored out at sea. It looked like a wreck that had been dragged up from the ocean floor, skeletal and sinister. Green glass lanterns hung along its side, and its empty masts loomed tall and ghostly in the sunlight.

The boat bounced gently as it passed out of the shallow river mouth and out onto open sea. The thin guard stood upon the roof of the boat and flickered a second signal to the ship, using a circle of glass pressed against his palm to reflect the light of the sun. One of the ship's green lights winked in reply, and the boat cut swiftly toward it.

Kate and Edgar held on tightly to the guardrail as dark water, fathomless and deep, surrounded them. The closer they got to the ship, the clearer it became. There were people on board, moving around on the deck, and the skeletal shapes Kate had seen from the shore were damaged sections of the ship that had been singed by fire arrows or cracked by catapults. Most of them were badly patched, leaving scars that made the ship look battle worn and barely seaworthy.

"So . . . do we have a plan?" asked Edgar.

"We see what they want," said Kate.

The men on the ship slung ropes down to the boat as it bumped gently against its hull. Once it was secure, rope ladders followed.

"Prisoners first," said the leader.

Edgar was first to climb the ladder, and he turned to help Kate step up onto the deck behind him. There they were met by unsheathed blades, letting them know exactly who was in charge on that ship.

"Prepare to set sail," said the leader, stepping expertly up from the boat. "We have what we came for."

Two officers quickly bundled Kate and Edgar through a trapdoor in the deck, pushed them down a flight of steps, and forced them into a small room with a tiny window that was split in half by a wall of bars. The dark-haired guard prodded them through a door set in the bars and stood blocking the doorway.

"Won't be long now," he said. "I'll be glad to leave this rat-bitten rock of a country behind."

"I'm sure it's glad to see the back of you, too," said Edgar.

The guard grinned. "For now," he said. "Not for long."

"You're going back?" said Kate.

"That depends on how good a little witch you are, doesn't it?" The guard, stepped back, slammed the door, and locked it tight. "You'll stay quiet in there, if you know what's good for you."

The ship raised anchor, the sails were unfurled, and Kate felt the great vessel lean and pitch as it began to gather speed, heading east toward the Continent, out into the unknown. Kate and Edgar could not talk freely with a guard standing right outside the door, so they spent the journey in nervous silence, neither of them knowing what to expect on the other side.

The farther the ship sailed from Albion, the more distant the veil became until Kate had difficulty sensing it at all. It felt as though a deep noise had been reverberating in her mind for weeks and had suddenly stopped, making her realize how quiet the world was without its relentless hum. The air grew colder, drawing steam from her breath, and she knew they were entering cooler waters when scratches of ice began scraping along the length of the hull.

Kate curled up on a narrow bedroll. The hours passed slowly, but there was no way she could sleep. While Edgar slept restlessly beside her, her mind kept wandering to memories of Silas and the dark, creeping edges of the half-life. She did not know how long they had been traveling, but the door lock finally scraped back and a dull bell tolled somewhere in the distance, chiming out the hour. The dark-haired guard entered the room, and Kate reached over to shake Edgar awake.

"Rest's over," said the guard. "We've arrived."

# 19

# BLOOD
# WORK

Silas couldn't see. The veil was not answering him, and every one of his senses had failed. He was sealed in. Trapped in darkness. Powerless to do anything except hold on to his thoughts, let go of everything else, and drift. If he had been an ordinary man, death would have been waiting for him in that emptiness; instead, there was nothing but the dark.

Memories flickered over one another, erratic and out of his control. The strange pressure of the veil stripped him of his sense of time, dampening every part of his being until he was not even certain that he was still thinking. He felt lost, empty, and forgotten. Perhaps this was what Dalliah had been talking about: his form of death. An ending with no end. Nothingness. Unable to move or speak with only darkness smothering him, separating him from the world, sealing him within his own corner of the veil, silent and alone.

A flurry of light burst into his thoughts, and for a moment he *glimpsed the living world through his crow's eyes. Then the link was broken, the image lost. His crow was there, the world was still there, and it offered him a thread of hope. He still had a connection to the living world. It was weak, but it was his.*

*Silas focused upon his crow, trying to regain that connection, but part of him held back; part of him did not want to fight to escape that place. The veil was already claiming what was left of his spirit, binding him tightly within its web, and he was starting to forget. Fragments of his life were breaking away, stripping back his memory beyond his days as a warden and a soldier, spreading back into the few distant memories he had of his family: his mother, father, and sister. He saw their faces and remembered the sparkle of silver as a warden counted a handful of coins into his father's hand.*

*That was a memory he could never forget: at ten years old, he had been sold to the wardens for less than the price of a carriage wheel. Twelve coins were all his life had been worth then. Twelve coins that would be spent feeding his sister, the sister he had loved enough not to complain when his parents walked him to the meeting place and sold him into a life of order, discipline, and death. He concentrated upon the last time he had seen his family, the promises they had made that they would see one another again, and the haunted look in his mother's eyes when the warden led him out of sight.*

*The veil could not strip that memory away, and he held on to it, using it to focus his resistance. He had spent years crushing* that memory into the back of his mind, seeing it as a weakness. Now it had become his strength.

The veil could not draw any closer. Its hold upon him faltered, and in the midst of the emptiness he heard the crow screech out a short call. Heaviness pressed down around him. Pressure sealed him in, constricting him. He saw flat stones laid out at an awkward angle in front of his eyes and felt the chill of the solid ground as he became aware of his body and his chest tried to heave in a single choking, spluttering breath. The veil fell away, his eyes opened, and he saw Bandermain standing over him, sword drawn, circled by candlelight.

"I saw you die!" said Bandermain, looking at him as if he had just crawled out of a cold grave. "You were dead for hours! Your skin was cold!"

Silas's hand closed secretly around the hilt of the stolen dagger in his belt. His flesh felt alien to him; his fingers, clumsy and unfamiliar. The confines of his body clung around him like a metal cage, and it was even an effort to move, but still, that feeling was better than the draining emptiness of the half-life. He got to his feet, making Bandermain step back. His chest still prickled. The veil had healed the damage that had been done to his lungs, but it was only a matter of time before the disease took his body to the brink of death again. He had bought himself some time; now he had to use it.

Silas struck before Bandermain had time to react, stabbing

the dagger blade deep into his thigh and drawing his sword, ready to fight. Bandermain roared with pain and dragged out the bloodied blade. Silas watched him, waiting for him to react. Bandermain's confusion bled into rage, and his sword swung, metal striking against metal as Silas parried the blow.

Strike after strike scraped and slammed along the edges of the blades, the sounds of battle clanging from the walls as Silas shifted from defense to attack. His sword was lighter, quicker than Bandermain's, and it found Bandermain's skin enough times to draw blood and grunts of anger from his enemy; but the battle was more equal than Silas could have anticipated. Bandermain's blood fury willed him on, pouring every ounce of frustration into his sword blows, fueling them with adrenaline and fierce desperation as his illness weakened him. Silas's strength and skill thrived upon facing an equal opponent. Every hit was hard earned, every block powerful enough to shudder his bones. Decades of hate between the Continent and Albion welled up between the two men. It did not matter why they were fighting, only that they should.

Silas could feel the energy of the circle draining him slowly, sapping his strength as the battle waged on. The blood-filled vials shone upon their cords all around him as Bandermain launched another attack, wheezing and wavering as blood returned to his lips. Silas knew then that he was fighting the wrong enemy. Those vials were used in blood work. He had seen Da'ru Marr use the energy in a person's blood to weaken his body, trap his spirit within the veil, or bind it to a certain place. Bandermain and Silas were as helpless as each other under Dalliah's influence. She had sprung her trap, and she was using them both.

Bandermain roared with rage as his sword swung back for a mighty strike. Silas anticipated it, but instead of blocking the blade, he dodged to one side and landed a hard kick to the back of Bandermain's injured leg. The momentum of his swing threw Bandermain off-balance as his knee buckled, the sword crashed from his hands, and he fell to the floor. Silas stood over him, blade pointed down at his throat, and Bandermain looked up with determination.

"You won't do it," he said, whistling in each difficult breath. "You won't risk angering her. You need Dalliah as much as I do."

"You are a leech," said Silas. "You feed from her skill with the veil, while she feeds from your connection to it. Without her, you will die. She has given me nothing."

"You came here for answers, exactly as she said you would," said Bandermain. "You will not throw that opportunity away."

"You are beaten," said Silas, pressing the blade closer to Bandermain's skin. "Your life is mine to claim."

"No," said Dalliah. "It is mine." The door to the courtyard had opened, and she was already walking inside. "You are stronger than I expected, Silas," she said. "The veil should still have you."

Silas could already feel his blood thinning and his muscles beginning to ache. He kicked Bandermain's sword away and swung his own weapon up through the air, slicing through the cords holding the vials closest to him and smashing them to the floor. Blood crept out of the shattered glass and spread eerily toward the center of the room.

"Smash them. Crush them. It makes no difference," said Dalliah.

Silas sliced through more of the strings, raining glass and blood around the room as long as his strength remained.

"You want to feel you are doing something. I understand that," said Dalliah. "You will not admit that you are no longer in control. But I am not your enemy. This blood the Blackwatch took from you is not truly yours. It is as good as Winters blood now. Kate's essence lives within every drop. You did well to find her, but you cannot protect her from me. She is as much a slave to the forces of Wintercraft as you are. The veil has shown me her future. You cannot stop fate."

"You will not subdue her with tricks like this," said Silas, snatching a vial in his hand and throwing it to the floor. "She will resist it."

"She has not resisted me so far," said Dalliah. "The right thought, the right memory presented to her at exactly the right time . . . she is already mine. You gave her to me. The blood link between you allowed me to influence her mind. She had no defense against me. Even if she had tried to resist, it would never have been enough. She trusts too easily, and her greatest mistake was in ever trusting you."

Silas took a step back as the blood pooled around his feet, spread into shallow grooves on the floor, and traced the faint outline of a skull cut into the stone. It was so faint that he had not even noticed the carving until the blood filled its curves like poured ink. He looked closer at the floor around it and saw the faint ghosts of more carvings—a skull, a bird, a wolf, and a flame—and beneath his feet was a snowflake, the mark of the Winters family. They were the same symbols as those found on spirit wheels within Fume, and the more he looked, the more he found, spread in a carved spiral around the room.

"Kate has protected *Wintercraft* well," said Dalliah. "She has kept it close to her, and she has studied it. I recognized your loyalty to her long before even you did. You let her live for a reason. You knew her life meant something, and you know that what I am doing is right."

The energy of the veil vibrated in the air. Silas could feel Kate close by.

"Your work is over," said Dalliah. "This room will help you do what is right. It is here to help you, as it will help Kate."

"I know what this room is," said Silas. "It is a prison."

Dalliah smiled. "You should have used your mind more often than your blade. Perhaps then you would not have found yourself in this situation. You might still have been free."

"You cannot hold me here. My blood is not bound to yours. Only Kate can work a circle in that way."

"And she *is* working it," said Dalliah, touching one of the remaining vials of blood and making it swing upon its string. "Kate has barely begun to understand what Wintercraft truly is. I can manipulate her connection to the veil in any way I see fit. I can open her eyes to the black heart of the veil . . . let her see its horrors for herself."

"No," said Silas.

"Have you looked into the darkness? Have you seen the place where your spirit lies?"

Dalliah snapped the vial from its cord and trickled a line of blood over her fingertips. The last time he had seen someone attempt blood work was the day his spirit had been broken, but this was something very different. Silas's eyes clouded white, and a high-pitched screech pierced through his mind. Bandermain got painfully to his feet and watched with interest as Silas struggled to block out a sound that only he could hear. It was the screech of lost souls, a cry of torment and desperation.

Silas knew that sound. He had spent the first two years of his new life hearing those voices every day, drowning out every other noise and haunting him in his sleep. It had taken him a long time to ignore them until eventually he had learned to block them out almost completely. Souls bound so deep within the veil were beyond the reach of all but the most skilled Walkers. They were the truly lost, every one of them abandoned, forgotten, and sealed away with no hope of release into life or death.

Echoes of his soul's prison still bled into Silas's life every day. Now Dalliah had used his blood to break down the barriers he had built between himself and the truth, throwing the door in his mind wide open once again. His knowledge of that place gave him some defense against it. He was ready for the wave of anguish and pain, but his was not the only blood Dalliah was working with. Somewhere inside the veil Silas heard Kate scream.

The guard pressed his hand across Kate's mouth, muffling her scream that had begun the moment their carriage passed through the last of Grale's back streets. They were traveling through a dark, frosted forest, following a trail so narrow that branches snapped and scratched against the windows as the carriage rattled past.

Edgar was sitting in the seat opposite Kate, watching as her eyes blackened and changed into white, swirling with the clouded energies of the veil. "What's happening to her?" he demanded.

Kate grabbed the carriage door handle, but the guard held her still. Edgar had never seen her act that way before.

"We were warned this could happen," said the leader. "It will pass."

"What do you mean, 'it will pass'? It shouldn't be

happening in the first place!" said Edgar. "Look at her!"

"It will pass," the leader said again. "We will be there soon."

"Kate!"

Kate shivering, opened her eyes, and saw Edgar crouching in front of her, clasping her icy hands. The two Blackwatch officers were watching him, the atmosphere in the carriage was heavy with danger, and for a moment it was hard for her to tell if she was still inside the veil or not.

"You're all right," said Edgar. "You're back. You're safe."

No words came anywhere close to the terrifying void Kate's mind had just been shown. Emptiness. Lifelessness. Nothingness. She had entered the half-life before, but even it was nothing compared with the empty terror of what she had just seen. It was the worst kind of prison, a prison of the mind and soul, and she never wanted to see anything like it again.

Silas was the only person who had ever been able to draw Kate's mind into the veil against her will, but she knew he was not the one responsible. She could feel the shadow of a woman close by, watching her within the veil.

The trees parted outside the carriage windows, giving way to a high stone wall broken by a pair of open gates. The land within those walls was filled with death, thick with the memories of many lives that had been ended too soon. Kate glanced out of the carriage window as the wheels rattled slowly across the cobbles and caught sight of a large house on the other side of a wide courtyard. She recognized its twin spires, its boarded black windows with candlelight flickering behind them, and the sense of cold isolation, as if nothing existed beyond its walls.

The driver pulled the horses to a halt in front of a small circular building, beside a door made from glass and iron. He opened the carriage door and stepped down first, then held out a hand to help Kate to the ground. Kate jumped down without his help, and a woman stepped out of the shadows beside the door. If she had not stepped forward to greet them, Kate would have believed she was a statue, she looked so lifeless and still. Kate had the same feeling that she had had whenever she stood near to Silas, a feeling of empty menace that could come only from people with broken souls.

The woman pressed a bloodstained hand to her chest and bowed slowly. "Welcome to my home, Kate," she said. "I have been waiting to meet you for a very long time."

## ←— 20 —→
# BLADE &
# CLAW

Now that Kate could see the woman for herself, she had no doubt of who she was. She was the same person she had seen in her vision through the spirit wheel. She might have been older, but for someone who had to have lived for centuries she did not look very much different from the young woman Kate had seen in her vision of the past, the woman who had condemned so many of the bonemen to death. She had the same sharp eyes, the same aura of dominance, and a sense of secrecy that made Kate think she was missing something that had been put out in the open for her to see.

"You knew the bonemen," said Kate, not caring how impossible her words seemed. "You ordered them to kill each other, and you bound their souls into the spirit wheels."

"Very good," said Dalliah. "Few people's minds are open enough to accept the truth of my existence during our first meeting. Even Silas was uncertain, and he and I are very much alike."

"You're not like him," said Kate.

"I'm surprised you think so, given your history," said Dalliah. "In certain ways you are right. Silas was blind to the truth of this world before his eyes were opened, whereas you and I were born with the gift of sight in our blood. The veil has shown me what has been and what will be. You may learn to do the same, in time." Dalliah reached out her bloodied hand to Kate, who did not take it.

"Why are we here?" asked Edgar.

Dalliah looked at him as if a dog had just opened its mouth and spoken. "We are standing at the edge of a new world. She stepped aside and gestured to the door. "Please," she said. "Silas is waiting for us inside."

Kate went to step forward, but the Blackwatch leader held her back.

"Our work is done," he said. "What news do you have of Bandermain? Is he alive?"

"He is close to death," said Dalliah. "Had you taken much longer it is doubtful he would have survived. This girl will give him the help he needs."

"Where is he?"

A man's strained voice carried from inside the building. "Let her in!" it said. "The girl. Now!"

The Blackwatch leader handed Kate over at once. "Take her," he said. "We have done as ordered. I trust it will be enough."

"As do I," said Dalliah. "Wait here with your men. You two, come with me."

With three of the Blackwatch and Dalliah Grey surrounding them, Kate and Edgar had no choice but to walk through that door and face whatever was on the other side. Determined to lead the way, Kate went first. The veil, which had seemed faint and erratic since she had set foot upon Continental soil, was alive in that place, her connection with it strengthening with every step.

She stopped just a few steps in and saw the bones lining the walls, the hanging vials, and the dimly glowing carvings on the bloodstained floor that her sensitive eyes could see clearly in the candlelight. The air was thick with energy, but there was no listening circle there, no half-life, and no shades. Something inside that room was different, more primitive, and infinitely more powerful.

Edgar whispered beside her. "Now that is something I never thought I would see," he said.

When Kate saw what he was looking at, it took a few seconds for her mind to take it in. Silas was lying on the floor on the other side of the room, with the red-coated man standing over him, holding the blade of Silas's own blue-black sword to his neck. He was conscious, but only just. His eyes were shot with blood as they turned slowly to meet hers, and his body was still.

"Silas," she said, her nervous voice barely more than a

breath. She tried to cross the room to reach him, but Edgar held her back.

"Don't do it, Kate," he said, looking around the bone-covered walls. "There's something wrong in here. Don't . . . move."

Kate caught the flicker of a warning in Silas's eyes, and she stayed still, clenching her fingers into fists as Dalliah stepped between her and Edgar.

"Bandermain, what are you doing?" demanded Dalliah.

The red-coated man looked almost as ill as Silas. He was clutching his chest, his voice thready and breathless. "I have to know," he said. "I have to be sure."

"He is not here to satisfy your curiosity," said Dalliah. "Your men have delivered the girl. You have earned my trust. It is time for you to receive your reward."

"No." Bandermain held the weapon calmly against Silas's throat. "If you can do this to him, what is to stop you from doing it to me once I am changed? Look at him! You caused this. His life may be endless, but *that* is no way to live."

"He is a danger to me," said Dalliah. "You are not."

"But I *will* be." Bandermain's voice was growing louder, and the strain of his words made him cough hard. "No one should have that much power over another life."

"What's wrong with him?" asked Edgar, taking a few steps back.

Bandermain snapped his head around to glare at him and

then turned his spit-soaked lips toward Kate. "I knew Silas Dane long before you and your kind got your hands on him," he said. "His life was his own. He fought and bled for his country, and it was an honor to stand against him. Now all it takes is one witch to set him on his back! One witch to poison his life!"

Dalliah stepped forward, pulling Kate with her. "This is what you wanted," she said. "The girl is here! Do not turn your back on what we have achieved together."

"I will take no pleasure in taking the life of an unarmed enemy," said Bandermain. "But if what you say about Silas is true, he will survive. If not . . . I must know how far your witchery goes. A swift slice to the neck and I will hold Silas's head in my hands. Let us see if he is still breathing after that. Let us see if this suffering is worthwhile."

Bandermain leaned forward and pulled Silas off the floor by his bloodied shirt. "I will give you an honorable end," he said, raising the dark blade high over his shoulder. "Death by the sword. If you survive, I will accept this path I have been offered. I will take this gift and start my life again. To face death—the ultimate enemy—and live . . . let us see if that truly is a battle Silas Dane can win."

Dalliah stood in silence, watching as the sword reached its height, but instead of doing something to stop Bandermain, she looked interested in what he was about to do. She wanted to see what was going to happen next.

"No!" Kate and Edgar shouted together as the sword flashed down toward Silas's neck. Edgar looked away, and Dalliah stared wide-eyed.

What came next happened in a single moment.

Silas's sickly eyes looked up at the sweeping blade. He snatched hold of the hand holding his shirt and twisted it hard, snapping Bandermain's wrist and forcing him to let go. Silas fell back, out of reach of the sword, and Bandermain struggled to recover his balance as the glass in the door exploded in a burst of black feathers and splintering shards. Silas's crow slammed through it and flopped onto the floor, dazed and unsteady on its glass-dusted wings. Its claws scratched the stones, and it launched itself, screeching and fluttering over Edgar's ducked head, toward the man attacking its master.

Bandermain did not see the bird coming until it was too late. He brought the sword down hard, desperate to deliver a mortal blow, but Silas dodged and struck him hard in the throat, making him buckle and fall. The crow took its chance and flew at Bandermain's face in a feathered frenzy of beak and claws. The sword slid from his hand as he tried to break his fall, and Silas reclaimed his weapon, sweeping it up as he got to his feet. Bandermain yelled in fury as the crow scratched at his face, barely managing to keep its snapping beak away from his eyes.

"Crow." Silas said the word quietly, but the bird still heard him. It ceased its attack at once and fluttered awkwardly onto

Silas's shoulder, out of reach of Bandermain's grasping hands.

Bandermain glared at the bird with a crazed look of fury. "Keep that filthy thing away from me," he said, drawing a dagger from his belt with his good hand and spinning it in his fingers.

"Get used to that feeling," said Silas, glaring at Bandermain from beneath his eyebrows as his own neck twitched with pain. "You want to know what it is like to live my life? Well, now you are living it. For weeks you have allowed this woman to take you to the edge of death and claw you back from it. You fear death. I see that. But what she has done to you is a far greater cruelty than simply watching you die. You are a tortured man, and you do not even see it. You believe that my life is a reward to be handed out for a job well done, but you do not yet know what it truly means to fear something, Celador. No one should live as I do. No one should be denied the death that is rightfully his. That is cruelty. *That* is pain."

"I could have killed you," said Bandermain. "No one can survive a blade to the neck. Not even you."

"Perhaps one day someone will put that theory to the test," said Silas. "But not you, and not today. You wanted life. I am proof that you can have it, but it does not come without its price. Do you still want what I have? Do you want to look into the current of death and turn away from it forever?"

Bandermain looked at the people around him and pointed his dagger shakily at Kate. "You," he said. "You can heal me. You can take this sickness away."

"She cannot heal this disease," said Silas. "No one can."

"She *will*," said Bandermain.

Dalliah pulled Kate closer to the sick man, so close that she could smell the scent of blood upon his breath. "She may not be able to heal you," said Dalliah, "but she can *save* you. You are a worthy man, Celador. I will have need of you when the veil falls."

Bandermain looked weaker every moment, until he barely had the strength to hold the dagger, and as he weakened, Kate felt the energy in the room change. Silas noticed it, too, and whatever it was, it was having a direct effect upon Bandermain. Kate did not know what to do. Silas had had his chance to take his life, but he had held back. She did not know if Bandermain was truly an enemy or not, but she could not stand by and watch a man die without doing something.

"Let me try," she said.

"No," Silas said suddenly. "Stay away from him."

"The only thing Kate will do here is what *I* tell her to do," said Dalliah. "If he will not accept the binding, there is nothing we can do for him. It will be a shame to see him die like this. But if he wishes it . . ."

"No!" Bandermain grabbed Kate's arm in a weak grip. "Do it," he said quietly. "Let me have what Silas has. Let me live. I do not want to die like this."

Bandermain's face was wild and terrified, but Dalliah

was smiling, enjoying his torment. She wanted him to beg for his life.

Kate tried not to look at Bandermain. She looked instead toward Silas, who was trying not to show how ill he was. Bandermain had attacked him just moments ago, but it was difficult to separate who was an enemy and who was a friend in that room.

"You have the book with you," said Dalliah, close to Kate's ear. "*Wintercraft* will tell you what you need to do. All you need is a blade."

"Take mine." Bandermain handed Kate his dagger, hilt first, and when she took hold of it, she clasped his uninjured hand in hers. She could feel the muscles quivering beneath his skin and could sense the veil hanging like a silvery aura around him, waiting for death to carry him into its current. He did not have long. As soon as she touched him, Bandermain began to breathe more freely and the bird claw scratches faded a little upon his skin. Kate heard the crack as his broken wrist snapped back into place, and Bandermain stared at it as if it were the most amazing thing he had ever seen.

Kate could see Silas questioning her with his eyes, unsure of her plan. But Kate did not have a plan. She had read about the binding secretly during her time with the Skilled. She knew the theory. All she needed now was a strong enough connection to the veil. The building they were standing in may not have held a listening circle, but that did not matter.

Listening circles were created to channel the veil at places where the barrier between it and the living world was at its weakest. There on the Continent the veil was so far away that it needed to be attracted toward a circle, not pierced by one.

With all the bodies buried beneath her land, Dalliah had re-created her own miniature version of Fume, a graveyard inhabited by the restless souls of the dead. Kate could sense hundreds of those souls gathering across the land outside, their presence tingling like eyes on the back of her neck. Every one of them was bound to that place—to the blood that had seeped into the soil and to the memory of their deaths still hanging over them. Those souls carried the veil with them as Bandermain's spirit reached out for death.

Kate reached deeper into the veil, letting it flood across her in a way that was different from what she had felt within an ordinary listening circle. The power of what was happening within that building just outside the reach of normal sight overwhelmed her. The candlelight that had glowed gently when Kate first walked in now revealed itself to be a carefully crafted lie: a distraction created by Dalliah to hide the raging maelstrom of destructive energy brewing underneath. Kate did not know how she had not felt it before. If Silas had known what he was walking into, he never would have entered that room.

Opening her mind in that place was like lifting her head out of a gently flowing river and being dragged under by the pounding force of a raging waterfall. The full extent of the veil's attracted energy plummeted down around her, raw and disorganized, primal and wild. Listening circles were built to harness those energies; they tamed the veil and allowed it to be manipulated safely, but this circle simply called it forth and let it slam into its stones, fierce and uncontrolled. Kate braced her mind against it, defending herself against the awesome power of something far greater than any single life. The veil was one of the world's greatest secrets, one of the unseen threads that held the world together. Standing there, staring right into its essence, she could see that it was falling apart.

Memories flickered within the misted glaze that hung across her eyes, belonging to the living people standing within that room as well as those of the Blackwatch waiting patiently outside its doors. Kate glimpsed the minds of everyone there—everyone except Dalliah herself—and through it all she saw Edgar just standing there, calmly ignorant of the invisible forces thundering down around him. To his eyes that room was just like any other room with bone-clad walls and bloodstained carvings on the floor, and for that moment she envied him. He did not have to see what she could see. He did not have to struggle with the veil every day and be persecuted for something he could not control. Even Silas could not see the full truth about that place, and its influence was affecting him and Bandermain the most.

The racing energy scrubbed through the air, making it impossible for anyone except a Walker to connect with the veil.

It was moving too fast, being absorbed into the earth, rejecting the lost souls that were not yet free to pass into death and then retreating back toward Albion. As it moved, its absence left a vacuum in its place, preventing Silas and Dalliah from being able to heal and hastening the progression of Bandermain's illness. Kate could not even begin to understand how Dalliah had created that place or how she was able to stand within it so calmly, conducting conversations as if nothing were happening when the ground was ready to open up and tear everything apart.

"Bandermain's spirit will be bound to me," said Dalliah, reaching out to Kate. "The blade. Give it to me." Kate handed her the dagger and watched her draw the silver twice across her palm, leaving two deep cuts behind.

Bandermain stepped closer to Kate, his strength failing. "Now mine," he said, as Dalliah handed the blade back to Kate, and he held out his own already scarred hand.

"This can't be undone," said Kate. "If I do this, you will never go back to the way you were. You will never get your spirit back."

"Yes, yes. I know all that," said Bandermain, impatience cutting through his words. "Get on with it!"

Kate hesitated then, allowing the memory of how Bandermain had received those scars to bleed into her mind. Dalliah had already tried to bind his soul to hers twice before, and she had failed. The silver in the blade hummed gently as Kate's energy ran through it, the knife ready to do something that Kate herself knew she would instantly regret.

*"Do it!"* said Bandermain.

Kate lowered the dagger just enough for Bandermain to sense that she was having serious doubts.

"You said she would do it!" he said to Dalliah.

Silas dug the point of his sword into the floor, helping himself stand. "Things are not as simple as they first seemed, are they, Celador?" he said.

"Quiet!" Bandermain's eyes flickered briefly to Edgar, who was trying, and failing, to get Silas's attention. He lunged for him, grabbed Edgar's neck, and locked it beneath his arm, holding him off-balance so he could not squirm away. Edgar flailed his arms, trying to wriggle free, but stopped the moment one of Bandermain's daggers pressed against his back.

"It is a simple enough task," said Bandermain, panting to catch his breath. "Do it now, girl. Or I will show you how blood spilling should be done!"

# 21

## LOST

Bandermain's anger flooded into the veil, and Kate started to lose control. All she was seeing and feeling started to blend together: the veil, the memories, and everything that was happening in the room throughout its past, present, and future, until she was no longer sure what was happening and what was not. The vision the spirit wheel had shown her dominated her thoughts. Nothing made sense. Her head was splitting with pain, and then Dalliah was beside her again, a calm face within the growing darkness as her mind began shutting down, desperate to escape the confusion.

"You are a true Winters," said Dalliah. "Your connection to the veil makes you more a shade than one of the living. But like so many of your ancestors, you lack the tenacity to get things done."

"She is not one of your experiments," said Silas's voice.

"But I will use her, exactly as you did," said Dalliah. "We

must take what we want. Do not pretend that what I am doing is beneath you. You have done far worse."

"I showed her what she was," said Silas. "Nothing like this."

"And I am showing her what she will become. There is no difference."

Kate saw Silas walking toward her, a black shadow against the veil's silvery light.

"Do not interfere!" said Dalliah. "This must happen. You cannot stop it now."

Kate could hear Dalliah's words, but she could also hear something else underneath them, a whisper creeping through the veil. It was Dalliah's voice, but it sounded different—more distant.

*"Bandermain can help us repair what has been broken,"* she said. *"Save his life. We need his strength."*

Kate looked over at Edgar, standing completely at Bandermain's mercy. All she wanted was for everything to stop and give her time and space to think. She wanted her mind to be clear again, but even there in the midst of all the confusion there was one thing of which she was perfectly sure: even if she could bind someone's soul, she knew that she could never bring herself to do it, and that certainty was more than she'd had to hold on to for a long time.

"No." She said the word out loud. "I can't do it. I won't do it."

Bandermain's sickly face turned as red as it could manage, twisting with rage and disappointment. And even though Edgar was scared, he smiled proudly at Kate, letting her know that she had done the right thing.

Dalliah was unfazed by Kate's refusal. "How will you learn how capable you are if you do not test yourself?" she asked. "This is your chance to become more than just the girl who made the Night of Souls real again. I will show you how to complete the work your ancestors began centuries before you were even born. They knew this time would come. The bonemen had their chance to reveal the truth about our world. They had an opportunity, and they turned away from it. You have already revealed the veil to so many closed minds. Soon you will be able to show them a side of life that they could never have imagined. We need Bandermain and his men to carry out that plan."

"I don't care about your plan," said Kate.

"The Skilled should have helped you instead of holding you back," said Dalliah. "Will you continue to deny what you and your family have always been? Or do you want to accept it?"

"What . . . is *happening*?" demanded Bandermain, struggling for breath. Death was close. Kate could not see it; but she could feel it, and so could he. It was coming for him.

"Quiet!" Dalliah glared at Bandermain, but this time he refused to be silenced.

"If no one here . . . is willing to help me . . . I will not . . . enter death alone!"

Somewhere inside her, Kate knew the moment was coming. The spirit wheel had warned her of it, Bandermain had already threatened to do it; but when the moment finally arrived, she could not quite accept that it was real. The confusion of the veil pulled back from her eyes as she focused completely upon Edgar, whose brave smile melted into shock and pain as Bandermain's dagger sank deep into his back.

Kate stared as Bandermain pulled out the bloodied blade, and she stood in horrified silence, unable to react as he pushed Edgar to the floor. Silas shouted something and stepped toward Bandermain, but it was too late. The dagger fell from Bandermain's hand, and he crumpled to his knees, unable to speak, unable to breathe, as the creeping lung finally claimed what was left of his life.

"Kate!" Silas turned to her as Bandermain slumped wide-eyed to the floor. "Get out of here!"

But Kate could not move. She was staring at Edgar lying still upon the floor. His blood trailed into a carving of a bird cut into the stone, and her eyes stung with tears.

Dalliah held Kate still as something moved across the floor. It looked as if the stones were rippling outward from Bandermain's lifeless hand, moving toward Edgar. Kate could tell it was not a trick of the veil, but it had to be impossible. Silas snatched a candle from a cord hanging from the ceiling and threw it between Edgar and the creeping stones. The flame crackled and spat, and the moving floor changed direction, spreading around the source of burning heat. Only then did Kate really know what she was looking at. Tiny insects were seeping out of Bandermain's body and spreading across the floor in search of a new host. The floor was crawling with them, their tiny forms barely visible to the eye, moving across the ground like a cloud of dust.

Kate reached up, grabbed three ceiling candles, and dropped them in front of her. Then she grabbed two more and clasped them in her hands ready to protect herself as the creatures spread.

"The physical body is so frail and weak," said Dalliah. "The mind is where true strength lies. Bandermain was weak. We will find a way forward without him."

"Shut up!" Kate shouted, dropping another candle as the bugs spread her way. She had to get to Edgar.

Silas saw what she was doing, unhooked one of the few oil lamps, and threw it into the center of the creeping mass. Glass smashed, oil spread, and flames burst into life, searing the tiny creatures before they could advance any farther. Silas threw another lamp toward Edgar, setting fire to the sleeve of Bandermain's red coat, and a third smashed at Kate's feet, forcing her back, away from the growing flames.

"Stop!" Kate screamed as Silas smashed a fourth lamp dangerously close to Edgar's head, sending glass shards sprinkling across his wild dark hair. "He's not dead! He can't be dead!"

Silas's skin was slick with sweat. Between the creeping lung and Dalliah's manipulation of the veil, he was not thinking clearly. The crow flapped its wings restlessly as Silas grew weaker, but Bandermain's body had to be burned. Nothing else mattered but making sure every last one of those creatures was dead.

Dalliah pulled Kate toward the door. "Listen to me," she said, her voice pouring into Kate's ear like poison. "As long as you are alive, the people around you will always be in danger. You do not want that. I can see that your friend's pain disturbs you, but you are not strong enough to help him here. Leave him, come with me, and I will help you bring an end to this. You do not belong with him anymore. You belong with me. I will show you the way. Let me help you. Let us do what needs to be done."

Kate struggled to keep her eyes open as Dalliah's words washed over her, and her cheeks were damp with tears. "I have to help him," she said. "I have to bring him back. Edgar!" She could hear Dalliah's veil voice whispering quietly beneath her spoken words, seeping through the smoke that had begun to spread around the room.

Silas fell to his knees, willing himself to stand but no longer possessing the strength. Whatever Dalliah was doing, Kate knew she held all of their lives in her hands. She was the only one who could stop this. Kate could give Dalliah everything she wanted, all she had to do was say yes.

"I couldn't bind that man's soul," said Kate. "It wasn't right. I couldn't do it."

"Everything can be overcome," Dalliah said carefully. "No plan rests on the shoulders of one person alone. We will not suffer too badly for his loss. It was wrong to ask so much of you so soon."

Kate turned to face her. "I'll come with you," she said, firmly wiping her tears away. "I will. Whatever's wrong with the veil, I want to help you put it right. Just let me help him!"

"No," said Silas, his voice rasping but still strong. "She is lying to you, Kate. Do not listen to her."

"Your ancestors wrote *Wintercraft* for you," said Dalliah. "But you have not seen everything it has to teach you. There are secrets within its pages that you will never discover without me. I will teach you. I will hide nothing from you, Kate. Silas has had his time. He is the one who destroyed your life. He stole everything from you. Do not allow him to steal your future as well."

As Dalliah held Kate's hand, her mind began to clear again. She began to feel comfortable and safe, and Dalliah's presence gave her a feeling of belonging that was intoxicating.

"Come with me."

Kate allowed Dalliah to lead her toward the door, away from Silas, away from Edgar.

"It is too late for them, but their spirits will not be lost. They will remain bound to this place, just like all the other souls I have collected. This is the way it is meant to be. You can trust me, Kate." The veil voice echoed Dalliah's words. *"Trust me."*

Kate found herself nodding slowly in agreement. Dalliah stepped carefully across the symbol-etched floor, crossed the carvings that glowed in firelight, and pulled Kate out into the open night.

The Blackwatch officers and their carriage were waiting outside. Dalliah forced Kate into the lead officer's hands, and he held her tightly, preventing her from going back inside.

"Where is Bandermain?" he asked. "Did the girl succeed?"

"Your commander is dead," said Dalliah. "The girl is not to blame. His disease was too far advanced. If you had found her sooner, he would have stood a better chance."

The officer signaled for his men to investigate. One of them entered the smoke-filled building, holding his sleeve over his mouth and nose. He emerged moments later.

"Three bodies," he said. "Blood everywhere."

"Bodies?" Kate's voice was a whisper. He was wrong. He had to be wrong.

"Your commander fought with his last breath," said Dalliah. "He lost one battle, but he will carry a greater victory into his grave. He claimed the life of Silas Dane. Celador Bandermain is a hero."

The Blackwatch officer considered Dalliah's words and bowed his head with respect. "Then I must thank you for your efforts," he said. "Your attempts to save his life will not be forgotten. Bandermain's name will live on."

"I'm sure it will," said Dalliah. "He was willing to do what had to be done for the good of his country. Will you continue the work we planned together in honor of his name?"

The officer stood to attention. "Of course."

"Good. Then order your men to burn this place down. Burn the house. Burn everything. Our plan remains unchanged."

"You can't do that! Edgar is in there!" Kate struggled to free herself, but the two Blackwatch guards were already lighting fire torches and crossing the courtyard to set fire to the grand house. "No. Wait!" she cried. "You have to get them out! *Silas!*"

No one was listening to her. A thousand thoughts were battling for her attention at once, but all Kate saw were the flames licking higher and smoke pouring out of the domed building's door as Dalliah turned her back upon it.

"I need your carriage and your ship," said Dalliah.

"Yes, my lady. My men will assist you any way they can."

"Then we sail today. I shall require horses and a messenger bird once we reach Albion's shores. Do you still have your men positioned within Fume?"

"Yes, my lady. Everything is ready."

"Then let us begin."

The Blackwatch leader forced Kate up into the carriage, and he and Dalliah climbed in on either side of her as the great black house glowed with inner firelight.

"We can't just leave them!"

Dalliah rested her hand on Kate's wrist. The veil voice crept through Kate's mind, and she felt herself giving in, watching the house's windows bursting in the heat of the growing flames and listening to the crackle of the circular building as its wooden frame split and burned.

"Edgar," Kate whispered, but Dalliah's touch slowed her thoughts until she was no longer sure why she had said his name. She did not know why she was crying or why the rising flames made her stomach knot with fear.

She looked out the carriage window as the two Blackwatch guards returned, walking straight through the pouring smoke like ghosts, and climbed up into two seats at the front of the carriage.

"We shall reach our homeland soon," said Dalliah, her voice gentle and eerily reassuring. "It has been many years since I set foot upon Albion's soil. This time I intend to stay."

Once the two guards were back on board, the reins snapped, and the horses sped swiftly to a trot, pulling the carriage away from the rising fires. They stopped just once to let the dark-haired guard open the gates and climb back on board, and then they were off, heading out deep into the forest. Kate watched the icicle-laden trees flash by in the evening light, their icy fingers sparkling like crystal as the carriage disturbed them, knocking them loose to smash upon the frozen ground.

The moment Dalliah passed out of the gate her connection with the energy in the circular building was broken. The energies fell, and Kate looked back as fire engulfed everything in the distance until all she could see was the glow of the flames.

"Do not worry about the past," said Dalliah. "We carry everything we need with us wherever we go. We require nothing else. Do you understand?"

"Yes," said Kate, but the word was alien to her. She felt as if she were forgetting something, but she no longer knew what.

"Work the horses harder," Dalliah ordered. The Blackwatch leader relayed the message to the driver, and Dalliah smiled at Kate as the forest swallowed the burning buildings and Kate turned away from the window at last. "I want to be at sea within the day."

# ← 22 →
# FATE

As soon as Dalliah's link to the circle was broken, Silas's injured spirit plunged back into his body, and he forced his eyes open. He was on his side, lying beneath a thick layer of darkening smoke, and something was pecking at his nose. Firelight flickered gently across his crow's black feathers as it tried to wake him, and flames were devouring the wooden walls, leaving bones scattered and singed on the floor as the cords holding them burned and snapped. Close by, Bandermain's clothes smoldered upon his lifeless body. His red coat was fully ablaze, his face turned toward a dark shape that was sprawled across the floor.

Silas got to his feet, his body recovering slowly as it came back under his control. He tested his injured lungs and found the pain had lessened considerably. His chest was clear. Whatever influence that room had over him had been broken by Dalliah's absence. She had used the power of his own blood against him, and he could no longer feel a single scratch or bite as he breathed in the hot black smoke. The injuries that had driven him into the darkness of the half-life had felt sickeningly real. Any doubt Silas had about the extent of Dalliah's Skill faded in that moment. She was a formidable woman. She had defeated him easily, and she expected his body to burn, leaving his broken spirit lost within the veil for eternity.

There was enough of the veil's influence left within the room to help Silas resist the ill effects of the smoke, and he walked straight through it, making his way over to the dark shape lying beside Bandermain. He walked around his enemy's burning body and crouched down beside Edgar. The boy was not moving. Silas lifted one of his arms up, hoisted him over his shoulder, and carried him to the door. One hard kick was enough to send it splaying out on its hinges, feeding more air to the fire inside.

Silas carried Edgar out into the courtyard and saw Dalliah's black house being torn swiftly apart by flames as he laid Edgar on the ground.

"Owwww . . ." Edgar groaned, and his eyelids flickered. Silas pulled his eyes open with his thumbs.

"How many of your nine lives do you have left now, Mr. Rill?"

Edgar coughed weakly.

"Keep still," said Silas, carefully inspecting his dagger

wound. "You have lost a lot of blood. I can stop the bleeding, but I cannot heal you here. You hit your head when you fell. I thought you were dead."

"Where's . . . Kate?"

"Gone," said Silas, opening Edgar's bloodstained coat and tearing strips of fabric from the sweater underneath.

"Dalliah took her?"

Silas pressed the fabric strips against the dagger wound. "The wound is a clean one," he said. "If the blood clots quickly enough, you should survive."

*"Should?"*

"We have more important concerns."

"I'd say this was pretty important! Ow!"

*"I* will find Kate. You will stay here."

"I'm all right!" lied Edgar, trying to stand. "I can walk."

"I have done all I can for you. Good-bye, Mr. Rill."

"What? Wait!"

Silas left Edgar on the ground and strode through the smoke toward the open gate.

"Silas!"

Edgar's shouts carried across Dalliah's land. Silas ignored him. The boy was unimportant. All that mattered was reaching Kate before Dalliah took her out to sea.

Silas's boots thumped into the gravel, carrying him out through the gates, where he stopped and searched for something he hoped would still be there. Movement to his right made him turn, and a large eye blinked at him from the darkness. The horse he had stolen from the stables in Grale was standing calmly in the trees. His crow took flight, flapping up into the branches overhead while Silas stepped toward the animal and rubbed its wide nose. "A beast without fear," he said. "I was right." His touch calmed the horse, and he climbed smoothly up onto its back. "So much for fate," he said, guiding the horse swiftly back out onto the path.

The pair of dead trees loomed over him as he rode toward the crossroads leading back toward the town. He still had time. All he had to do was ride, but then his thoughts turned to Edgar, an injured man of Albion, left bleeding and alone on enemy land. Throughout his years spent fighting Albion's war, Silas had never once allowed an injured man to be left behind. The horse gave him an advantage. It gave him speed. No matter what else was at stake, his conscience and his honor as a soldier would not let him abandon a good man now.

Edgar heard the echo of hooves pounding across the ground, and he blinked into the darkness, half expecting the Blackwatch to have sent someone back to finish him off. A great beast thundered toward him. He managed to stand; but the dagger wound blazed, and his head swam. He had done his best. He had tried to help Kate. If he were going to die there, he would at least die on his feet, knowing he could have done no more. Then the rider slowed the horse to a walk and circled him, holding an arm out for him to take.

"You may not be able to run, Mr. Rill," said Silas, "but you can ride."

Edgar could not believe what he was seeing. He reached up, grabbed Silas's hand, and let Silas heave him up onto the back of the horse.

"Hold on," said Silas as Edgar clutched the belt of his leather coat, clinging on tightly.

The horse turned back toward the forest and raced into a gallop, speeding toward the trail through the trees. The path to Grale ran downhill most of the way, and at the few points where the trees were thinnest and the trail ran due west, Silas caught brief glimpses of moonlight sparkling upon the surface of the sea. Dalliah's carriage had gained a head start; but his horse was well rested, and its hooves thumped into the dirt at a thundering pace. The track wound tightly between the trees, and the horse raced on, finding extra speed as Silas guided it down the path.

The sky lightened into a mist-filled morning. The horse slowed to a steady pace, but by the time they reached the edge of Grale, Dalliah's carriage was still nowhere in sight. Silas knew the Blackwatch would be watching the main routes into the town, so he took a sharp turn off the forest road, sending the horse plunging through the trees and out into Grale's back streets. Edgar's grip grew weaker as they rode over a river bridge, heading for the dock, until his fingers slipped completely at a tight corner and Silas had to grab hold of his arm to stop him from sliding off. He could not afford to slow the horse, but Edgar was unconscious. His condition was far worse than Silas had thought. The dock wasn't far. He could hold Edgar until then, but if he died before they reached it, the delay he had caused by helping him would have been for nothing.

Behind Silas, in the distance, plumes of smoke and flame reached toward the sky from Dalliah's burning house. He looked for his crow and spotted it flying high above him, matching the horse's speed. It circled down, close enough to hear Silas. "Follow the girl," he said. "Do not leave her side."

Edgar was slipping farther from the horse, and Silas had to make a choice: stop and help him, or let him fall. The crow flew over the rooftops, heading for the ship, the sails of which were already being unfurled. The carriage must have reached the dock, but the ship would not set sail immediately. There was still time.

He pulled the horse to a stop, lowered Edgar to the ground, and slid down beside him. Edgar's breathing was shallow, and his back was wet with blood. "This is not the best time for you to die." Silas glanced up at the ship as he rolled Edgar onto his side, and his fingers tingled with cold as the veil gathered around them, preparing to take Edgar into death. He pressed his hand to Edgar's neck, trying to channel what little energy he could reach to help the wound heal. Nothing happened.

The veil was too weak, his connection to it thin and fading.

Silas tried to concentrate, but he was distracted. He could leave the boy and make it onto the ship before it sailed. He was all but dead anyway. Nothing would be lost. Letting him go would be the sensible thing to do, all he had to do was walk away, yet he still kept his hand against Edgar's neck, cursing the boy's weakness under his breath, his impatience building with every second his body remained still. At last the veil answered. The blood within Edgar's wound began to clot, and the flesh knitted slowly. Edgar's body trembled, his chest began to move, and his pulse quickened to a steady pace.

Silas grabbed hold of Edgar's shoulders. "Can you hear me?" he asked. "Can you move?"

Edgar opened his eyes, his strength returning, as a clear bell rang from the dock and the Blackwatch ship began moving into open sea. Silas stared out toward the ocean. He was too late.

"Where's the ship?" asked Edgar.

"Where *is* it?" Silas struggled to contain his anger as the boat turned to the west. "It's out there!" he said, pointing to the moving sails. "Where we should be!"

"It's gone?"

"I should have left you to die. You were all but gone anyway. I should never have returned for you!"

"Don't hold anything back," said Edgar. "Just say what you mean." The bloodied rags had fallen off, the blood had stopped, and the wound was healing. "I didn't ask you to come back for me. I told you to go find Kate."

"I could have reached the ship," said Silas. "I could have stopped her. If you were not so weak, this could have been over."

"Don't blame me for this," Edgar shouted. "I was quite happily dying on the back of that horse before you decided to help." He lowered his voice a little. "Thanks for that."

Silas glared at him. "I should kill you myself," he said. "Do you have any idea what Dalliah is going to do with Kate? Do you know what will happen if they succeed in making the veil fall?"

"That won't happen. Kate wouldn't do anything like that."

"Kate does not know her own mind! Not anymore."

"If you stopped shouting and thought about this for a second!"

The Blackwatch ship's lanterns illuminated one by one as it sailed deeper into the night with the black speck that was Silas's crow trailing dutifully behind. Silas's hands tensed into fists, and Edgar spoke quietly.

"I'm just saying, how far can they get?" he said, pointing out to sea. "They're right there. If you wanted to do something to the veil, where would you go?"

"Fume," Silas said at once.

"And are you saying that in this whole town there is not

one person who will sell us a boat? This can't be over. I've been stabbed, threatened, chased, and I pretty much died right over there. Now I'm stuck here with you, and the Continent is planning to invade Albion. You might want to stand here and beat yourself up about all this, but I am not going to let an ocean stop me from helping Kate. If I have to swim across the bloody thing myself, I will!"

Silas smiled wryly. "But a boat would be easier," he said.

"So let's find one and get out there!"

Silas looked down at Edgar. "The wardens would have liked you. You would have made a fine officer."

"Thanks . . . I think."

"If you insist on staying alive, you can at least make yourself useful," said Silas. "Sell the horse, quickly. We have an ocean to cross."

Kate stood on the deck of the Blackwatch ship, looking back toward the Continent as the land slowly slipped away. Dalliah was busy giving her final orders to the crew, and the great sails heaved above them, carrying them through the freezing sea toward Albion's shores.

"You will be home soon," said Dalliah, walking up beside her. "You will feel better as we draw closer to Albion. The veil will welcome you back again, and any confusion you are feeling will pass."

Kate stayed quiet.

"Fume is not what you believe it to be," said Dalliah. "It was never meant to be a city, and it was never just a resting place for flesh and bones. Its purpose is far greater than that. Wintercraft will open your eyes. It will reveal to you the truth that lies beneath the stones, exactly as it was meant to do. The circle you opened on the Night of Souls was only the first key in a far greater lock. It is up to us to open the others. Do you understand me, Kate?"

Kate looked at Dalliah, her silver-tinged eyes reflecting the light of the moon.

"Good." Dalliah turned her away from the ocean and led her toward a cabin at the back of the ship. "You may rest now. And try not to think about anything that has happened before today. The memories will fade quickly. None of it will matter soon."

Kate walked into the cabin alone, and Dalliah locked the door behind her. *Wintercraft* felt heavy inside her coat. She took the book out, sat down on a narrow bed, and placed it beside her. Just touching its cover made her head feel a little clearer, but the clouded feelings did not completely pass. She carried it over to the tiny cabin window and opened the glass, bracing herself against a blast of icy wind as she looked back toward the Continent, unable to shake off the feeling that she was leaving something important behind.

Something outside the window caught her attention: a black shape gliding just above the waves. Kate looked closer. There was a bird out there. A crow, shadowing the ship with motes of frost speckling across its beak. The crow looked at her and called out once, before lowering its head and settling back into its steady flight.

"Silas," she said quietly, but she could not remember why the name mattered. Whenever she tried to concentrate upon it, the memories slipped away.

Kate watched the crow for a while as the ship cut swiftly through the icy waves, but something about its presence made her feel empty inside. Eventually she closed the glass against it and lay down beside her book, trying to sleep.

The world outside that cabin was cold, the sea dark and empty, as ghosts of ice drifted secretly by the window in the night. Kate dreamed of fire, of daggers and blood. Her spirit was caught in a dark place created by Dalliah to keep her thoughts locked in, but dreams were not enough to free the memories that were sealed within her mind. She was too tired, and she no longer trusted her own thoughts. All she knew for certain was what Dalliah had told her. She had a responsibility to uphold. She had important work to do, and she would not turn her back upon it. She would not let her family down.

That thought kept Kate company upon the long journey, and she hugged the book close as the sun began to rise across the sea. She did not see the crow settle upon her window ledge or hear it tapping on the glass. Dalliah had set her mind adrift upon the veil, and out there on the ocean all Kate felt was completely and powerlessly alone.

# HOW WILL KATE'S STORY CONCLUDE?
## READ ON FOR A PREVIEW OF

# WINTERVEIL

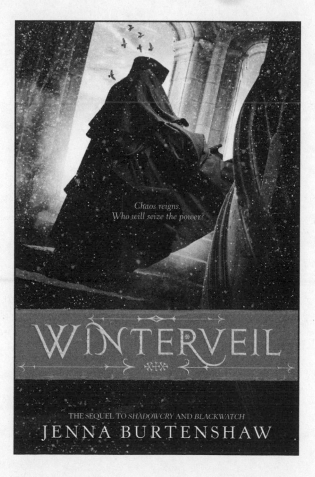

*Chaos reigns.*
*Who will seize the power?*

# WINTERVEIL

THE SEQUEL TO *SHADOWCRY* AND *BLACKWATCH*

## JENNA BURTENSHAW

# ⤙ 1 ⤚
# GRAVEDIGGER

High above the chilled waters of a sunlit sea, a dark tower rose like a wizened thumb from the crags of a blackened cliff. It cast a broken shadow across the rubble-flecked land behind it, standing crooked but strong in the rising daylight as it kept its ancient watch over the waves below.

The waves crashed against the foot of the cliff, their rhythmic surge echoing along the eastern coast of Albion, but few human ears were there to hear it. There, in that isolated place, a man climbed out of a hatch in the tower's roof and carried a small wooden crate draped with cloth up into the open air. He left the crate near the hatch and walked to the edge, where a spyglass stood upon its stand, pointing out across the sea. His stubbled face was half hidden beneath a wide hat, and his hair hung tattered across his shoulders as he cleared the lens and pressed his eye to the eyepiece.

Tarak had spent months freezing in that tower, watching ice drifting sluggishly across the horizon. That bleak seascape had become his world, but not—he hoped—for much longer. He knocked his hat back, exposing deep green eyes. The sword he kept propped beside the spyglass had claimed the life of the man who once guarded that place, and a mound of earth near the tower's foundations marked the spot where the body now lay.

This was the day he had been waiting for. Everything was going according to plan.

As the sun rose higher, a distant shape on the water drew his eye. He adjusted the lens until he could make out every wave on the surface of the sea, raised the spyglass's eye to the horizon, and settled at last upon a dark, welcome sight. A ship, heading toward the coast, with a mass of black sails raised high and full.

"The *Gravedigger*," Tarak whispered, his face softening into a satisfied smile. At last, his time in that vermin-ridden place was coming to an end. He buttoned up his coat and set to work.

He crossed the tower roof and dragged the cloth from the crate. Powerful wings beat hard against the latticed sides and four beady eyes blinked up at him as he carried it to the wall. He cooed gently to keep the birds calm and carefully unlatched the lock before reaching in and lifting out a pigeon. He tucked the bird under his arm and slid a prepared note into a ring attached to its bright pink leg. "It's time to do what we came here for," he said.

The bird wriggled excitedly, sensing the freedom of the open sky. Tarak held it out and sent it fluttering into the freezing air, where it settled into a smooth glide and flew across the water heading toward the Continental lands that lay beyond the icy sea.

Tarak watched it swoop past the dark sails of the oncoming ship. He had spent many months of his life stationed on that weather-beaten deck. The black hull bore the scars and burns of countless battles, and just seeing it again brought back memories of combat, war, and death. Enemies often underestimated the deadly power carried beneath those sails, but the *Gravedigger* was the strongest vessel in the Continental fleet. It had earned its name many times over.

He prepared a second note and attached it to the leg of the remaining bird, which sat peacefully in his hands as he held it out over the side. The pigeon flapped into the air the moment he let it go, circled once, and settled in the opposite direction to the first bird, heading deep into Albion territory, straight toward the distant graveyard city of Fume.

Tarak closed the crate. With the ship in sight and his messages sent, his work in that tower was done. He waited until both birds were no more than dark specks against the sky, then grabbed his sword, headed for the roof hatch, and descended the tower steps two at a time. He spiraled his way down past the living quarters and out onto an overgrown patch of land that was half buried in snow.

His horse was where he had left it, inside the tower's single tumbledown stable. He slid the blanket from its back, saddled it quickly, and led it outside. Salty wind whistled past the tower's stones as he mounted the beast, flicked the reins once, and rode along a gravel path, following a narrow trail that ran along the cliff top, traveling south.

Winter still held Albion firmly in its grip, and the clear morning sky was already under threat as heavy clouds massed on the horizon. Tarak glanced out to sea and spotted the winking light of a lantern signaling from the ship to the shore. He worked the horse harder, forcing its hooves to slam into the crumbling cliff, traveling past long-abandoned buildings that stood perilously close to the edge. The watchtower had not always been alone. It had once stood guard over a coastal town that had almost finished crumbling into the sea. Now only a few forgotten houses were left to mark the inland edges of the vanished settlement. The ground here was riddled with old tunnels, weakening the cliff and making it a dangerous place.

Tarak led his horse into a sheltered spot between two buildings, tied the reins to a bare tree, and picked his way on foot through what was left of the town. He headed for an exposed patch of land, perilously close to the cliff edge, and walked slowly until the ground sounded hollow beneath his boots. There he bent down, scrubbed away a thin layer of earth, and heaved open a hidden door, revealing a steep flight of steps cutting down into the cliff.

Two threads pinned across the entrance were undisturbed. No one had passed through that door in days.

Tarak followed the steps down into a twist of old cellar tunnels, and the glare of the low sun dazzled him at the point where the base of the cliff met the shore.

The tunnel's mouth opened out into a small cove, with the watchtower's crags on one side and a curving face of jagged rock on the other. A small, battered fishing boat lay abandoned within a low cave close by. Smugglers sometimes used that place, and it was not unusual for them to leave things behind.

Tarak crossed the cove quickly, tugging at a leather cord hung around his neck. A circular disk of polished crystal slid from his collar and sparkled in the sunlight as he pressed it into his palm. The ship's lantern flickered again. He held the lens up to catch the sun and flashed a signal across the water, letting the crew know that their landing place was secure.

The *Gravedigger*'s crew pulled in the sails. Ropes snaked out over the ship's starboard side, and a boat with a curved roof was lowered slowly down onto the water. It was hard for Tarak to see anyone in it clearly, but he knew whom to expect.

A woman and a girl were due ashore that day, accompanied by armed officers wearing their distinctive uniforms of red and black. Tarak straightened his shabby coat. He would be glad to clean himself up, cut his hair, and wear the colors of his true station again. Those men were his comrades, his brothers, every one of them honored to be part of the Continental army's elite force known as the Blackwatch.

He was standing proudly at the water's edge, waiting to welcome the boat ashore, when the sound of a whistle carried down from the top of the cliff. He looked up to where a man was leaning fearlessly out from the cliff edge, flickering a signal. Tarak raised a hand in reply. The horses had arrived.

He turned back to the sea and watched the boat advance slowly toward the shore, until thickening clouds swept over the sun and sharp spits of hail began to fall. The wind churned, and the air filled quickly with swarms of stinging ice, while storm clouds swelled like a bruise, filling the northern sky. Tarak stood braving it out, until the hail became too heavy to bear. He had hoped to provide a dignified welcome, but if he stood there much longer, he would look like a fool.

Cursing the weather under his breath, he headed to the cave for shelter. He pulled up his collar and made for the hollow where the fishing boat's prow jutted out over the sand. His hand had just touched the cave's clammy wall when he hesitated. Something about the boat looked different. There was a red net draped over the side that he was sure had not been there before. He edged closer, until his boot pressed down on something firm just beneath the sand.

A strained cry rose up from the ground, like the whimper of a wounded animal. He raised his foot and saw what looked like four long fingers curling upward, but the moment he saw them they were gone.

Tarak drew his blade, not sure what he had just seen. He tested the ground again, pinpointing the muffled sound, then bent down and sank his fist firmly into the sand. His fingers met something that felt like cloth. He grabbed hold of it and dragged it out. The cloth was a dirty sweater, and wearing it was a young man who spluttered loudly as his sand-covered face and mop of black hair were revealed.

"Who are you?" demanded Tarak.

The boy was too busy coughing to answer. Tarak was about to question him again when he felt something cool and sharp press against his throat, and a deep voice spoke into his ear.

"Release the boy."

A trickle of cold fear ran through Tarak's blood. He had been threatened before; he had been close to death more times than he could remember. His fear had nothing to do with the blade at his throat but everything to do with the person who was wielding it. He hesitated for a few seconds before releasing his grip. The boy scrambled away from him.

"Drop your weapon," said the voice. "And turn. Slowly."

Tarak did as he was told, letting his sword fall flat upon the sand. The blade of a dagger played gently around his neck as he turned to face a pair of dead gray eyes.

He was standing in the presence of a man whose height towered far above his own. Those lifeless eyes stared down at him with no hint of emotion. The rugged face gave away nothing but indifference as his ambusher held a rough dagger in one hand and a sword made of blue-black steel in the other.

"Silas Dane."

Fear pulled the name unwittingly from Tarak's lungs and out into the air. This man's reputation had spread farther than he could imagine. People on the Continent called him a man without a soul, a perfect warrior. The soldier who could not die. Tarak was trapped in the shadow of a predator that could not be outfought, outwitted, or outrun, but he would not flee and die with a blade in his back. Pride kept him standing tall, knowing that all he could hope for was the mercy of a swift death.

"The ship," said Silas. "How many of the crew are coming ashore?"

Tarak remained silent. He would not betray his men to the enemy.

"How many are above us with the horses?"

Silas's blade bit a bloody mark into Tarak's flesh, but still he said nothing. How had he not noticed that the fishing boat's hull was damp from recent use? Why had he not stayed by the water, braving the weather, rather than venture close to the cliff?

No matter what happened to him, his birds were already on their way. Not even Silas Dane could stop what was to come. He rolled his shoulders back, forcing himself to look his enemy in the eye. If he was to die, he had done his duty. There was no dishonor in that.

Silas gave him time to answer, letting the silence stretch on. "If you will not talk," he said at last, "I have no time for you."

In one quick move the blade cut deeper, slicing swiftly through the pulse beating in Tarak's neck. Warm blood spilled across cold skin. Tarak felt the weight of his body slump heavily to the ground; his life stolen away in a single cut. Darkness and pain closed in. The warm current of death swept through him, and then his spirit was gone.

Silas looked down at the body in the bloodied sand, then stepped over it and watched the sea through the swirling hail. The young man with him was a shabby seventeen-year-old named Edgar Rill, who stared at the dead man, not sure what Silas expected them to do next.

"Bury him," ordered Silas, cleaning his dagger on a patch of sand grass. "And stay out of sight."

"More Blackwatch are heading in on that boat," said

Edgar. "We don't have time. Have you seen how close they are?"

"I have eyes. Dig."

Edgar grabbed an oar from the fishing boat. His stomach, which had been growling with hunger just a short while earlier, squirmed with discomfort at being so close to the dead man. He used the oar to scrape away a hollow in the sand beside the body, working as quickly as he could. "Are you going to help?"

Silas had tucked the dagger back into his belt and was listening silently to the ice-filled wind.

"I'll take that as a no." Edgar's hands were shaking. Through fear or cold, it was impossible to tell. In the past day alone he had been stabbed, dragged back from the waiting hands of death, and ferried across a frozen sea. His only company had been a man whose conversation stopped at giving orders. Silas's presence still made the hairs bristle on the back of Edgar's neck, despite his having been the one who had saved Edgar's life.

"Next time you can be the bait," said Edgar, digging quickly. "What if he had decided to kill me as soon as he grabbed me? What then?"

"I would have stopped him."

"Why couldn't I have hidden in the boat?"

"Dragging someone out of a boat makes them an enemy," said Silas. "Dragging them out of the sand makes them a curiosity."

"Well, I'm glad that logic works for you. Feel free to step forward a bit quicker next time."

Edgar knew the makeshift grave was not yet deep enough to fully hide a man, but the Blackwatch were getting too close. He had to finish the gruesome job quickly. He jabbed the oar into the sand and decided to improvise. Two drags—one on the man's shoulder and one on the knees—sent him rolling into the shallow trench, where Edgar spotted the bright glint of a crystal lens light hanging around his neck. Something like that was too useful to leave behind, so he tugged it loose and pocketed it.

"And the coat," Silas said, without turning around. "He has no use for it anymore."

Edgar's own coat was torn, filthy, and drenched through. He was surprised he had survived so long in that state. He may not have liked stealing clothes from the dead, but Silas was right. He dragged the patched garment off the man and claimed it for himself. Sliding his arms into the wide sleeves, he realized with a grim shudder that they were still warm. He whispered an apology, covered the man's face with his hat, and kept working.

It took less than a minute for Edgar to pile a mound of sand on top of the grave, while Silas kept his eyes upon the ocean, completely ignoring his efforts.

"I'm assuming you have some sort of plan?" asked Edgar.

Silas said nothing, and Edgar knew better than to ask again.

As soon as Edgar finished, he joined Silas within the shadow of the cave wall, watching the boat moving closer to the shore. Whatever plan Silas had in mind, Edgar would be ready when the time came. Until then all either of them could do was wait.

# JENNA BURTENSHAW

has been writing since she was a child, and she divides her time between her writing, her dogs, and her rescue rabbits. She is the author of *Shadowcry, Blackwatch,* and *Winterveil.* Jenna Burtenshaw lives in England.

www.jennaburtenshaw.blogspot.com

**FOLLOW JENNA BURTENSHAW ON**

For exclusive information on your favorite authors and artists, visit www.authortracker.com.

Also available as an ebook.